ONE LAST PRAYER FROM THE QUEEN

THE LION THAT LIONS FEAR BOOK II

SALUTE, CELEBRATE, AND SAY GOODBYE

DAVID HUNTER ELLIS

HUNTER ELLIS PRODUCTIONS, LLC

To request permissions, contact: davidhunter.ellis@gmail.com

ISBN:979-8-9853767-3-9

This is a work of fiction. Any references to real people, historical events, or places are fictitious. Names, characters, and places are products of the author's imagination.

Book Cover by DAMONZA

Edited by David Ellis Jr.
Author Photo courtesy of Dai-zha Ellis 2025

First print edition 2025.

http://www.davidhunter-ellis.carrd.co/

PROLOGUE

Indeed, the sight of the sun breaking through the gray clouds occasionally brings a smile. Of course, some raise their hands, not to do the impossible and reach the unreachable, but to praise the Lord's work. And maybe, just maybe, in a moment of weakness, question the still-unanswered hope for brighter days amid the struggles of our oppressed Colored lives. Or, even grimace at the slight relief from pressure—like a tiny pinhole in a water balloon. Its reprieve is so minor that it only reminds us of the trials we continue to face, as if there weren't people eager to tell us we have no place, no space, and no time for fairy tales to distract us from reality. A rainbow appears, and I stare—dare I doubt my prayer? Was it a Wonderful Life? This holds my glare.

CHAPTER ONE
MISSISSIPPI ROOTS

DEBRA-ANN WAS A child who knew and lost love early in life, a blessed daughter of the colored South moving through the hate-filled, blood-soaked landscape of 1941 Mississippi without proper guidance. She forged her path through the dense, less-traveled backwoods and the hazy, body-snatching rivers in a world that now had little use for her. Debra-Ann's gift for fishing and hunting was as legendary as her grandfather's, surpassing the skills of the town's best, both black and white. With the mastery of a man twice her age, she harvested the land's bounty, skillfully casting fishing lines into schools of fish like shooting threes, hitting nothing but net, and liberating collard greens from white sharecroppers, selling the meat and skins to support herself and her dreams of life far away from the hell she was born. Debra-Ann exemplified generosity in honor of her beloved Grand Michael, sharing most of her hard-earned earnings with the elderly and those in need, radiating a warmth that illuminated her otherwise solitary existence. Only on Sundays did she dare to indulge in the fleeting joys of childhood—a rare escape laden with danger for a pretty, young black girl navigating such a tumultuous town. This particular Sunday would be etched forever into the memories of the townsfolk, marking the last time they would see her bright, infectious smile.

The musical chimes of the church bells pierced the morning air, their resonant bongs weaving a dissonant tapestry that startled flocks of birds from their nests, sending them flapping into the cerulean sky. At the same time, frightened chickens scurried in a flurry of feathers from their feeding spots. For the bleary-eyed residents, reluctantly roused from their slumbers, the booming chimes heralded the arrival of Sunday morning: a sacred ritual for the hellraisers, fervently clinging to their blind faith in justifiable bloodshed, thanking God for their blessings. Yet for those who bore the weight of oppression, these chimes served as a bitter reminder to be grateful for simply surviving another week.

In Hush, Mississippi—a town steeped in a legacy of deep-seated prejudice—the blurred lines that separated good and evil were continuously crossed by men and women, colored and white. Evil held no conscience, feeding off both communities, one cloaked in insecurities and self-hatred, and the colored folks struggling to survive the cruelties of oppression, while not becoming the likes of their oppressors. Beneath the seemingly quaint exterior of Hush, marked by its dilapidated train station that once transported slaves and livestock to be auctioned off side-by-side to the inviting storefronts, filled with trinkets from around the world. Every Sunday, shopkeepers hung "Closed" signs. Meanwhile, *Knight Raiders,* too old to saddle a horse, reclined lazily on creaking rocking chairs, sipping sour mash moonshine and casting bleary-eyed, pestering stares at passing foot travelers, their faces reflecting a mix of curiosity and contempt for the ones they once terrorized. On this unusually hot Sunday morning, the dirt roads morphed into a dusty canvas of brewing tension, and reality stripped to bare truth provided color folks with a deceptively rare opportunity to lift their tormented eyes from the ground as they cautiously traveled through the town. It wasn't that the white folks set aside their prejudices for one second; instead, they paraded their Sunday best, flaunting their superiority like unsullied badges of honor.

Meanwhile, the colored townsfolk avoided eye contact, fearing they might inadvertently invite trouble. It was customary for nearly thirty colored individuals to walk in solemn procession, their eyes fixed no higher than the wheels of horse-drawn buggies that rattled by, the creaking wood echoing the weight in their hearts. As they moved along the sun-drenched streets, an oppressive tension held the air captive, manifesting in squinting eyes and flinching bodies as whips cracked sharply above the shuffling hooves of horses and mules. Yet, as the colored folks approached the majestic ninety-foot red maple tree, a weight voided and their bodies relaxed, its vibrant autumn leaves carpeting the ground in a swirl fitting the hope-filled sighting of rainbows in the sky. In the cool shade of the church, they found comfort in the tree's connection to Mother Earth, a seedling now a monument planted by their descendants, a source of strength amid the tormenting winds of sorrow and strife, offering a spark of hope in defiance of the harsh realities of their lives.

The church at the far end of town, at the crossroad, a modest yet sturdy structure frequented solely by the colored folk, stood as a heartbreaking leftover of days gone by. Once a glorified box for storing cured meat to sustain the early settlers through merciless winters, its beaten façade—worn and cracked—bore witness to a history long forgotten. The pitched roof, sagging slightly under the weight of time, could hold no more than twenty-five souls within its walls, with just enough room for five more to lean against the creaky, splintered wooden planks that offered shelter and sanctuary. Young Pastor James filled this church with an unwavering spirit, cleverly weaving prayer and preaching into the very fabric of each lesson. The Pastor's intense 'out of the mouths of babes' stories brought tales to life. He compared their trials and tribulations to those in the Bible that tapped deeply within the hearts of his congregation. Even the insurmountable weeds that pushed through the cracks in the eroded floor stood as a statement to their shared commitment—a symbol of a nurturing life that thrives despite the hard edges of their world. "Mornin'! Mornin'," the pastor greeted with a broad, welcoming smile, illuminating the dim entryway. The fresh scent of cut grass clung to his clothes, a sweet remnant of the weeds he had recently pulled from behind the pulpit. As he shook hands and counted parishioners as they entered, anticipation of this week's inspiring sermon filled the air. Churchgoers shuffled eagerly toward the front, vying for the best seats, causing the patchy red and white drapes—once repurposed from chicken feed sacks—to flutter playfully in the warm, inviting breeze.

"Y'all hold dem ends and remember, no more than three raise at the same time. Sermon cn healin' next Sunday," he instructed with a tinge of anxiety in his voice while eyeing the makeshift benches—simple planks of pine, precariously balanced on tree stumps, threatening to topple with even the slightest movement. "Seventeen... eighteen... Ah, pardon me. Hello there, Miss Mary, Miss Emma! What a joy to see y'all!"

"Mornin', pastor," replied Emma and Mary in unison, their voices a soothing harmony.

"Sit where you see fit; the last pew in the back of the church is mighty comfortable. You got the wall to lean on," the pastor suggested, his warm demeanor wrapped around them like a comforting embrace. Mary and Emma weren't regular churchgoers anymore, though they both felt the pull of the Lord, especially when the call was strong enough to stir their spirits. As young girls, later vivacious young ladies, they had always danced to their rhythm. However, the weight of the past hovered over shame and guilt like a scarlet letter. Most kinfolks they knew had long left for the coldness of the grave, while others had turned away due to the sinfulness of their personal lives. Mary's petite frame contrasted with Emma's statuesque five-foot-nine height, making their presence all the more conspicuous. Within the church walls, memories were shared like sacred verses; Mary felt much like the woman marked by a scarlet letter, burdened with her history.

"Thank ya kindly, pastor. Come along, Emma, he at eighteen. Ain't two seats together up there. Besides, my back can use dat wall," Mary stated firmly, a slight tremor of resolve in her voice. Emma understood Mary's shame but was unfazed by it. She rolled her eyes playfully at Mary, then glanced up to see the pastor's gaze gloomy with concern as he studied the ominous gray cloud hovering above the church.

With a resigned sigh, Emma remarked, "Dat frilly cloud ain't gonna shed no tears; it's got an angel on it lookin' to stir the pot." Pastor James chuckled softly to himself, clearing his throat before responding, "Yes, yes. Amen, sister."

His eyes widened as if grappling to comprehend the weight of her words before turning to greet the next church-goer. "Good morning, uh, Sara—*Sister* Sara," he stammered, slightly flustered. With her lips pressed into a thin line and brows arched in scrutiny, Emma held her chin high, cutting through the congregation with a piercing gaze. Each step resonated through the worn floorboards, demanding attention. She was no frail elderly woman; she was a force capable of matching any man's strength in hard labor when the need arose. Emma dared to lock eyes with anyone who dared cross her path. Mary settled herself in the far corner of the church, beckoning with an inviting gesture.

"Emma! Emma! Over here," she called with confidence. Emma's eyes flicked from Mary to the bold red hen emblazoned on the curtain above the seat, its vibrant design suggesting an aggressive pecking motion near Mary's head. Whispers and muffled snickers trailed behind Emma like shadows as she moved to sit beside her friend. With a heavy sigh, Emma arrived, fully aware that it wasn't Mary's aching back weighing on her spirit. It was the persistent loathing that lingered in this community, among both Black and White folks, that continued to suffocate even after all these years, hovering over her like a dense, oppressive cloud. The subtle hints of murmured rumors—the belief that they loved each other like a man has feelings for a woman.

Mary's eyes drifted along the church aisle when a figure abruptly captured her attention, sparking a sense of familiarity. She braced herself, her mind full of wonder as the woman walked cautiously, her posture bent and uneven, favoring her left leg as she maneuvered through the lively crowd. A sharp wave of recognition struck Mary's heart—this woman resembled the mother who had once held her tenderly, even though she appeared too young to truly be Mary's mother. The peaceful sight of this woman's struggling walk to worship awakened memories of Mary's past, the kind-heartedness within a community, and the longing for the family she had willingly left behind—discarded not by death but by shame-filled choices that had banished her from their lives. With her back flat against the splintering wooden wall, Mary felt the years of unsettled sadness settle in as she pondered the stark reality of her existence. Over the years, she had tried to come to terms with the decisions that had forged a rift between them. Yet deep within her was an unquenchable longing for acceptance of her choices and those she had once treasured. Emma's muffled squeals of delight pierced through Mary's reflective reverie, pulling her from the sea cliff of regrets she stood on and back to the present as they spotted Debra-Ann, number thirty, gracefully entering through the door. As she stepped inside, a chorus of smiles greeted Debra-Ann, showering her with the warmth that accompanied memories of kindness shared through food and coins. She had grown; the women marveled at how much, and maternal instincts kindled as hopeful dreams tugged at Emma's heartstrings. Debra-Ann glided past their row, and the simplicity of her sky-blue dress spoke to the calmness that Sunday mornings brought. "Look at her! She favors sky blue, Mary," Emma whispered excitedly, her voice reserved, still swishing the air like a gentle breeze. Mary's budding smile challenged her, a bittersweet blend of joy and sadness welling inside her as she watched ghosts and legends reemerge, stepping back into her life in the form of a beautiful little girl. With the doors left ajar, the echo of Pastor James's footsteps filled the space as he hurried after Debra-Ann, his hands clapping urgently. Startled, she sprinted toward the front of the church as if engaged in a playful chase, her heart pounding as she pressed against the wall. She embraced the moment, fully aware that the children would always part ways with their elders.

"Amen, amen! Can I get an amen?" the pastor thundered, positioning himself triumphantly behind the pulpit. The congregation, roused by the pastor's reading of Revelation, clapped with triumphant vigor, 'divine truth,' soon to be revealed, urging them to their feet. In contrast, exhausted from the excitement of the juke joint the night before, others sat, their moaning voices synchronizing into a soft blended chorus of "Amen." The lifted spirits buzzed with interest, each word igniting a sense of unity that lingered in the air like a 'surviving the whip and the day' slave hymn. Pulling the ribbon from her hair with an almost reverent touch, Emma focused on Debra-Ann, concern etched across her features.

"Look, Mary, this sky-blue ribbon would look mighty nice in her hair. Don't you think? She's about ten or eleven now—such a big girl," Emma remarked, holding the ribbon delicately in front of Mary's line of sight, its vibrant hue catching the light. Mary let out a soft sigh.

"Emma, let dat child be," Mary harshly whispered, a note

of weariness in her voice. "You missin' some years. Dat child is some fourteen years now." Emma folded her arms, the weight-iness on her spirit leaning heavily as she observed Debra-Ann, the wanting to reach out becoming an almost overwhelming tide.

"Just a sight, that little girl is such a beautiful child," Emma mumbled, her voice bubbling with pride. "I just can't shake this notion..." Mary sighed, her head shaking slowly in frustrated recognition of the tone and weight of the words Emma would utter next. Emma exhaled slowly, a wave of uneasiness swelling within her as she leaned forward, softening her tone to express her concerns. "Mary... that poor child is troubled; she's been touched." Mary's shoulders slumped slightly, a wave of understanding washing over her as she recognized the depth of Emma's concern.

"Emma, you're trying to carve a place in dat child's life, but she's nearly grown," Mary replied softly, her voice struggling to match that of a whisper. Emma's voice surged with newfound strength, drawing the attention of those nearby like a beacon slicing through the dim church air.

"What colored girl, with no male kin to speak of in your time, Mary, who ain't been touched? They's sheep... easy prey for these wolves," Emma asserted, her tone a blend of fierce know-it-all and heartfelt worry. Despite the agitated brow furrowing with murmurs from others around her, urging her to quiet down, her conviction remained strong. With a slow, dramatized gesture, Pastor James raised his hand, pointing upward, his eyes sparkling.

"Y'all notice that gray cloud resting over our church?" he asked, his voice laced with humor, a sense of certainty evident.

"I reckon rain might be on the way. Or maybe, thems angels watchin' over us, waitin',' seeing if we share a little kindness to our neighbors." The pastor's gaze settled on Debra-Ann, whose eyes widened with surprise at the sudden attention thrust upon her. "Y'all see that little girl over there? Not used to seeing her without men's pants, totin` a shotgun, huh," he chuckled as he gazed into the eyes of many seated before him. "That child be sharin' fresh game wit you all; not seekin' praise, prayer, or pay. So, why don't y'all take a moment to come together, share a kind word with the fella or missus sittin' next to you now, and maybe some greens and salt pork later, can I get an amen?" A nervous murmur rippled through the congregation as whispers and pointed fingers traced across the church like a hurried breeze.

"Remember," the pastor cautioned, his voice steady and deep, "angels surely could be watchin', but *He* most definitely is," he proclaimed, his arms stretching wide as if embracing the entire room.

Mary fixed her gaze on Debra-Ann as the congregation stood clapping their understanding, examining her with a focus that implied she was attempting to interpret a hidden message in the child's posture. Cautious about Mary's harsh tongue, Emma sat stoically, taking sharp breaths while observing Mary's seriousness, keen to grasp her thoughts. Shifting before standing confidently, Mary resembled a dancer poised for a graceful finale, her chin raised with assurance. Emma tilted her head, her broad smile gradually erased from across her face, like curtains drawn at the end of a Saturday matinee. Mary's hand moved to her hip as other parishioners kept rising around her, praising the pastor's preaching. "Hear me now," she leaned in, her neck stretching closer to whisper in Emma's ear, "May their tortured souls find peace... that child over there is the daughter of Michael and the cherished granddaughter of Grand Michael," Mary firmly exclaimed, her eyes shimmering with heartache for her mate. Once radiant like the northern star, Emma adopted a steely expression of determination as her mind wrestled control over her emotions. Disturbed, she directed her gaze to the floor for the rest of the sermon, her body swaying involuntarily as waves of pain washed over her. Her tormented memories of a wicked mother matched violently with the destructive image of Debra-Ann's mother, Helen.

Pastor James's sermon calmed stirring souls like the Lord's gentle kiss to a powerful summer thunderstorm across the open plains. Exhausted, he moved through the aisles, sweat racing down his cheeks. A woman darted forward to hand him a cup of water, and with a spirited shake of his tambourine, he unleashed a wave of enthusiasm that rippled through the crowd. After a quick sip, he returned the cup, stepping back behind the pulpit, where his voice—hoarse and nearly spent—softened into a comforting balm. "The devil comes in many colors... not just white!" he proclaimed, his voice resounding like a clap of thunder through the pews. "They may not all be good, but they ain't all bad... Can I get a witness?"

"I don't know, pastor, the cream in this town mighty bitter," a voice bellowed from the back of the church. Chuckles and the soft hum of whispered debates made the pastor giggle as he pressed the handkerchief against his lips. The Pastor strode down from the pulpit, hat in hand, like a maestro commanding the orchestra of faith, his heavy boots thumping against the creaking floorboards—his personal rhythm section.

"Giving is a blessing, amen!" he pressed as everyone left. His head nodded as each coin fell into his hat as they exited. Wearing a crooked smile, the pastor made eye contact with each church member, adding a touch of guilt to inspire generosity. The congregation remained lively as they made their way onto the street.

"Was a fine sermon, Pastor," Mary said warmly, her bright smile accompanied by the soft jingle of two shiny coins dropping into his well-worn hat. The pastor cleared his throat, a broad, grateful smile spreading across his face as the coins chimed together.

"Thank you, sister. Hope to see you ladies next Sunday, amen," he replied, beaming with delight. Emma stood with her arms crossed, tapping her foot impatiently, her gaze scanning the dwindling crowd that began to filter outside. "Did I hear you singin' along with the choir, Miss Emma? You should join our church choir," the pastor suggested, his tone encouraging. But Emma's thoughts were elsewhere, fixated on the flurry of dresses outside, hoping to spot the distinctive sky-blue dress Debra-Ann wore. Mary gently patted Emma's leg, bringing her focus back.

"I hear him. Dat was Mary singing," Emma replied, her voice filled with indignation, her brows furrowing slightly with irritation. "I hum. Know the songs, not know the songs, I hum. Ain't got it in me to sing, done it in the field to pass the time—it made colored folks shed tears, is all," she added firmly, placing two more shiny coins into the pastor's outstretched hat to alleviate any unintended disrespect. Just then, a spirited voice rang out from the distance.

"Lancelot, where ya at, ya ol' hound dog?" Debra-Ann

called, emerging annoyingly from around the side of the church. "Dat old hound is probably sneaking up on some jackrabbit. He knows better—he's long in da tooth, can't catch his tail, never mind a rabbit! " I told him we go huntin' in the mornin'!" Debra-Ann worried, her frustration dancing on the warm breeze as she strolled up the road, and Emma's attention instantly snapped toward the familiar voice.

"Debra-Ann! Debra-Ann!" Emma called out. The little girl startled and stilled in her tracks, twirling toward the voice, her dress flaring outward. Emma took a firm grasp of the rail and Mary's arm before slowly, cautiously pacing her steps down the splintered pathway to the wooden stairs of the church. The stirred-up spirit of kindness embraced within the sermon seeped from the lingering congregation with the ease of a peeled banana—their convicting eyes and whisperings dipping into murmurings of disdain about a woman's choices without knowing the woman. Mary felt a knot of urgency swell within her as she rushed to the now half-sprinting Emma's side, aware that the path ahead was uncertain.

"Best we be getting on our way, Emma," Mary called out, her voice tinged with anticipation and caution for the unfolding scene. But Emma, seemingly unfazed by the warnings around her, ignored Mary's subtle plea, leading them both into an unknown that lingered ahead as they approached Debra-Ann.

"I see this ribbon right here goes nicely with dat dress," Emma exclaimed, her eyes sparkling with delight. "I thought you might like to put it in dat pretty long hair of yours," she beamed. Mary looked to the growing crowd that paused their after-church shopping to gawk, stress shifting her weight from one leg to another, her heart pounding throughout her body—a sea of narrowing eyes and curling lips twisted into mocking sneers greeted hers. The air thick with unspoken judgments grew, each added unfriendly face amplifying the tension around them. Unconcerned with the ignorance surrounding her, young Debra-Ann relished the company of kind elderly folks. She reached for the ribbon Emma held with a warm, gentle smile stretching across her face. As the soft fabric slipped through her fingers, it became a soothing reminder of the beauty the outside world offered amidst the harshness that engulfed her home life. As anger and disgust festered, the joy on Debra-Ann's face sparked a sliver of hope in Emma's eyes.

"Thank you kindly, ma'am," Debra-Ann said, her voice a soft breeze of innocence. Holding the ribbon close to her chest as if protecting precious gold, she exchanged friendly nods with the elderly ladies. As she turned to leave, she felt the air buzz with comfortable familiarity.

"You like this blue because of the sky; feel free, no troubles, right?" Emma exclaimed, her words bubbling with enthusiasm as she tried to prolong the moment a little longer. Debra-Ann paused, a radiant smile spreading across her face like sunlight breaking through clouds. She cast another glance at the woman, whose eyes sparkled with joy. Emma clasped her hands together, her excitement palpable, and her eyes gleamed with delight and unshed tears as she looked skyward, catching a glimpse of a soft, cerulean canvas. "I knew your Grand Michael... and your Pa... some," Emma continued, her voice dancing with nostalgia and vibrant energy.

"Dat right, ma'am!" Debra-Ann beamed, her heart swelling with pride. Emma moved closer, gently touching Debra-Ann's hand, her face aglow with a broad grin that seemed to light up the dimming afternoon.

"Sure is! It was me, Mary, and Michael—your Grand Michael—back when he was as young as you! Maybe even a little younger, right, Mary?" Emma's laughter rang out, a melody of shared memories that weaved them together in that moment.

The air was tense as onlookers from the crowd and casual passersby swelled with indignation. "Dem old heifers pitching woo to that little girl," a distressed woman cried out, her voice slicing through the murmur of the gathering like a razor. Mary's body quivered involuntarily at the sound of the scornful remark; her wide, unblinking eyes met Emma's for a fleeting moment before snapping back to the swirling whispers around them, the words igniting the atmosphere like a spark in dry tinder. Urgency surged within her as she nudged Emma with a firm yet whisper-soft touch.

"We have much to do before sundown; best we get home now, Emma," Mary urged, her voice low yet insistent, carrying an undertone of protective desperation. But Emma remained unfazed by the rising tide of commotion or Mary's plea. She yearned for a relationship with Debra-Ann, shooting daggers at the crowd, before she took another step toward Debra-Ann, a grin spreading across her face.

"Maybe a little surprise for you, Debra-Ann," Emma declared playfully, her voice tinged with excitement. "I gifted your Grand Michael that old hound dog of yours—named him Lancelot, after a knight from a book I learned to read. He's about eight weeks old, right, Mary?" Emma laughed, her sound bubbling with warmth. "That little pup would bark at anyone who dared to come close until your Grand Michael showed up as if he'd chosen him himself! I remember how Lancelot spotted Grand Michael from across the yard, trotted right over, and did his business on his boot—just to get noticed. It was like he was claiming him, his right then and there!" Emma continued, her eyes sparkling with recollection. "Mm-hmm; your pa was about your age now—half-grown, just like you. It seems that hound pup tamed the wild right out of him some." Her gratitude and pride radiated as she reminisced. *Yet beneath all this colorful remembrance, there was so much Emma had left unspoken, so much yearning to express. Wanna to say, "I be your grandma," but the weight of that truth felt too heavy for today.* Each time Emma's heart flared with the pain of unsaid words, Mary gently pressed her arm, a silent reminder to stay grounded and keep moving forward through the haze of emotions.

A striking figure emerged from a sea of pale faces, each contrasting sharply with the deep ebony of his skin, which seemed to cradle the sun's golden rays. He towered above the crowd in stature and the mysterious aura surrounding him. The crown on this ebony king was a wide-brimmed black straw hat, hand-woven by him, accentuating the smoothness of his bald pate. The hat cast a darker shadow over his sharp features, which were defined by high cheekbones and a strong jawline—a blend of determination and grace that was impossible to ignore. The only reflection of age was the wavy, Santa-white goatee framing his smile, which hinted at stories filled with wisdom, warmth, and a playful twinkle, suggesting a life rich with adventures yet to be recounted. His physique was lean yet muscular, a testament to a life spent engaging with the world under the sun, defying typical assumptions about his years—perhaps fourscore, or even more. Each step the man took was carried out with assured self-pride; the air around him blessed him with vitality, throwing down the gauntlet to time itself. As he crossed the road, dust swirled around his feet like a sparkling halo, lifting into the sunlight filtering through the leaves above, creating an enchanting dance of particles. The heavy thud of his boots echoed off the road, steady as a heartbeat, mingled with the distant murmur of the crowd, daring them to look away.

The crowd was fraught with mixed thoughts about this man, aside from their loathing for the moment and the women before them. He carried the weight of suffering and the promise of countless untold stories. "Emma!" Mary shouted, her body jerked, her fingers digging into the palm of Emma's hand, compelling the man to turn his gaze their way. His eyes drifted upward to the ominous gray cloud above the church as if it bore silent witness to the unfolding drama below. A sly smirk trickled at the corners of his lips, a tell that the cloud was not there to release rain, but shared a knowing. Emma's hand flew to her mouth in disbelief. At the same time, next to her, Debra-Ann's expression brimmed with excitement, her eyes nearly bulging as they followed the direction of Mary's frantic look, caught in a headwind of bewilderment.

"I see him, Mary!" Emma finally exclaimed, her body vibrating with anticipation as she prepared for the whirlwind of emotions about to unfold.

"Straw Hat!" Debra-Ann shouted excitedly, arms spread wide as she ran toward him. Leaves swirled around her feet as she dashed past the majestic maple tree. With an explosive leap, she hurled herself into Straw Hat's arms, the impact ringing out with a hearty grunt that erupted in surprise and unmistakable familiarity. It had been far too long since they had embarked on their hunting and fishing adventures together, especially after the void left by Grand Michael's absence. In that instant, Straw Hat's rugged, beaming grin illuminated his face while crinkling the corners of his eyes and filling the moment with an intensity that crackled in the air. "You seein' that, Mary?" Emma gasped. Her voice was low but laced with jealousy. "She knows Straw Hat. A bit too close... feels like family, I'd say." A pang of longing tugged at Emma's heart, heavy with the swirl of her emotions, as she grappled with the bittersweet beauty of the moment.

How can Straw Hat share such joy, holdin' my grandchild in his embrace while I stand apart, longing to touch her hand for the first time?

A burning sensation stabbed Emma in the chest, and a green monster was growing inside her. "How you be knowin' this old Billy Goat?" she asked, her voice trembling slightly like a leaf caught in a gentle breeze. Debra-Ann nestled her head against Straw Hat's sturdy side, her fingers woven tightly around his waist as if seeking solace in the moment's warmth. Her soft, drowsy voice fluttered like a delicate whisper through the air, betraying her reluctance to pull away from this cherished reunion.

"Some years back," Debra-Ann began, her smile fading as her gaze drifted to the worn earth beneath her feet, memories flooding her mind with vivid clarity. "Straw Hat took my pa down from that big oak tree by the riverside before me, and Grand Michael stumbled upon it all. He cleaned him up afterward—made him look as if he were merely napping before bringing him home for a proper rest."

Debra-Ann fought back tears as she guided the conversation, her heart aching with the weight of remembrance. "That hound dog had been Straw Hat's friend first; he had followed Lancelot down that twisted road, only for Lancelot to return two days later, drenched in blood, though none of it his own."

"After that, Straw Hat turns out of nowhere like a shadow. I get into a fight at school; he there like he had known it was gonna happen, showin' me fightin' moves, guiding me on what punch to throw. Soon, he was just family to me and Grand Michael." Debra-Ann's face brightened with a smile as she gazed up at Straw Hat, her heart swelling with gratitude. Emma's expression shifted as she glared at Straw Hat and marched closer, determination etched on her features.

"How you be... down from dat angry mountain so early in the season?" she demanded with piercing fierceness. Straw Hat held her unwavering gaze, then subtly nodded toward Mary before shifting his gaze to the brooding gray clouds lingering above. The intensity in his eyes softened as he turned his attention back to Emma, choosing not to dwell on the snow-white strands of hair atop her head that mirrored his chin; instead, he focused on the once-little girl perched on his back. He wrapped her in a gentle embrace, enveloping her in warmth, and whispered soothing words to calm her racing thoughts.

"She is ready for whatever comes her way, just like her grandmother; she is strong and only growing stronger," Straw Hat grinned as he spoke close to her ear, a flicker of pride in his voice. "She got the spirit of a warrior, fights like a man, and can think like one when the need arises."

Debra-Ann observed the troubled look etched on Miss Emma's face. Her heart felt heavy with the weight of unspoken sorrow. The burden of grief lingered in the air, palpable and thick, yet the tension began to dissolve as Miss Emma nestled her head against Straw Hat's chest. Her arms hung down at her side, her body slack. She stood there, his heartbeat was comforting, pulling her back to cherished memories. Debra-Ann laced her fingers under her chin and frowned. "You be a might bit friendly with Straw Hat, Miss Emma?" She shifted her gaze to the dusty ground as she waited for a response, the corners of her mind racing with thoughts. Debra-Ann gaped at the two, a fluttery feeling striking her belly, "You two family, ain't ya" she exclaimed. Standing nearby and rubbing the back of her neck, Mary shifted her weight from one foot to the other.

The air crack'ed with a strange mix of anxious anticipation. A cold tremor shot down Pastor James's back, slamming the heavy church doors shut with a force that raced through the bustling streets like a clap of thunder. Mary hurried to Debra-Ann's side, casting a cautious glance back as she moved, her heart racing. Most of the colored congregation scattered like startled birds, wings flapping in a panic, while others averted their gazes, choosing to fix their eyes on the ground as if trying to escape the charged atmosphere. Everything was muffled, except for the rhythmic thud of hooves pounding in Straw Hat's eardrums. His ears perked up, and the hairs on his forearms stood at attention. Emma stepped back from Straw Hat, her complexion turning ghostly as her motherly instincts surged. She placed herself between Debra-Ann and the danger, who stood wide-eyed in the middle of the brewing storm, unaware of the threats just beyond their fragile bubble of safety.

A large, burly man swaggered down the cobblestone street, his imposing frame draped in layers of leather that creaked with each confident step. His glossy black Mustang gleamed ominously in the fading light. The polished pony pranced through town with an air of defiance, its sleek form a fitting steed for the man rallying his eclectic posse comitatus. His imposing figure bobbed to the Mustang's trot, hood that struggled to contain the wild waves of his vibrant auburn beard. Each exposed strand caught the golden glint of the setting sun, creating a fiery halo around his rugged features as he led a motley crew. Straw Hat watched intently from the corner of the bustling square, his keen, observant eyes tracing the ragged edges of the dingy white robes and hoods draped over the eerie, faceless figures trailing behind the burly man. As the group drew nearer, Straw Hat tilted his chin from beneath the wide brim of his well-worn black straw hat, allowing a confident grin to escape; it shone with a mischievous glimmer, thanks to the gold tooth that flickered like a clandestine jewel. For a fleeting moment, their gazes locked—two titans sizing each other up in the dimming light. The burly man's ears reddened, and he lifted his chin a notch to stare down at the colored folks like bugs he wished to smash. His hand rested comfortably on the revolver holstered at his hip. Nearby, Emma and Mary both sighed as they laced their fingers together, standing between Debra-Ann and the parade of hooded cowards. Straw Hat remained fixated until the last horse in the strange procession faded from view, leaving a swirling trail of dust dancing in the wake of their departure. Finally, breaking the evening hush with a steady and commanding voice, he spoke, "I see Lancelot, I send him home, Debra-Ann. Now, you women folk best be on your way; this town's about to become a hellscape come sundown." His words hung in the air, heavy with a sense of impending doom, urging them to leave before darkness swallowed the streets.

CHAPTER TWO

NO GOOD MOTHER

EMMA'S HAND ROSE to block the brightness of the midday sun. She hissed urgently to Mary, drawing her attention to the sight of Helen, Debra-Ann's unpardonable mother, entering the General store. She gripped Mary's arm, almost piercing her skin while marching across the bustling road. Manhandled, Mary dug in the heels of her patched-up soles. Still, her feet plowed gravel and soft dirt, mule-driven, her arm flailed like a child not wanting any part of the school. Emma's battle was won when they reached the steps before the store's door. They gathered among other colored folks, all with their heads down, hoping for no trouble.

"Stop, Emma," Mary's eyes blazed, snatching her arm back to her bosom and clutching the gathering of her dress's collar around her neck in her fist. *Mary wanted to protect her dignity and body, but it was too late. They had drawn the dark, hateful eyes of three old white men, engulfed in the haze of their stench of armpit and stale tobacco, flies dare not travel through. Perched in rockers on the store's porch, these men looked down and held colored folks back with stare and stench.* Wanting no part of the ruckus the two old ladies created, the gathered colored folks separated like the Red Sea, exposing Emma and Mary. "We can't go in there," Mary mumbled, then cut eyes at the old men. One of the old men, Elmer, who wore suspenders over a tattered, stained armpit undershirt, moved to the edge of his seat. He pulled his corncob pipe out of his mouth, peered down at the two old ladies, and smirked.

"That's right, darkie. Listen to your friend," Elmer hissed. "Only one of you thievin', stank niggers at a time." He looked contemptuous, his lips curling into a sneer, and he sighed heavily. At the same time, he directed a sharp gaze at the man sitting to his right. His friend, Fred, a frail elderly man with a toothless grin and a slack-jawed expression, slowly returned Elmer's intense gaze. The only sound in the stillness was the rhythmic creaking of Fred's old rocking chair, its wooden frame protesting with each sway. Fred's vacant stare drifted across the shaded porch, highlighted by the soft smacking of his gums—a sound that hinted at his growing annoyance.

"What?" Fred pleaded, his voice barely above a whisper, yet at the brim with dumbfounded frustration.

"Stop rocking, yah ol' fool," Elmer shrieked, his frustration bubbling. He sprang to his feet, exaggerating the motion as he tucked his thumbs under the frayed edges of his suspenders. He strutted back and forth like a proud rooster on display. A deep crease formed between his brows, shadows darkening his furrowed forehead.

"I'm tryna keep my eye on these black heifers," he added,

gesturing with irritation as he spoke. Fred's cheeks flushed pink as he jerked back in his chair and pointed at a sign above his head.

"Only one nigger, one red skin, or one Mexican at a time, yah dumb niggers," he shouted, then looked at Elmer for reassurance. His gruff voice rumbled through the air, causing the gathering of black folks to quiver with unease. Many of them shuffle away, their movements portraying frustration and fear. Emma's head drooped in annoyance, which she masked as best as she could, while Mary's head hung low out of sheer terror. I don't see why we wait until sundown to have fun, wear hoods... we the law... we the righteousness, Elmer lectured. He stopped his pacing and glared at Mary and Emma. Heads still bowed, the two slowly retreated, like the others, to follow the path they knew Helen would take to get home.

"White folks take jobs from us, not want before that Great Depression hit, gotta spend little money we got in they store, huh? Think we don't know they make us pay more for same?" Emma mumbled as she slowly stomped up the road. Mary's footsteps clawed against the dirt road, her stride brisk and purposeful, yet she lingered a step behind Emma.

"Damn it, Emma, slow down," Mary fumed. Her eyes flashing, her mouth twisting into an ugly sneer, as she watched Emma's dress ride up, revealing more of her legs than fitting for their surroundings. Her eyes widened in disbelief as the dress continued to rise, exposing her buttocks.

"Miss Emma," Mary called out sharply, her voice a mix of urgency and concern. "This ain't the time or the place for that. If it can't wait, you'd best make your way to the tall grass."

Emma glanced over her shoulder at the old men once, then

back to Mary. Emma's eyes glazed over with a haze of relief. She grinned.

"I believe the breeze is gonna carry right nice, yah ol' coots." Emma grimaced once, then again, before her body relaxed along with a satisfied smile. "Them be the beans we ate last night. Emma beamed at Mary, who covered her nose and mouth with her hand. That stank right there, gonna burn their nose hairs." Mary rushed to walk a step ahead of Emma as they continued.

"You gonna get lynched, Emma! Me too," Mary hissed. Emma began to measure Mary with her eyes as her lips slowly curled upwards into a grimace when the general store's door slammed, drawing her attention.

Helen's head bowed as soon as she left the store, tightly clutching her heavy bag filled with salt pork, lard, rice, flour, sugar, and candy for Charlie's insatiable sweet tooth. She skittishly made her way across the road, carefully timing her steps between passing horse and car. As Mary observed Helen approaching, she murmured to Emma, "Here she comes."

Her thoughts swirling like the gentle tune she hummed, skillfully steering the treacherous stretch of road where horse manure and cow pies littered the ground, resembling uneven cobblestones strewn carelessly across asphalt. With her head down, she quickened her pace, entirely focused on her path, intentionally avoiding eye contact with the two women nearby,

"Afternoon, ladies," Helen greeted them as she scurried without slowing down. Emma's hand instinctively twitched as if to strike Helen, but Mary held her back.

"Ladies!?" Emma replied. Her eyes flashed, and her mouth twisted into an ugly sneer, "We near raised you grown; helped your grandmother raise *your* mother. You stop and show us respect when you see us." Helen's head drooped to its lowest as she mumbled,

"Sorry, ma'am. I just need to get home and have dinner ready; Charlie likes salt pork in his greens." Desperately, Helen looked up, hoping to find understanding in the eyes of the two women, but her plea fell on deaf ears.

"You ain't no slave; Lincoln fix that some time now. Dinner be warm or not," Emma insisted. Helen inched forward like she wanted to be the first off, the line in a foot race. Mary touched Helen's shoulder;

"Child, them chains on you ain't real, not on Debra-Ann, yet," Mary begged Helen's wit."

Emma sneered as she dressed Helen from head to toe. She knew Mary's word went deaf; saw how broken Helen's spirit was; it would let the world and everyone in it walk all over her, and she had no time for it.

Emma stepped closer to Helen, placing herself between her and Mary. Emma's eyes met Helen's directly, staring, tethering to her soul if possible. Still, Mary continued.

"I know you see it in Charlie, child. That man of yours has the evil nature of dem slave owners shackled to his soul. He jes like'em, doing the same evil," Mary said, her words begging from a place of knowing. Still, Emma just glared. *She believed her granddaughter had been touched.* "They took women, men, took children, from their beds, from the fields, raped them, left 'em broken, left me broken, can't be fixed. Charlie that! You see it," Mary roared.

Helen's shame pedaled her feet backward until she thought herself safe. Only then would she turn and run off, disappearing down the road without glancing back. Emma's stomach heaved, and her morning meal teased her to cough back up. She staggered off the road, absorbed by the dense, swaying green grass. Mary held Emma's waist, a steadfast presence amid the unrest Emma, bearing wounds and crying from the weight of injuries that spanned more than half a century, felt as though the pain was unfolding in the present moment. Emma gazed up at Mary,

"Your words cut deep. Ran her off, you see." Collapsing, Mary knelt beside Emma and cradled her fragile form. Mary gently brushed away the strands of hair and wiped the tears that covered Emma's face. Emma's voice trembled with desperation as she asked,

"My blood don't know me, never gonna know me, what do I do now?"

Mary sat quietly, her jaw clenched and her body rocking. A flicker of agony passed behind her closed lids. "This world stole my true nature, who I aim to be. Hold my tongue on many things, tryna keep us safe and alive, while you let go… well, much as a colored woman can. *Mary gazed in the direction Helen ran.*

"I thought 'do it for love'. It be love… fear more, same fear in Helen; It gonna send her to hell, she needs to know who leads her. Don't think you know any better, Emma…Give a colored child away… In this world!? We know they a nigger, gonna hear it their whole life. A colored boy… should look up and see his mother's love smiling back at him, first thing. Not a Helen ready to spread her legs, thinking that be love, Mary scolded.

Emma's head slowly rose from Mary's lap. Mary's eyebrows

arched upwards. *Her cheeks puckered as if she'd tasted a sour lemon.*

"Calm those feathers, woman. I ain't no better." *Mary's voice resonated with a deep, growling timbre as if she were channeling every ounce of strength within her to project an imposing presence. It was the voice that could rattle the bravest of souls, meant to intimidate, much like someone preparing to confront a formidable Grizzly bear. Each word rolled out with a weight that suggested she was not just speaking but summoning a fierceness that demanded respect and attention.* "Knew you were wrong, but I said nothing. Kept my mouth quiet, even to you, like a good nigger. Close my eyes, I be Helen sometimes." Mary sighs, "I was beside myself when you lay with Grand Michael, and…was like the sting of the whip when you gave him that child you two made six weeks deferred. Pondered it for a long time… said nothing. Woulda gone but being like I is." Mary brushed the tear rolling down her cheek like she was flicking a fly. "It was me that boy smiled at after he off your teat, every day… cleaned him, while you lay in dat bed mending.

"He was my kin, too, Emma," Mary shrieked.

Mary's quivering bottom lip betrayed her inner strength as she repeatedly pounded the ground beside her. "Thought we had time, someday tell Michael and Debra-Ann we kin, we loved them first," she sobbed. The grass was uprooted; loose dirt dangled from her clenched, raised fist. Tufts of loose soil cascaded from her fingers like dark confetti, as the rich scent of damp earth filled the air around her.

"I was there, Emma!" Mary confessed, her eyes narrowing to slits as she spoke. Emma's nose scrunched up,

"W-what you talkin' bout," Emma asked.

"Saw Michael swinging from that tree," Mary quickly answered, "...Cut him down while Straw Hat held him." Emma's face grew pale, and she grabbed her neighbor's arm to brace herself to sit. Mary wincing at the touch, before a deep sigh.

"Helped clean him up, then hid behind a tree in the woods when Straw Hat bring him home to Grand Michael." Shaken, Emma's hand flew to cover her mouth. Her words were muffled as she whimpered.

"My baby," Emma repeated while rocking back and forth.

"Every time I lay eyes on Debra-Ann, I hear that scream she made seeing her pa, dead. Goes through me. Can't tell you, I hurt, but I hurt," Mary continued. "It chills me, that scream does; I reckon she was beside me." Mary's tears streamed as her rocking slowed. "I was alone in them woods, Emma. Hugged that tree like it was you. I looked around it and saw Grand Michael. His rage... just beneath his eyes, but he stayed quiet. Saw him kiss Michael's forehead like he was the baby he just put to bed. Then, Grand Michael sat in his rockin` chair staring into the woods, blood boiled as he is rockin' in that chair. I know more death comin', his or who hangs his child. Can't say what said, reckon Straw Hat reminds him Michael be his blood, too.

"See Straw Hat reach in his coat and pull out a white hood, drop in front of Lancelot. Posit he tells Grand Michael he gonna make it right before he turns, and he runs off behind that old hound."

"Emma?" Mary whispered, "Grand Michael's rage, my rage. I be tracking Straw Hat when Lancelot found the white men's camp."

Ducking beneath low-hanging branches and leaping over scattered rocks, Mary felt a surge of terror, as if she were chasing her freedom that seemed just out of reach. "I could hear bullets cut them down like a sharp blade through tall grass," Mary said. All of the color once again drained from Emma's face, and she desperately searched for something to support her. Beads of sweat trickled down Mary's flushed cheeks, and her heart pounded in her chest, keeping pace with the rhythm of her hurried breaths. As she finally burst through the dense forest some ways behind Straw Hat, "I see him standing over the last white man alive, " she confessed. "Can't say what's said, reckon he begs for his life," Mary rasped.

The white man had already been dead by the time Mary reached the camp, leaving only ghosts of their encounter in the hushed twilight. Still, Straw Hat yelled at him, "Go back in time! Save my blood from hanging! Do that!"

Mary steadied herself to one knee, her heart racing as she scanned the landscape around her. The tall grass swayed ominously in the wind, creating a fluid dance that sent shivers down her spine. "Best we be gettin' home," she said, her voice firm despite the unease coursing through her. Resolved, she rose to her feet and started walking, her shoes crunching on the gravel, giving the impression that more than just the two of them were on that road. Struggling, Emma made it to her feet, hop-hurried to catch up the pace, before matching Mary's steps.

"What is it, Mary?" Emma asked, her voice laced with curiosity. Mary glanced nervously, as dark imaginings filled her head. Shuddering uncontrollably, she leaned in closer, her voice dropping to a ghostly hush.

"I tell Straw Hat, we strip dem men down, make it look like they be a bunch of dogs in heat for each other. Only one of the men gets away; he been squattin` behind a tree doing his business when Straw Hat surprise dem others. Lancelot sniffed him and followed the trail back to the man's home. There, under the moonlight in that stable, Lancelot jumped, let loose his rage like a lone wolf closing in on its prey, I tell ya. *The air filled with the sounds of struggle as he mauled the man, flesh tearing like rags swiftly and decisively, leaving no doubt about the gravity of his pursuit.* "That man was long dead when Straw Hat pulled Lancelot off… was like Lancelot feel our hurt," Mary whispered lower and more seriously than before.

"Lancelot loved Michael and Grand Michael like they be a pack, I knew that from the first… that be his rage, his hurt," Emma firmly said.

The setting sun greeted the two elderly ladies with a warm and tranquil sensation as they strolled hand in hand down the winding road. The gentle crunch of gravel underfoot was the sole sound interrupting the tranquil quietness that extended for miles around them. Emma's brow furrowed with thought, and she momentarily froze. Her gaze dropped to the ground, "So, that story about those white men—white folks trying to cover it up—couldn't be true?" she mused. Her voice was tinged with curiosity. "And the white woman they hang? Say she crazy?" Emma's question left the air around it fetid, heavy with concern. Mary released Emma's hand and folded her arms beneath her bosom. Mary sighed, taking two more steps before coming to a stop. Slowly, she turned toward Emma, her face set in a cold stare, which unnerved her.

"The cracker Lancelot ends in that barn… Well, Straw Hat

steals his wife's dirty clothes and shoes; say, 'we gonna make for sure mess don't come back on Grand Michael or no colored folks.' Have me put on them stank clothes; … shoes bout my size. I marched from that house, through the woods, rubbing her stench on every tree, rock, and bush on my way back to that camp. The grind of twigs underfoot, thought someone, followed with every step. Straw Hat have me stomp all around that camp, stand over them men like that white woman, got evil intent, catch'em sinning, shoot'em all dead. Make some tracks back to that barn, burn them clothes and that barn, and leave them shoes on the porch. Next morning, hounds go looking, find that white woman, not a vengeful nigger.

Emma blinked out of her daze as if being pulled from a deep, dark ocean, the weight of her thoughts lifting. *A lance of light burst, comforting notions once placed in Mary and Straw Hat, sending a shiver* coursing *down her spine.* Catching a glimpse of Emma's reaction, Mary furrowed her brows tightly together, concern etching lines on her forehead. "You can eye me down cold, Emma," Mary said, her voice steady yet soft, "But don't burden yourself with judgment; let that rest with the good Lord above." Mary chuckled, "You think I done wrong by that white woman? She ain't no better than the rest of them; seen her kind, too." Mary's head shook violently. "Anytime a woman thinks like a man, always be a bad one; it leads her down a troubling path." Mary squeezed her eyes shut, a wave of pain washing over her. She scrunched her nose in a reflexive grimace, her lips forming a delicate pout. Tilting her head to the side, she sought to lessen the discomfort, her brow furrowing in concentration as she tried to find a moment of relief, only to fail.

33

"But they got women's feelings, so it don't work," she callously added.

Emma stopped walking; her stance was stiff, and her eyes narrowed in concentration.

"Still, Mary," Emma yelled. "It should have been me. What if you got caught?"

Mary snorted and threw her hands up, turning to face Emma. Her voice carried a hint of frustration, and her head shook in disbelief. "After all, I just tell you, you think I fear death, Emma? I caught, I dead. You caught, you dead. I ain't fightin' to hold on to this world. Ain't made for colored folks." Mary's shoulders slumped. So, it don't matter who is dead first," she resigned. Her feet felt heavy, dragging along the uneven path to their shabby shack nestled in the woods. Emma let out a weary groan as she climbed the creaking stairs ahead of Mary.

"I get dinner you look plum tuckered. Guess, twas' all that pain you been holden all dem years." Emma said. Mary's heart clenched at Emma's dejected tone, causing her to pause midstride just two steps behind Emma. Mary placed one hand on the third step, hesitating, then chuckled as she brushed away the settled dust with her other hand.

"You feel that white woman was wronged, think she not deserve what comes her way? Think maybe you don't know who I is?" she mused, her voice laced with disdain. Mary gathered her dress, tucked it neatly against her legs, and sat down. With a cheeky smirk dancing on her lips, she gave a subtle nod and gestured invitingly to the space beside her. "Sit," Mary requested… "Seems like you think only men do us wrong." Emma sighed while doing the same, smoothing her dress before sitting next to her. Emma glanced at Mary, whose face glistened in the last light of the setting sun. Her chin lifted invitingly, as if she expected a kiss; Emma's brow knitted with concern.

"You pining over some man, Mary?" Emma suspected. Her hand went to her waist as her foot tapped in judgment.

"Not like you with Grand Michael," Mary snapped. "No snake ever slid through my grass, but I hold dear a man, well 'boy,' sometime back..." Mary's smile briefly challenged the sun as she remembered a boy, Daniel, who had given her a hug she still feels. Emma joined in watching the setting sun, captivated by the fiery hues that painted the sky in shades of melting oranges, yellows, and pinks. The air between them filled with unspoken thoughts until Mary cleared her throat, breaking the silence that had settled like a gentle fog around them, and finally found her words.

"When I's just a child, bout five years old, ol' Massa John bought some men slaves from this plantation in Kentucky. This one slave, named Daniel... tall, with muscles big from working the fields," Mary marveled. "Still, looking into his eyes, you could tell he was a boy, maybe 16.

"Well, that wagon parade dem men slaves around the plantation like they be prize stallions. Daniel jumped off the wagon like he gonna run away, only he run to me." *Tears stream down Mary's cheeks.* "He took the whip while holding me tight, calling me 'Mary.' Was only when he dredged up it be six years last time he saw Mary, his sister, she be bout thirteen, that he let me go. Fittingly, over time, I grow fond of him, seeing as I had no one. Ol' Massa John's wife grows fond of Daniel, too, only in a different way. Seeing I spent most of my free time with him, she had me shuffle him out to the stable night after night. I know he be dead before winter comes, and he knows it. Every time I fetch him, he tells me, 'Don't look in dat barn, just two animals, nothin' more.'

"She is with his child; she says Daniel attacked her; she is scared to tell. That's months later when the baby comes out as dark as me. The night before he run, he comes to me, say, God, let me feel love again, the first day he saw me." He tells me his name, Daniel, means, "God is my judge," say, always let that be it with me." Mary sighs. Daniel caught a free man in Delaware and walked behind a wagon back down here. Ol' Massa John says, 'hanging too good.' Daniel, they feed him to the hogs while he is alive." Tears streaming down her cheeks, Mary continues, "Them Missus' evil, keep their wicked hidden till they get caught, then say they try to fight off but still taken by a buck." Disbelief sways Mary's head from side to side. "They gonna be Daniel's, always."

Emma's eyes fall to her feet, the sun's shine resting above her shins. She looked up at Mary, her head slowly shaking like the answer to a question not asked was no.

"Mary, your name is always Mary, named after your momma," Emma asked.

Mary nodded, "Yes." "Cut the cord, lay me on my momma's chest. They tell me, I feel her loss... I stop crying. I believe the same ache, the same pain that settles deep in my chest as my momma when Daniel is gone," she said. Mary smiled, but her eyes glistened with an unspoken sorrow. *Daniel was my uncle—a man whose presence lingered in her warm and bittersweet memories.* Emma stood, looking down at Mary as the last of the sun settled. Her voice was filled with shame and sorrow when she spoke,

"I see to dinner," Emma whispered.

"Emma," Mary called out. Emma paused as she reached out for the doorknob. "I will be joinin` you tonight when you feed Lancelot and peek in Debra-Ann's window."

CHAPTER THREE
HELEN'S CHOICE

DEBRA-ANN TRUDGED ALONG the familiar dirt road that wound its way toward home, her hands resting defiantly on her hips, prepared to deliver a well-deserved scolding. "Where on this side of Mississippi is that ol' hound?" she muttered, her voice laced with concern. "Must be finishing off some jackrabbit."

Lancelot was tough, unlike most hound dogs his age, who were little more than skin and old bones. The thought brought Debra-Ann a flicker of relief. Still, a heavy sigh escaped her lips. "Lancelot, Lancelot!" she called out repeatedly, her voice piercing the quiet evening as she walked further down the well-trodden path. Only the unsettling silence loomed, gnawing at her insides. Never had she faced a day without Lancelot by her side, and as she scanned the surroundings, her gaze flicked nervously from the dusty road, waiting for the familiar sight of his paws, to the vast blue sky above, searching for any ominous signs, such as circling buzzards. A heavy weight settled in her chest, a self-assured feeling that something was wrong. *They ain't gonna pick his bones if that be it,* urgency quickening her pace.

Standing on the top step of her porch, Debra-Ann watched as a gray cloud chased the vibrant hues of sunset across the horizon. Her voice, weary from calling for Lancelot, hesitated when Helen's words sliced through the still air, cold and unforgiving as her expression pulled her attention from the woods. "I can hear you hollering as soon as I come off the main road, child; that old hound ain't come by now; he dead."

Hot tears streamed down Debra-Ann's cheeks as Helen continued, "It's just a dog… just an old hound dog, three legs in the grave, child," she sneered, bitterness spilling from her lips like poison. Debra-Ann wiped the tears away with the back of her hand, their source unknown to her—maybe her fears, she thought. Helen knew her words held no power. Yet, still, she tried to sting Debra-Ann with the same venomous truth Emma had used against her, and the jab was evident. Debra-Ann's eyes, sharp and piercing, met Helen's with an intensity that rendered her silent.

"Lancelot, be the only family I got in this world. And ifen he be dead, I glad he finds rest from your evil." Although saying the words churned something deep within her, her voice held firm. Debra-Ann kept her cold stare on Helen until Helen turned away. Love for most things was lynched along with Debra-Ann's father, even her childhood. Shame didn't touch her most days; this day was no different. Helen shook her head in exasperation as she retreated to the front door, tossing her words back over her shoulder like daggers.

"You done beat up, scare off every boy dat comes roaster around here for ya. Maybe you like dem old witches Mary and Emma," she taunted, a mocking snicker escaping her. "Get in here and skin those potatoes. Charlie, be home soon," she ordered, slamming the screen door with a force that rattled the frame. Debra-Ann's head drooped as if the world's weight had settled upon her shoulders. "Want me to be like you, Helen, blackeyes and bruised? Got you more raccoon than a raccoon," she shouted. Debra-Ann fell forward slightly, clutching the porch rail, a surge of pain welling up inside like a storm about to break as she glanced over to the corner at her Grand Michael's rocking chair. "That be my Grand Michael's door you slam; his house, his land—not Helen's, not Charlie's. Now it be mine," she whispered, the words barely escaping her lips as she felt the loss and longing swirl around her.

Some hours had passed since sunset, and the shack was now faintly lit by two lanterns. Still, Helen sat with her hands clasped in her lap at the dinner table, three plates of food untouched before her. Her body ceased the slight rocking it had engaged in to glare at Debra-Ann as she came in from outside, slamming the door with such force that the windows quivered.

"Come eat," Helen insisted, her voice sharp, firm, and unwavering.

"*You* eat!" Debra-Ann quickly responded, then marched to her bedroom, bolting the door behind her. "Eat... eat", Debra-Ann mocked.

"Heifer knows she gonna sit there and drool over her food. Want me to do the same?" Debra-Ann mumbled under her breath. The old springs of her bed groaned as she flopped down. "Huh. Must got some bees in her bonnet," she yells. Helen sat at the wooden table, absorbing her daughter's words washing over her like cold water pouring down her back. Nevertheless, her gaze remained fixed on her plate, and although her stomach growled with hunger, she understood the unspoken rule of waiting for Charlie to join them at the table. She didn't mind the hurtful words; it was the swollen, shut eyes that blurred her vision for weeks at a time. Her mind drifts through memories, much like a slave's dreams of freedom fading with time or the moment before death. Seated across from her, haunting her hunger, is an image of Charlie, his tall, dark-skinned frame smiling, daring her fork to touch food before he says. The muscles in his arms were thick and robust, forged not only by labor but also by the burden of his truth; their twitch was her flinch.

Every thought that flickered through Charlie's mind and every word he spoke felt like deceiving shadows, wrapping themselves around the truth in layers of haziness. Only in their imposing stature did he find common ground with Debra-Ann's father; otherwise, they were worlds apart. Suddenly, the bolt on Debra-Ann's door rattled free, swinging open with a creak. "Make you two plates, eat one, and stare at the other!" she shouted before the door shut. "Woman's belly is growling so loud that mine is answering," Debra-Ann muttered angrily, her voice fading as she stepped away from the door. Yet, it still carried a bittersweet humor that lingered in the air, even as her worry for Lancelot subsided when he huffed and plopped down under her window. "Too old to be roosting up with them hounds, you got enough kin to fill you a town," she kidded.

CHAPTER FOUR
STRAW HAT IN HAND

STRAW HAT STOOD at the heart of the winding road; his eyes fixed on a solitary gray cloud drifting determinedly along the horizon. He trailed behind, sensing it had a life of its own, floating down the road, swirling over the sparkling stream, and billowing across the colorful meadow. Straw Hat froze in his tracks as the cloud began to change shape, size, and shades of gray, almost approaching black. He was sure the cloud carried a message; an unsettling thought nagged at him that something terrible might have occurred or was about to. Yet, he followed the cloud's divine path, pausing frequently, questioning its intent as he called out for Lancelot. Each shout startled the wildlife, causing them to freeze or flee before dissolving into the peaceful surroundings. With no pack alerting howls from his four-legged companion, he grew weary, lifted a hand to wipe the sweat from his brow, and reflected on Lancelot's fate and his own as sunset approached. "Hmmm, there be a miracle, mayhem, or perhaps a blend of both tonight," he mused.

It was long rumored that Straw Hat was a child slave, forced to fight like a rooster in a cockfight or a dog in a pit, battling against larger boys some two years after emancipation. He bears scars of heavy lashes laid thick across his back, resembling a tiger's stripes. Still, his body was not broken; it lay with muscles bulging through his shirt. Years later, he appeared much younger than his actual age. Straw Hat's gleaming baldness made you squint, like trying to stare at the sun, dulled by the gray clouds. The clouds hovered directly above, slowly turning black before swallowing him like the "great fish" that swallowed Jonah. Amid the darkness, Straw Hat still searched for light.

"I have no tears to shed for a life I did not ask for, nor for this skin I learned to see as my curse," Straw Hat professed. His voice was steady and calm, a serene certainty shining in his gaze. "I've come to see this as the truth in a world of lies. So, if this is to be my end, I thank you for granting me my peace."

Amid the air-siphoning mist, Straw Hat sat peacefully, his wide-brimmed hat cradled gently in his hands. Closing his eyes, he surrendered to something more powerful than he, preparing to confront whatever destiny had in store. A metallic scent hung in the air, sharp and unsettling, as visions began to flicker before him. They painted a picture of him as a wild child, a feral creature, a savage ruled by primal instincts, merging past and present in a haunting dance of memories.

His body tensed, arching backward as if pulled by something not of this world, his wide-brimmed hat tumbled from fingers splayed loosely in surprise. It cascaded to the ground in a forgotten heap. In that moment, his body and mind surged back to a distant past, flooded with vivid and sinister shrines that begged to be erased. It was the paralyzing sting of the whip used to drive the beasts of the fields that spurred the child Straw Hat to combat. His feet shuffled reluctantly over the straw-covered floor of the makeshift fighting pit, where he locked eyes with the fierce, predatory gaze of older slave boys from nearby plantations. They were all too aware that they were merely entertainment fodder before the men slaves fought. Still, the savagery was the same, and death was a possibility. Straw Hat, prey for predators yet fierce in spirit, embodied the essence of an agile cat caught in a dogfight. Remarkably agile, his blows were comparable to 'death by a thousand cuts.' The crowd roared their approval for the violent hearts he represented, and every match culminated in a flurry of coins raining down into the ring for the victor. Straw Hat would stuff his shirt and pants with straw as he collected the coins. The frenzied action was seen as the nonsense of an untamed slave child.

"The nigger child has done gone mad. His master will have to shoot that stupid nigger. When he starts losing, they taunt him. "Guess they hang him out in the cornfield to scare the crows," the drunken crowd of gamblers jested, their voices mingling in a chaotic blend of cheers and curses, the air thick with anticipation and the scent of spilled drinks. And in that course of discourse, he earned the moniker "the Scarecrow" long before he became widely recognized as "Straw Hat."

Now, becoming infamously known as Scarecrow pained him beyond the experience of enslavement. Yet, still a boy, he was feared by other slaves, unable to enjoy the fleeting moments of wonder that they took for granted. Straw Hat emerged from the increasingly brutal battles as a fierce warrior, marked by a legacy that spanned across lands and people separated by a generation and a vast, turbulent sea. The farther north he was taken to battle, the more he learned about the difficult roads they traveled, the blind spots under the bridges they crossed that slave catchers overlooked, and the peculiar gray cloud that seemed to befriend him as it hovered above. This silent guide appeared to shadow his every move, surrounding him with an aura of mystery. Straw Hat welcomed the distraction and whatever might come of it.

Only Straw Hat understood the irony of packing his ragged clothes with straw, using it as padding for the grueling, bone-jarring journeys in the back of the rickety wagon. In the stillness of the night, that same gray cloud remained, studying him as he studied it. And, as a chill settled around him, Straw Hat would lie beneath, learning the vast expanse of twinkling stars, his breath misting in the cold air. He found solace in gazing up at the luminous moon while each dawn brought a flickering warmth from the rising sun in the east, wrapping him in golden rays. And when it rained, it hid his tears. Straw Hat stared at the clouds and prayed for forgiveness and lightning to strike him dead in the same breath.

Straw Hat: guilt-ridden, battle-weary, and lonely, he desperately wanted to somehow make atonement for his acts of violence against his people and began crafting the most exquisite straw hats to screen field hands from the scorching sun as a hoodwinking of their masters and the overseer that did their bidding. Straw Hat used the same crimson straw stained with blood that lined his clothing as a testament to his unwavering hope and determination for his people to achieve independence. He wove hidden maps pointing east or north to Pennsylvania and Canada, guiding the enslaved on every plantation he traveled who dared more than cry freedom.

Only a fourteen-year-old child, Straw Hat, was tall, and his body was lean with muscles from countless hours of forced training and fighting. He stood resolute, ready to face death in the pit, a bloodstained battleground where he now faced men, proving his mettle with every clash. He no longer carried the burden of the traitorous Scarecrow, the soulless boy warrior; he embraced a new identity: Straw Hat, a black Freemason, a symbol of hope and help among the slaves.

In that moment, Straw Hat knelt on all fours, his fingers sifting through the cool earth, desperately searching for his beloved hat. When he finally found it, he stared down longingly, brushed off the dirt with reverence, and carefully placed it atop his head. He hoped to escape the terrifying reflections that patrolled the darkness like a slave catcher with a hound. He gazed skyward to catch a glimpse of a solitary star, its light shimmering faintly through the thick veil of fog. A smile crept across his face, but it faltered as his eyes dropped to the rough ground beneath him. "Are you now my Pharaoh?" he bemoaned; his voice tinged with bitterness. "What do you command of this humble, Hebrew slave laboring in the heart of 'your' Egypt? Must I now make bricks without straw?"

The air buzzed with crickets chirping, hinting that it was night outside his prison. A calming scent of fresh country air hung heavily around him, taunting him with the promise of freedom that lay just out of reach. Deep within, an ache coursed through Straw Hat, weighed down by the betrayal from the cloud he had once regarded as an ally.

"We were torn from our people, stripped of our freedom; whipped, raped, enslaved to serve, then bow at your feet. This was the only path left for me!" he cried, combating the oppressive silence. As the weight of his inner pain overwhelmed him, he sank to his knees.

"Why did you go away …? Leave *me*?" he pleaded into the dark hollowness, his voice breaking in the stillness of the night.

The ominous black cloud swelled around Straw Hat, clenching him in its suffocating embrace like a hand slowly but deliberately closing into an angry fist. He held his breath, eyes tightly shut, standing tall and rigid, every muscle in his body coiled with tension, bracing against the impending pressure. When he could no longer contain it, he exhaled slowly, his brows creasing as his gaze snapped into sharp focus. The image before him from his pass revealed an old white man trembling with intense fear, a tremor that seemed to resonate between them. Their intense gaze locked in a charged standoff, filled with unspoken emotions and a certainty that a power shift hung heavily between them. The white man's fury erupted like a storm of entitlement, his voice hoarse and frantic.

"I know you, nigger! They call you *Scarecrow*," he shouted. Straw Hat bared his teeth; it was the snarl of a wolf before its bite. Then, a grimacing grin slowly unfurled across Straw Hat's face, his gold tooth glinting in the flickering light of the crackling campfire, casting a warm glow on the shadows that danced across the dead bodies around them.

"You spill my blood, I spill yours," he calmly replied, a smile widening to reveal the full brilliance of his gold tooth. The old man's short, sharp breath spoke of desperation; his eyes, wide with terror, betrayed a flicker of recognition as he raised trembling hands, pleading for mercy.

"Sure do! My pappy made a fortune betting on you in that pit! All of it came to me when he died." The man's voice cracked with emotion, his initial bravado fading like smoke in the wind.

"Send me to school up north... Tell me... what can I do for you to spare my life?"

His clemency denied without a voice, the white man leaned forward. His face buried itself in his hands, where sorrow flowed freely. Straw Hat raised his gun; the tick of the hammer locking lifted the old white man's head to glare at Straw Hat. It was as if the devil himself were staring. Straw Hat shot the man dead and stood, an imposing figure, as he shouted,

"Go back in time! Save my blood from hanging...Do that!" Tears welled in his eyes, glistening in the firelight like droplets of pure anguish. The gunshot continued to bounce across the sky as Mary rushed forward, her hand gently resting on Straw Hat's shoulder, her voice soft yet urgent.

"He can't hear you," she appealed, pulling at his arm, urging him to step back from the sea cliff of emotion. Straw Hat repeated his plea with a heavy sigh, his voice thick with longing.

"Don't matter, going back in time be easier than show-ing a colored man respect... They sacrifice them wives before they show a colored man respect," he conceded. Straw Hat's eyes fluttered open, his body instantly struggling against an immovable force around him. He felt an overwhelming sadness that wasn't his; it wafted through the cloud like an unpleasant stench.

"This is why you abandoned me," he grumbled, his tone infused with defiance and sorrow. "I do not regret!" Straw Hat boldly asserted. He confronted the ethereal figure before him, his desperation apparent in every word. "If this is true, then expose the shame within this fog... the shame that falls like rain, the tears I can now taste... Gabriel." Suddenly, an invisible weight bore down upon Straw Hat, dragging him to his knees, then forcing him flat against the cold, damp earth as if a heavy boot crushed him into the soil. Straw Hat strained against the pressure, his arms quaking under the burden, desperately trying to rise. "I remember this from my youth, before the whip from my white master," he chuckled. "... Show me... your burden... Gabriel!" he groaned, determination flaring within him. With a fierce inward resolve, he squeezed his eyes shut tighter, every muscle in his body tensing as he was slammed back against the ground, fighting against sorrow as profound as the depths of the sea.

Straw Hat's brows furrowed as the crackling sound of the campfire filled the air. Yet, his eyes remained closed while the rich tang of moonshine lingered enticingly on his lips. Then, just like that, it all faded into a void of silence.

CHAPTER FIVE

AN ANGEL'S SHAME

WITH A JUG of moonshine clutched tightly in both hands, Charlie staggered unevenly down the winding dirt road, kicking up dust and bellyaching to every sturdy tree, curious rabbit, croaking frog, and rustling leaf that danced in the gentle breeze. This Friday evening, his complaints flowed as freely as the liquor he consumed before this journey began, each word dripping with frustration about how he'd trained the next white man destined to become his boss. That Saturday, a fraught and tense mood filled a shack built on land owned by another man, now a ghost, yet haunting Charlie's manhood. And, well into the night, whimpers could be heard by a little girl bolted behind a door of safety.

As dawn broke on Sunday morning, Charlie sat in restless silence at the table, his heart simmering with frustration. It wasn't the stifling grip of his boss that ignited his anger; it was the women in his life, particularly those in a home that would never be his. He realized that by Monday, he would once again have to wear the façade of the happy nigger's mask, a make-believe smile that concealed his true self, with his shame laid bare to two women. Helen couldn't help but inwardly question the strange absence of her husband by her side, walking through their place of worship. Usually, Charlie would strut into the church like a peacock, ready to flaunt himself and catch the eye of yet another woman he would ultimately betray with. But today was different; he had chosen to heed the devil's whispers of temptation, thoughts that had taken root in his mind's most sinister, darkest corners. Urges once thought shredded by the snare of a hound dog's protection.

So, instead of seeking the counsel of God's children, Charlie meandered down the winding dirt road, glancing warily over his shoulder as he approached a familiar marker—a weathered, broken jug of moonshine half-buried in the dirt beside a gnarled tree stump. The old stump, massaged by slaves' hands in years past, bemoaned to him like haunted treasure; it represented a superstition deeply rooted in the history of the first enslaved who had courageously made their way to this underground camp to plot their daring escapes. He pushed through the encroaching weeds and thick brush towards a camp not far from a juke joint that defied the sundown raids; the undergrowth before the campsite nearly swallowed him. The air was thick with free expression in the camp until twigs snapped beneath heavy footsteps, sending sharp pulses through the dimming light. It raised chins; eyes widened like startled deer. While some instinctively moved to cradle the cold steel of shotguns, others lightly brushed their fingers over hammers and triggers, ready to draw guns from holsters. Cautiously emerging from behind a massive oak tree, Charlie lifted two jugs of moonshine high above his head as he awaited a stamp of approval for entry, his voice a mere whisper, "It's me, Ol' Charlie." The camp, filled with tense silhouettes, watched as he took slow, deliberate steps forward. Gradually, he saw the stiffened postures relax, hammers disengaging, and fingers loosening their grips as they recognized him. He nestled himself among this group of grizzled old men who preferred the warmth of corn liquor and hearty conversation by a campfire to the cold sobriety of church worship.

By nightfall, the distant strains of gospel music, clashing with Charlie's spirit, were drowned out by the lively music bellowing from the juke joint hidden deeper in the backwoods, along with the chatter and clinking of what seemed like endless jugs of moonshine. He wasn't a regular among these old men; they didn't like him at all. They could barely tolerate him, and he felt the same way about them. But with a jug of corn liquor in each hand, it was all it took to earn a welcoming smile. Soon, their weathered faces closed in around him, and the stories about him came full circle. Charlie eyed every crooked smile and grin filled with loathing; he joined in the knee-slap laughter while it relentlessly reminded him of his and the hound Lancelot's first encounter. To Charlie, this encounter, this night, was not by chance. He likened it to fishing, with his pole enchanted by fish waiting in line to be hooked. Charlie's laughs, some heartier than those around him, formed a plan, the fuel that fed the hellfire of his evil deeds already in motion. He was branded as thick-headed, mistaking his powerful physique for a path to favor from everyone he encountered. "My strong back and hands get me what I want," he often bragged, which opened doors to work, women, and a measure of respect in town. That was until that hound made them all laugh at him. Everyone who witnessed his fragile ego was at ease and eager to belittle Charlie.

"The muscle between your ears is smaller than a squirrel's nuts," an old man, overlapping his hands on a cane across the campfire, raised his chin to yell. His thought, locked and loaded for some time, was a shot across the bow, ignored. As Charlie recognized his blind truth, it was that hound dog Lancelot who had humiliated him, provoking laughter from those he still sought acceptance from. Charlie desired retribution against that hound and Debra-Ann, his master.

Now, this simple-minded man had done just that to ol' Lancelot, got the best of him. It took less than half a jug to turn the conversation to what he wanted to talk about. A grin spread across Charlie's face as his eyes darted around the camp.

It's time!

"That old Lancelot done lost his touch since he nearly tore a chunk out my ass," Charlie testified. "Ain't seen him all day, not surprised if that old hound done died up under some oak." A chuckle escaped his lips. Instantly, a whirlwind of teasing and tales erupted around the flickering campfire.

"You right, boy," another chimed. "Sure, it was funny, you standing there, with your black ass out...Pissed my pants laughing so hard!" Pissed your pants cause you old, nigger," his friend seated next to Charlie chimed. With his teeth grinding together in frustration, Charlie stared aimlessly, nodding with a forced smirk as the teasing stings hit him like the cold night air.

The eyes of that dog looked more human than animal; they

*raged as the hound stared me down, less a man. And the hairs...
all down the back of Lancelot's neck stood on end; drool streamed
from his jowls as his head swung violently from left to right. He
seemed ready to commence tearing my flesh from the bone if not
for a pat on the head from Debra-Ann,* Charlie sighed.

*I got it, "don't fuck with my family;" it was like he could smell
my cravings.*

Charlie raised the bottle of moonshine to his lips, savoring
the harsh bite of the potent liquid as it slid down his throat.
He recoiled from the liquid delight. Then, with a satisfied
grunt after thought. Charlie lowered the bottle. He quickly
brought his arm to his mouth and wiped the remains with
the sleeve of his worn gray flannel shirt, still, a glistening trail
caught the fading light. A sinister grin spread across his face,
showcasing a hint of mischief and the thrill of the night ahead
as he glanced around, his eyes gleaming with a mix of deviance
and excitement.

*Little did they know that old bloodhound, drunk on wild
berries like moonshine to a dog, his favorite in his old age, was
deep in the woods, tied to a tree, waiting to be slaughtered, field
dressed, and served to his master and these old men.*

Young Buck was anything but young; he was an old man,
some fifty-five years beyond that name. He was one of the
last two survivors to bear the marks of the shackles that had
bound them on that fateful ship, the Clotilda, which made its
last journey in the years preceding emancipation. Eager to join
the lively conversation, he poked his head out from behind a
gnarled tree, his movements unsteady as he wobbled through
a two-step while relieving himself.

"Ol' Lancelot, a special hound, once took down a black

bear who mistook him for dinner!" he hollered, his voice carrying through the night air. Teetering on his feet, Young Buck staggered back toward the men circling the dancing campfire. He settled onto a weathered stump beside Charlie, grinning with a slight twitch to his upper lip as he stared intently into his eyes, "That Lancelot was the prowling black panther you never saw coming."

"That dog has the devil in him, I swear," Charlie exclaimed, taking a swig, his voice laced with defeat. The jug slipped from his grip. "Just toss him bones to gnaw on. He never shows me an ounce of kindness—always snarling, like a lion eyeing its next meal." Charlie raised the jug to eye level, squinting at it in contemplation.

"Hmm... Them words make me his bitch, huh?" Charlie presumed before he chuckled. An elderly man, his parched lips chapped and cracked, suddenly lunged to the left, snatching the jug from Charlie's unsuspecting hands. A playful twinkle danced in his eye as he raised the rim of the jug to his nose, inhaling deeply. The rich, intoxicating aroma wafted up, wrapping around him like a familiar embrace as he savored the essence.

"Smells like pussy" the old man said, laughing as he leaned in, closing the distance between him and Charlie's face. Some snickered, while others burst into laughter. After a moment of hesitation, he raised the jug to his lips and took hearty gulps, the liquid glistening in the dim light as it disappeared down his throat.

"Ah, that was good," the old man said, savoring the smooth taste before turning to Charlie again. Although he swayed from drunkenness, his gaze was steady. Feathers ruffled; Charlie returned the gaze as the old man grinned. "Heard many tales of ol' Lancelot.. Seen him do things can't explain... You be his *bitch*," the old man said emphatically, and declared firmly. Laughter roared, circling the campfire. Charlie's anger burned within him like wildfire; his fists quickly clenched tightly at his sides as he staggered.

"When was the last time you smelled pussy, old man?" Charlie raged, silencing everyone. The old man chuckled as he observed the campfire's dance, then quickly turned his gaze back to Charlie. Charlie's eyes leisurely fell on the old man's hand, which rested on his pistol, the hammer cocked, and the weapon teetering between being in or out of its holster.

"Your *tone*, son," the old man calmly said. "We just jawing." Charlie knew the decision was his to get wrong. With a head that seemed to nod in mockery, the old man chuckled heartily, his laughter ringing like an old church bell. The old man scanned the faces of those surrounding him, some friends, others friendly, all carrying a seriousness about them.

"We have shovels ready," a deep, commanding voice proclaimed, breaking the silence. Six deep is how big a hole needs to be." The air was thick, the moment charged. Still, the old man's eyes sparkled with wicked amusement before settling on Charlie's frown.

"Your momma," he teased, his voice dripping with amusement. The old man's shoulders shook with laughter, the sound of a raucous cackle filling the air, until he could not contain himself. He dipped down, sitting on the tree stump beneath him, nearly toppling over with delight in himself. The moment and emotion mingled as Charlie's breathing hitched,

"My momma dead... some thirty years now," his voice

quivered, each word was laden with sorrow. The old man found shady humor in his tone and let out a chuckle, fake nostalgia bubbling in his laughter as he pretended to reminisce about a woman unknown to him. The elderly man's neck stretched like a turkey. He scanned his surroundings, his eyes shining with wonder and confusion. As he took in the astonished faces around him, he smacked his lips together, seemingly savoring the rich, delectable taste of a perfectly cooked steak from years past. Or perhaps the pungent, fishy scent of overcooked Mississippi flathead catfish still lingered, similarly distorting his expression.

"Thirty years? Sound 'bout right," the old man humorously pondered, a hint of fake nostalgia in his gaze. A smirk emerged on his weathered face, marked by lines that narrated tales of a rich and lengthy life. "You can call me *Pa*," he kidded, his tone warm and welcoming. His laughter rose from deep within, blending with that of the others. Just as the laughter began to fade, another older man shot a glare at Charlie, smacking his lips together and declaring, "Call me Pappy," his raspy voice reigniting the laughter among the men around him.

Among those present was one seated quietly, whom Charlie longed to hear from. This person was Debra-Ann's favorite elder, someone who also instilled a sense of fear in Charlie. He stole a look at Straw Hat, his heart pounding, nearly pulling him back to reality as Straw Hat remained silent and expressionless.

"Grand Michael called Lancelot 'the forest ghost' when they hunted black bears, deer, and rabbits. He says Lancelot come up from behind, scared them to death," Straw Hat declared.

"Can't say it be true; know I ain't never seen a bullet hole in any of those pelts he brought back."

A circle of murmurs and nods of agreement rippled through the camp as Straw Hat inched closer to Charlie. The earthy scent of marijuana from Straw Hat's corncob pipe and the air around him gripped Charlie by the collar as the crackling fire cast quivering shadows on their faces…I tell you this cause two things come to mind: if Lancelot be somewhere dead and a ghost, he is coming to get you; if Lancelot be somewhere dead and not a ghost, I be coming… to get you," Straw Hat whispered before he walked out of the camp and into the dark. With a swift motion, Charlie snatched the jug of moonshine from Young Buck just as it was handed to him.

"That's some *bullshit!*" Charlie exclaimed. "That hound… just a hound! Nothing special!" The old men paused their drunken chatter and stared at Charlie, waiting for him to convince himself of the myths or wonders surrounding Lancelot. Charlie stuttered, hesitated, and stammered without saying a word. Young Buck chuckled as he and the other old men, slow as they were, gathered their things, each waiting for the next.

Behind Young Buck, the old men stood silent, watching closely and unnerving Charlie. Charlie leaned forward, studying the men intently, his eyes straining to catch the outlines of their dark faces in the shimmering moonlight. This was how Charlie quickly understood the situation: no teeth, no smile, no joke. These were not just old men surrounding him; rings on their fingers glimmered by the campfire, and he was in the presence of Freemasons, a realization that added a layer of gravity to his predicament.

"Hear me now son: Big nigger, big hole," Young Buck

declared. The elderly men nodded sternly before walking away, following Young Buck as the gentle darkness gradually swallowed their figures.

Drunk on hooch, Charlie stumbled under the moon, now darkened by cloud cover. The still of the night left him alone with his thoughts. Soon, Charlie's thoughts, which resembled Lancelot's low, intense growls, were repeated back to him by the surrounding forest, halting him in his tracks. He gathered some courage, yet his zigzag up the road was still swift. A hair-raising growl echoed from the dark corners of the forest, suddenly freezing him. "That rope around your neck thick, you not breathe, sho' nuff not growl, just my head trickin` is all," he hollered. Charlie's steps are faster now, and he's hungry, not for food.

Finally reaching the ramshackle wooden shack, he climbed the creaky steps with a labored breath. That hound was some two hundred yards out. Turning back, he glanced anxiously at the murky woods across the road. Charlie took a deep breath, a smile emerging amidst his fear as he envisioned the slumbering bloodhound positioned far enough away to give him a false sense of security. I can take down that hound; he's still drowsy from those berries, Charlie thought, laughter bubbling up and making him stumble briefly before he steadied himself by clutching the aged post.

His gaze fixed intently on the forest some two hundred yards beyond the plowed field, he imagined it was Lancelot observing him. He first raised the jug of moonshine to toast over his head, then drank the last of the murky dregs. A wicked grin appeared as he wiped the remnants of the strong drink from his chin. "Nah... Maybe that hound's ears are big enough to hear screams," Charlie reflected with an unsettling sense of possession. "They all know I be the master, and I shoot that hound dead in the morning."

He burst through the door with a stumbling swagger, his eyes landing on Helen, who sat at the table, rocking back and forth in an anxious rhythm. Her gaze drifted from the three untouched plates in front of her, flies seemingly ice-skating on the stark white napkins neatly aligned, wanting the food beneath, almost mocking in their pristine presentation. The moment her eyes fell on him, recognition of his drunken state flickered across her face, mingling dread with resignation as she braced herself for what might come. Helen's stomach growled audibly, an urgency that clashed with the heavy mood in the room, and her gaze fell depressingly upon her plate. She let out a soul sucking, weary sigh, feeling the weight of her situation. "Clear that table, and get to bed," Charlie commanded, his voice a low growl punctuated by a dismissive gesture toward their bedroom. He stood rooted to the spot, observing as she hastily scraped each plate of food into a pail meant for the hogs, her hands trembling slightly. "Go on, woman, blow a kiss to that candle and get!" he added harshly. Helen hurried as instructed, stopping inside their bedroom to look back and see if he was coming along. With the door closed, her ears straining to catch the sound of his footsteps, she listened intently for the familiar creaks of the old floorboards. "Coming to bed, Charlie?" she called in the softest, most soothing voice she could muster, hoping to quell the tempests that brewed inside and outside her.

The doorknob in Debra-Ann's room rattled violently, like a warning bell sending a shiver down her spine. Startled, the little girl bolted upright in her bed, her heart racing. Panic filled her throat as she screamed Lancelot's name; her cries bounced around the tiny room and into the night across the countryside. The candle lantern, long extinguished, swung off its hook and fell to the floor. Moonlight crept through her window, casting a ghostly green light on every corner of the room. Suddenly, with a deafening thud, Charlie kicked the door with such force that it seemed to explode. There, Charlie, Debra-Ann's monster manifested and stood in the doorway—a silhouette carved from the moonlight, a marionette with tangled strings struggling to stay upright. Debra-Ann's dreamt shadowy monster had come to life. Her eyes widened beyond their measure; fear took control, stealing her courage to scream. Charlie patted the broken frame, the wood splintered, and the hinges uprooted. A low chuckle escaped his lips as he admired the damage, his gaze a mocking and amused look as he assessed the chaos he had created. "Gonna have to fix that... maybe not," he pondered casually, then turned his attention back to Debra-Ann, a depraved glint in his eyes making her heart race even faster. She quickly turned back, her head hitting the wall behind her with a painful thud. Clutching her pillow tightly with trembling hands, Debra-Ann curled up into a ball. Charlie's gaze flickered to the small window perched above her bed, where shadows danced across the glass in the dim moonlight. He could hear what he believed to be Lancelot— the sound, not a mournful howl, but something much more rage-filled, as if something was being torn apart with savage ferocity. Even through the haze of alcohol clouding his mind, a small sliver of logic whispered that it couldn't be the old hound; Lancelot was far too old and distant to make such an uproar. Charlie's weight crashed onto the old box-spring mattress, jolting it and Debra-Ann, creating a disturbance as it thudded against the floor. With every shift of his bulk, the old mattress offered no resistance, foraging a trench in the bed's sagging depths, dragging her closer to him like a relentless downpour cascading down a steep, unforgiving mountainside. Debra-Ann whimpered softly; the sound barely cut through the thick atmosphere heavy with tension and fear, as if the very air trembled around her.

Arms and legs flailing, she clawed at the loosened sheets gathering around her as she frantically tried to escape. Her limbs thrashed wildly as she desperately fought against the tangled sheets that trapped her like a suffocating web. Panic surged as she fought against the sinking mattress. Debra-Ann clutched the loosened blanket that threatened to pull her under. Each movement was filled with terror, fueled by an urgent need to escape the entrapment. Beneath a menacing smile, Charlie struggled to catch his breath, each labored inhale releasing the foul stench of mouth-decayed and moonshine into the air. A deep nausea churned within Debra-Ann, yet her stomach was empty, offering no relief. The sensation twisted and roiled, leaving her feeling hollow and unsettled. Charlie's eyes sparkled, and he grinned, knowing his prey never had a chance.

Recovering her voice, Debra-Ann screamed at the top of her lungs a name that had never crossed her lips until now. "Momma! Momma!" she cried out. Debra-Ann begged her mother to protect and save her. The woman who gave birth to her in the cotton field cut and tied the cord, allowed her to be taken, and then went back to picking cotton. She remained silent. The silence beyond Debra-Ann's screams brought tears streaming down her cheeks. In a heartbeat, Charlie spun Debra-Ann around, her rotation blurred into a flurry of colors, dizzying sensations overwhelming her senses, only stopping when she lay beneath him, breathless and disoriented. "Momma," she moaned, over and over, the word escaped her lips like a haunting prayer, a plea for help that no other creature must beg of their mother.

In that fleeting, surreal moment, a shadowy silhouette loomed against the shimmering backdrop of the moon; it was the angel Gabriel rushing from the cloud in search of his earthly warrior, Lancelot. Debra-Ann's screams and her desperate pleas that had alerted him were now frozen in terror. Charlie held her wrists above her with one hand while he tore away her night clothes and panties with the other. The screams returned with the powerful thrust of Charlie's thighs, escalating into an ear-piercing climax, a chilling sound that cut through the air with an intensity that froze the blood. It was a pitch so agonizingly high that only women who had endured this horror could truly understand the malice lurking beneath it. They alone could recognize the evil for what it truly was, a malevolent mocking of their past traumas. The hard pulse of his arousal intensified the agonizing pain, seizing Debra-Ann's body. Her screams and pleas for help, begging Charlie to stop, filled the air, now frozen in terror, anguish lacing every syllable as she reached out with hope. Her futile resistance to the raping of body and soul only inspired animalistic grunts and groans. Even in her despair, Debra-Ann could tell he took pleasure in her torment. A chilling silence enveloped her as she drifted away from consciousness. Debra-Ann's once vibrant eyes, now glazed over, stared into the darkness surrounding her, unfocused. Debra-Ann's body, stripped of strength, became limp; Charlie's frenzied laughter was the last sound she heard before she fainted.

The morning sun gently streamed through the shattered window above Debra-Ann's bed, scattering glass across her bedding and Debra-Ann. Abandoned screams for her mother to rescue her repeatedly played in her head like a dirty needle skipping on a vinyl record. Her once angelic face was battered and bruised. Her left eye was swollen shut, and a mixture of blood from a busted lip and drool seeped pink from the corner of her mouth. The eerie shadows of Debra-Ann's lost innocence have emerged. With her legs unsteady and barely able to support her, Debra-Ann slowly lifted herself from the edge of the bed, her senses still clouded and disoriented, as if she were emerging from a thick fog. The room around her swam in a haze, as her trembling hands reached out, grasping for the long-discarded sheets on the floor to cover her nakedness.

As she stumbled forward, Debra-Ann struggled to regain her balance and clarity, weighed down by confusion. Beneath her feet, shards of glass were scattered, sharp remnants that reflected her own vulnerability. Caught in the moment, her gaze was drawn to the glimmering shards, which seemed to capture not only the light but also her troubled thoughts as they surrounded her like a delicate but painful reminder of what had just happened. The floor around her was blood-spattered; however, it wasn't Debra-Ann's; hers had only begun streaming down her inner thighs. Her eyes curiously scanned the crimson-colored melee of pooled and dried blood until the sight of bloody pawprints froze her. "Lancelot," Debra-Ann gasped.

Terrifying, unfathomable visions surged through Debra-Ann's mind, each one more distressing than the last. Shadows of dread and anguish flickered like dark lightning, painting a vivid montage of her deepest fears and wildest nightmares. She dragged her feet across the floor, moving broken glass that didn't pierce her feet out of her way while carefully tracing the delicate pawprints etched into the wood floor, following them as they led her toward the doorway. Debra-Ann stepped through the threshold and into the main room. No signs of Lancelot left her dismayed. Her tear-filled eyes focused intently on the last blood-stained pawprint etched into the floor beside a shattered wooden chair, not entirely faded, and her heart hammered against her chest, amplifying her growing dread.

The absence of Lancelot made Debra-Ann's head throb. She griped the sheet tightly around her shoulders, wrapping it around her neck. Her gaze gradually shifted to the right without turning her head. Then, her eyes widened as she looked to the left, a blend of anxiety and anticipation flashing through her. She glanced at the front door, slightly ajar, and felt a flicker of hope that Lancelot would return safely and unscathed. Just then, low, rhythmic groans leaked from the kitchen, pulling her attention away. There lies Charlie, sprawled across the table, with flesh on his back clawed and deep canine puncture wounds on the back of his neck, revealing he nearly died in her protector's jaws. Helen stood over him, focusing on tending to his wounds. She remained entirely unresponsive to her daughter's presence; her gaze remained fixed on Charlie's back, never lifting her eyes to meet her daughter's. A sense of unease washed over Debra-Ann as Helen gently started humming a haunting tune, reminiscent of a sorrowful slave song, suggesting hidden struggles yet to come.

The front door nudged open, then swung shut, quickly drawing Charlie and Helen's curiosity. They both waited eagerly as sunlight crept through, wondering, with hope and dread, whether this was a reckoning or just the whisper of the wind. Just moments later, the front door slammed against the wall, flung wide by a sudden, forceful March gust. Charlie and Helen breathed a sigh of relief, but Debra-Ann's expression lingered with a hint of sadness, the weight of uncertain futures heavy on her mind. Pain tightened Charlie's voice as Helen tended to his wounds. Still, he assured and humored himself as he glared at Debra-Ann. "I hit that hound with everything I could muster; he was dead, a ghost." Debra-Ann sized up the tension in the room, her gaze darting between Charlie and Helen as she plotted their demise right then and there. Her eyes caught the glint of the small hatchet by the fireplace. Then her eyes locked onto the bucket used for washing dishes, a wicked idea forming in her mind as she noticed the long carving knife jutting out tantalizingly. Her pulse quickened.

In the doorway, Lancelot emerged like a phantom from a nightmare, his broad chest, powerful muzzle, and sturdy paws stained with the remnants of the fierce battle fought under the cover of night. The sun fought the fog that clung around Lancelot like a shroud, his keen gaze locked onto Charlie while Debra-Ann's heart raced in a whirlwind of emotions. Lancelot exhaled sharply, the misty fog swirling like smoke from a dragon's fiery nostrils. Debra-Ann trembled with relief and delight at the sight of her best friend, crying tears of joy as the old black-haired bloodhound marched in, his long ears and droopy jowls swaying at the same tempo as the frayed, heavy rope still around his neck. With each thunderous step across the creaky wooden floor, Lancelot announced his presence, his shiny black coat rippling like a dark wave as he huffed defiantly. It was clear he had returned to end Charlie's existence, Helen's, if she got between them. Lancelot paused at Debra-Ann's side; his claws dug into the wood floor like a runner's cleats into the ground before a race. Charlie watches the rope around the hound's neck, which now moves with the rhythm of his heartbeat. Or was it the breath heaving from the hound's chest? Each arc was filled with tension, the air around them charged, yet Charlie knew that even a twitch from him could reveal the hound's tendencies. Helen's steadfastness surged, and her loyalty was unquestioned as she positioned herself to defend Charlie's life with her own, just as fiercely as Lancelot intended to protect Debra-Ann. With swift determination, she reached into the wash bucket and seized the carving knife, its blade gleaming ominously in the soft light. Her knuckles around its handle grew whiter as it rested by her side. Taking her stance, she planted firmly in the narrow passage separating Debra-Ann from the menacing hatchet resting by the crackling fireplace. Lancelot, with a low, menacing snarl rumbling from his throat, advanced with an air of fierce protectiveness, his muscles tensed and ready for war. Debra-Ann, sensing the tension, gently tapped Lancelot's shoulder. He obeyed her subtle command and settled back onto his haunches, though his eyes still burned with a fierce desire to defend. This was the first time Helen laid eyes on her daughter and her disfigured face. She stared vacantly, neither blinking to break the deathly emptiness between them. Lancelot's snarl at Helen released them from their haze as he pressed forward. Lancelot huffed again, sending ripples through his layered, shiny black coat, as his trembling snarl revealed his canines before Debra-Ann's touch calmed the surge. In one motion, Debra-Ann grips the thick rope around Lancelot's neck and throws it at Helen's feet. Charlie's eyes followed the rope to its destination, then back to where Debra-Ann and Lancelot stood; Helen didn't flinch. Darkness in Debra-Ann's heart descended like a cloak; she had no fear of death or dying and was a warrior in the midst of evil surroundings.

"He dies by your hands or any other; you will have seen your last sunrise."

With a heavy sigh, Debra-Ann relinquished the tightly gathered sheet she had clutched around her shoulders, the fabric falling away as she straightened herself, resolute and determined.

"This is what that beast did to the flesh of your body… You mend his wounds, wipe the blood from his back, while the same blood from your veins still drips onto the floor where I stand, and you cannot shed one tear for me!" Debra-Ann screamed as she stood like a naked statue, bloodied and battered, before her mother, while Charlie leered.

"I suggest you hold your tongue now, child!" Helen snapped as she continued tending to Charlie's clawed back, her voice filled with tension. She stared at Charlie, her eyes fierce and protective. "He, my man; he will be my man even when you gone." Debra-Ann felt a wave of hesitation wash over her as she struggled to gather the sheet at her feet. It was a moment that revealed her reluctance, aware of the burden of the task and her emotions.

"You call me child; blood still running down my thighs… You have no love of God, no love of me in you," Debra-Ann declared, her voice steady but charged with tension, a daring challenge that hung in the air, still careful not to ignite Lancelot's fury. Struggling to rise, Charlie confidently declared from across the room,

"That hound good as dead once I mend." Lancelot bared his teeth in a fierce display, but Debra-Ann's soothing touch quickly calmed him once more.

"So, we wait till you mend before we finish this, huh?" Debra-Ann said, her head slowly tilting in confused disbelief, her brows furrowing as her tone became tense and serious. At this moment, she could embrace death as a warrior; her only fear was that Lancelot would die at their hands, which kept her words cautious.

"Ain't many who will believe or care what happened here, but my Grand Michael's friend, Straw Hat, or the Freemasons will. So, I say again, he dies by your hand or any other, it be your last sunrise. So, threaten again, with breath or gaze!" Debra-Ann serenely dared.

With a heart-wrenching cry, "No!" the distant crack of gunfire pierced the stillness of the night, each ricocheting bullet vibrating through the air like a ghastly reminder of the knight raider's chaos. The dark, swirling cloud that consumed Straw Hat rumbled softly, almost as if it understood his suffering, before finally dispersing and releasing him from its suffocating grip. As the mist gradually dissipated, he huddled, weeping in the tender embrace of a golden cornfield, where the tall, swaying stalks caressed him like a reassuring hand, all under the soft, warm glow of the moonlight. In that instant, Straw Hat understood that Gabriel's remorse and anguish had become one with his own, binding their hearts in a collective grief.

CHAPTER SIX
LEAP OF FAITH

THE MOONLIGHT POURED into the small sharecropper's shack, casting elongated shadows that danced across the worn wooden floor, reminiscent of the night two years prior when the beast first emerged from the darkness and tangled itself in Debra-Ann's life. It was April, the day after Easter; however, the joy of the resurrection had faded. But on this somber night, Debra-Ann, now 15, moved across the creaking wood floor where she had learned to crawl purposefully, each step guided by a mix of memory and determination. Her heart raced as she carefully rolled each foot heel-to-toe, evading the creak of loose floorboards, raised nails, and every other alarm that whispered the secrets of the sharecropper's shack she had inherited from her grandfather. Every inch of the shack was familiar yet foreboding, a relic of her past that now felt like a cage. Debra-Ann was determined not to awaken Charlie, who lay unwittingly asleep nearby. The cold steel of the shotgun felt reassuring in her grip. With every calculated movement, she prepared to confront the darkness that had taken root in her life. The carefully crafted plan was formulated some time ago; her bag was packed with a sense of urgency the night after Charlie raped and beat her half dead. Each item was chosen to remember her father, Grand Michael, and the good people of this tormented town. That night, Debra-Ann measured the beating; her body was black-and-blue, more than any beating she had ever endured from Helen.

This evening, Debra-Ann confronted the pain shrouded in darkness; yet, her actions, justifiable or not, directed her thoughts and guided her steps. She intended to point her Grand Michael's shotgun at Charlie while he and Helen slept. The pain of that night seeped through her being, reminding her of the despair that had driven her to make this choice. This night, payback. But for Charlie, the moment should come as no surprise; he saw change coming.

It started with the low muttering that slipped from her lips... a rebellion whispered just loud enough for him to hear. She shot him a piercing glance that said everything—she was unafraid, and the fire in her eyes made it clear she was ready to stand her ground. Being more of a country girl than city folk, Debra-Ann had the skills to shoot the wings off a fly. To her, Charlie was nothing more than the shit they landed on. She stood confidently in a shadowed corner of her tormentor's bedroom, shotgun firmly positioned against her cheek and shoulder, ready to take action. She waited for the perfect moment, observing the distance between Charlie and Helen. Her Grand Michael had been gone for more than four years, yet his lifeforce seemingly still guided her from beyond. Even now, she felt his wiry whiskers brushing against her cheek, his hot, ticklish breath a gentle breeze against her ear as he whispered instructions. His soothing voice, low and steady, would resonate in her ear, especially during their countless hunting trips. *Tighten up that grip, baby girl*, he'd say, a hint of excitement in his tone. This 12-gauge got some kick. Now, lead that jackrabbit, and hit with no more than five pellets like I teach you.

Moonlight glinted sharply off the double barrels of the shotgun, casting an ominous glow in the darkened corner where Debra-Ann concealed herself. Her heart raced, her vision blurred, and she struggled to calm her breathing. Debra-Ann wiped the sweat from her brow, squinted, and aimed, knowing she only needed to apply five pounds of pressure to the trigger. She squeezed, and the hammer pulled back. The night was about to ignite. Helen noticed the gentle moonlight shimmering on the edge of the double barrels before her gaze fell upon the white of Debra-Ann's focused eye. In this moment of vulnerability, she reached out for mercy, a woman unable to show compassion or love. Slowly and steadily, Helen's hand gently rose, her body followed, shifting to protect, cover her choice, her 'beloved', on his day of atonement. Undeterred by the blind love for this creature, Debra-Ann's finger gracefully shifted, gliding over to cover both triggers. The silent plea for mercy regarding Charlie's life drove Debra-Ann to numbness. Emerging from the shadows, Debra-Ann's nostrils flared, and her breath came in sharp bursts as the second hammer was drawn back. Helen's eyes widened in disbelief as fear surged within her, the dramatic moment frozen in time.

"You got something you want to say, Helen!" Debra-Ann's voice rang out, sharp and cutting through the tense air.

"Have mercy," she sputtered.

"For him? What about you?" Debra-Ann snapped, "He's flat on his back, drunk; he won't even know what hit him. You gonna see the hot lead comin'."

Helen's voice trembled as she stuttered, "This ain't you."

"Ain't me—you don't know me! You're not my mother, or are you just deaf… '*momma*?'" Debra-Ann responded with the same tone she had used the night before, while still managing to hold back her anger. "You never understood me… You never cared to know me, Helen! You found your voice to defend him, your bravery to shield him, but what about me?" The intensity of her pain-filled words pounded against the walls. "The only reason these heavy barrels never find their way under my chin is that God loves me, blessed me, my daddy, and Grand Michael," Debra-Ann shouted. A single tear rolled down her cheek, glistening in the dim light, splashing onto her bare foot as she blinked back more tears.

"You never saw the love my daddy labored to show you, unless you noticed a new hat or shoes. But you think this man loves you while he beats you? Beats on me? Love?"

The cold, hard barrels of the shotgun now rested equally upon Charlie and Helen, each a testament to their intertwined fates. Tears streamed down Helen's cheeks like condensation racing to the bottom of a cold bottle of Coke on a scorching summer day. Helen's chin dipped dramatically to her chest, lost in deep reflection, when suddenly, the piercing wail of a baby shattered the stillness like a thunderclap. As she lifted her head, A mother's smile calls for memories of better days. It was too far gone for Debra-Ann to remember. "Bye," Debra-Ann said. Her finger applied pressure across both triggers.

Debra-Ann let out a deep sigh as she stood on the porch of her grandfather's shack, dressed in her powder-blue dress. Her hair, resting on her shoulders, took flight with each gentle breeze. Her chest heaved as she inhaled, reluctant to let go of the scent, the only thing that made this place feel like home. The weight of the shotgun Debra-Ann had just fired lingered in her hands, a stark reminder of the moment that had brought her here. As she looked over her grandfather's land, his rocker swayed against the wind, knocking and tapping on the wall. It caught her eye, followed by memories of her Grand Michael rocking her to sleep, before a gentle smile crossed her lips. Put your shoes on, baby girl; you've got a walk ahead of you, his voice whispered tenderly in her mind. It brought a smile, even though the voice was in her head and didn't quite match the guttural tone she remembered coming from his giant frame. Debra-Ann saw herself as an old woman reminiscing about a silly little girl; her Grand Michael's voice able to crush the grass and bend the mighty oak when he called to her. It was only part of the bedtime stories he told his granddaughter that she remembered, but perhaps that little girl still believed. So, she entertained this voice; it was kind, and she missed him dearly.

The first stair was missing, so Debra-Ann jumped without her shoes on. The earth welcomed her bare feet as she landed. The rich, life-producing soil moving between her toes instantly brought a smile to her face. But as her gaze drifted back to the rocking chair, a wave of sadness washed over her, and her smile faltered, tears welling in her eyes. In a trembling voice, she whispered, "I don't want to say goodbye to this…, to you, Lancelot."

The old dog, roused from his resting spot by the gentle rocking—a place he first commandeered just weeks after leaving his momma's teat—leaped down to her side, a joyful spirit despite his age. Lancelot had been her faithful companion long before she could remember, and seeing him so full of life again brought back fond memories of days gone by—days filled with laughter and adventure lost in time. Go on, baby girl, the comforting voice urged softly as if wrapped around her like a protective blanket. That shotgun sound off across three counties this time of night... You gather my blood off this porch, and ol' Lancelot will walk with you for a spell.

Debra-Ann swiftly collected her belongings from the weathered porch, her heart heavy as she gazed at the familiar rocking chair, which cradled her thoughts and dreams. She turned, her first step hesitating as her eyes locked onto Lancelot, who sat a few feet away. For Debra-Ann and perhaps Lancelot, too, it felt like the moment before their first hunt alone after her Grand Michael's death. In that instant, Lancelot's eyes offered comfort, reassuring her that everything would be alright. Once again, only Debra-Ann's hesitation kept him rooted; his gaze stayed fixed on her and the shack where they grew up, as if capturing a moment for eternity. Just like their hunts, Lancelot took the lead, sprinting ahead, knowing exactly where to go. She was amazed because Lancelot had been here long before she was born; this energy had not been seen for more than two years. *His stride tonight was made of one looking out for danger; his pace was steady like that of his youth, never slowed until they crossed the tracks to the city. That's why Lancelot always took the lead;* she justified it. However, this night took a frighteningly different turn, with ol' Lancelot struggling to keep his legs under him after a mile. His pace slowed more and more, each exhale now a painful struggle as the miles dragged on. Lancelot halts, unable to resist the pull towards the open road. With a surge of concern, Debra-Ann's heart quickened. Her arms felt heavy with weariness, but she rushed to close the gap between them, her knees sinking into the cool earth as she knelt beside him. With gentle affection, she patted his graying head, whispering, "Come on, old friend. I'll get you something to drink the first chance we get, just like always."

Her smile was meant to reassure Lancelot, but she noticed the flicker of helplessness in his deep, soulful eyes. Lancelot gazed back at her, a silent conversation between them—his eyes brimmed with unspoken words, a mixture of love, loyalty, and an unshakable sadness. Lancelot's muzzle nudged the bundle in her arms. Perhaps it was a kiss, a tender farewell. Then the moonlight shone on his face, revealing Lancelot's sorrow and illuminating the tracks beneath his eyes in his fur. Tears had been flowing for some time. Although Debra-Ann wore a brave smile, she felt a deep ache in her heart. Her gentle strokes shifted from simple pats to long, soothing caresses as she lovingly traced his back from head to tail. Lancelot sniffs, breathing in the scent of his family, with some sniffs lingering as if he wants to take something extra for his next journey. Debra-Ann kisses the top of his head and does the same. Teardrops cascade onto Lancelot's head, causing his body to lean heavily against her; his hug, his goodbye. Her weeping was so passionate, a bittersweet goodbye that spoke volumes in the silence of the night. Debra-Ann struggled to stand and take steps as clouds obscured portions of the moonlight. Her cries were intense, tears streamed down her face like torrential rain as Lancelot disappeared into the dark, beckoning cornfield.

Panic surged within her as she rushed to clear her vision; she had to go after him. A couple of hesitant steps took her forward, but just then, a cloud swept across the moon, casting her in shadow. Her heart raced, and she twisted her head, rolling side to side frantically. "Lancelot! Lancelot!" she called out, the only sound in a world that felt so vast and empty without him. Suddenly, the moonlight broke through again, far off in the distance. In the dark, the sight and sound of resting birds startled into flight drew her attention, revealing the cornstalks swaying ominously.

The crows erupted into flight, their startled cries sending a shiver down her spine and pulling her gaze away from the long road ahead. Debra-Ann's efforts to move her feet were made more difficult by the weight of the bundle she carried; she chatted with her best friend as usual on this road, as if he were right there with her. Yet, as she trudged on, she couldn't help but speak to her faithful companion with a mix of weariness and determination.

"Grand Michael was right, Lancelot! You are the lion that lions fear!" she exclaimed, a spark of spirit igniting within her. Then, a vivid memory flashed in her mind, brightening her dreary trek.

"Remember the time you eased up from behind and howled at that black bear so loudly that he shits himself and bolted, I swear we 'all saw you laugh?" Laughter bubbled up from her depths, energizing her legs. "And thank goodness Straw Hat and Young Buck were there to witness your glory! Your bravery, your legend—I promise I will never let it fade."

Debra-Ann crept cautiously across the rusted train tracks, her heart pounding. She hesitated momentarily, glancing over her shoulder, though deep down, she knew Lancelot wouldn't be there. The streets were desolate, the sidewalks lifeless, except for the occasional creeping car and a handful of shadowy figures blending in with the drunks and drifters. The air was thick with tension, each corner hiding potential danger. Moments later, Debra-Ann climbed the train station steps and paused, her breath coming in shallow gasps as she stared through the grimy screen door, exhaling both fear and fatigue. A rat leaped from a bucket of garbage meant for the hogs, scurrying across the road, a starving alley cat chasing it, the sight raised anxiety through her body, her heart pounding with every creepy sound the night exposed. Lancelot's howl, the last time she would hear, was heard just as she struggled against the unwieldy doors of the train station. It slammed shut behind her with a deafening bang, reminiscent of the shotgun she had used just hours before. Debra-Ann smiled, embracing a newfound sense of freedom for herself and Lancelot.

Not long before joining my dad and Grand Michael on their long walks, she chuckled, then a smile spread across her face as she realized that Lancelot and she were both nearing liberation from pain and suffering.

The night cashier at the counter noticed the slamming door, cast a dismissive glance at the little colored girl, then returned to his crossword puzzle. The station was deserted. Debra-Ann scanned the dimly lit station, noticing its unpleasant smell and dusty corners, and welcomed the sight of the first uncluttered bench. A deep sigh escaped her lips like a slowly deflating balloon, followed by groans as gravity compelled her weary legs to fail. Seated, her gaze drifted over the posters lining the walls, and she realized her escape plan had faltered before a destination, prompting a sigh of frustration. She observed the cashier leisurely puffing on a cigar that dangled from his lips. It still had length, though more ashes than tobacco—a method he employed to endure the long nights. A heavy silence hung in the air, with neither of the two initiating a conversation, only occasionally interrupted by a cough, a puff of smoke, or a fart from the old white man at the counter. Cigar was hanging from his lips, and he squinted at his crossword puzzle, blissfully unaware of the storm brewing just outside the door.

The weight of her escape threatened to crush her spirit as she gazed forlornly at the enormous departure board, its dazzling array of cities and times seeming to mock her.

"Where do I go? Where do I go?" she fretted, shifting her bundle from arm to arm. Each move felt heavier than the last. With a determined flick, she brushed the dirt off her feet and put on her shoes, ready to choose when she reached the counter. But then the door slammed again, and all eyes—hers and the old cashier's—turned. He glanced her way, then returned to his puzzle, indifferent to the tension crackling in the air. Debra-Ann's heart raced as she caught sight of a familiar figure—the last person she wanted to see: Helen.

They measured each other from head to toe. Helen looked at Debra-Ann, a woman she now feared, and with that, she felt respect. Gradually, the attention of both Helen and Debra-Ann shifted to the bench. Each step matched; only Debra-Ann's were backward. Debra-Ann frowned as she grabbed her bundle, her head on a swivel, and stepped back carefully and cautiously.

"Why are you here?" Debra-Ann nervously questioned,

immediately regretting not sharing one of the shotgun shells with Helen, as her freedom was just a train's whistle away.

Helen looked down at her feet to steady her breathing before she answered. Her head lifted as tears streamed down her cheeks. Pain-filled anger rose in Debra-Ann. The only thing she has for Helen is a fuss. "You give me life; I spared yours. We even, Helen."

"Sorry," Helen smiled pitifully. "Please forgive me, Debra-Ann," she continued, her tone remorseful, wishing Debra-Ann would choose to return to the life she escaped. "Lord knows, child, I treat you better," Helen's voice trembled with fake sincerity. Debra-Ann scrunched her brows together as her head tilted to the side, her gaze piercing as a dagger as she pored over every tell on Helen's face.

"Did you say, 'Lord knows?' You right, He does. And so do I, Helen. Now, tears falling slowly because you want them to be seen," Debra-Ann shot back, her fury igniting into an inferno. "Everything ties me here gone; never saw love in your eyes when you cast them my way...never even felt 'like' from you. Just know we free, go," she conceded. Debra-Ann accepted her failure to be loved. Her voice was exhausted, and her tone lost its spite. Helen's trembling, blood-stained hands caught Debra-Ann's attention when she brought them to her mouth. She studied them, her heart beating dizzily as Helen pleaded with her to say goodbye.

The air crackled with explosive tension, each heartbeat a reminder of the storm brewing between them—as the cashier and the station seemed to hold their breath, waiting for the inevitable climax.

Helen hastily wiped away the tears streaming down her face, her hands slick with dried blood, rehydrated.

The vivid memory of Charlie's life pouring out replayed in Debra-Ann's mind, sending waves of panic coursing through her body. Debra-Ann's heart raced, thundering against her ribcage as she bolted to the counter, adrenaline surging through her veins. "Two tickets anywhere, please!" she cried, pouring every last cent onto the counter from her pouch with urgency and desperation Debra-Ann knew she would be cheated on the price; she just wanted it to end.

Ashes spiraled from the cashier's cigar, swirling like dark smoke signals as they danced around the puzzle before settling. The cashier's head snapped up, nostrils flaring in irritation as he glared down at Debra-Ann. Sensing the tension, Helen shrank back, her chin tucked into her chest, her eyes glued to the floor as if trying to vanish completely, as the white South demands. Debra-Ann stood her ground, heart racing, while the cashier begrudgingly counted each dollar bill and coin. "Go north," Helen murmured. Both the cashier and Debra-Ann looked at her strangely. His glare darted towards Debra-Ann, who felt the weight of his hostility like a heavy blanket. But Helen wasn't giving up. Her eyes locked onto Debra-Ann's. Helen's anguish silently pleaded to no avail.

Defeated, "Go north!" Helen said again, this time clearly, loudly, and firmly. The cashier's face twisted in anger.

"I don't care if that nigger is a bit touched in the head; she don't raise her voice in here!" Gathering courage, Debra-Ann turned her gaze to meet Helen's. Slowly nodding in understanding, she grasped the gravity of Helen's message.

"Orphanages up North take in you and your brother…

keep you all together!" Her voice was elevating, filled with determination, as she reached out. Her eyes rose to meet the woman, her daughter. She saw this for the first time, this last time, then back down to the floor, invisible once more before the cashier's seething anger. But just as quickly, the bravado faded, and she bowed her head again, shrinking back into the shadows, rendered invisible by the storm brewing around them.

With a heavy heart, Helen swayed as she moved toward the door. Debra-Ann watched her with nothing but contempt in her eyes as despair misted over Helen like a thick fog. She grasped the doorknob, eyes closing as she rested her forehead against the cool screen. "He's gonna live," she called out, her voice breaking through the silence, filled with hope and pain. "It gonna stay limp now," she said softly. Helen took a deep breath, her feelings in turmoil, before a soft smile appeared. "I had a hard time arriving; I came across Miss Mary and Miss Emma on a back road. I held up a lantern, saw the blood here, and told them Charlie was hurt. Miss Emma showed kindness, touched my shoulder, and assured me they would check on him. Miss Mary... she smiled at me as brightly as the morning sun, saying they would be there waiting for me when I came back." A small, humble smile emerged on Helen's face, her warmth offering a fleeting glimmer of light amid her sadness. "I truly believe they will help me, giving me what I need to heal my soul," she said, looking back at Debra-Ann as she left.

The cashier and Debra-Ann's eyes were fixed on the door, and they observed it slam shut behind Helen with a resounding thud, clattering throughout the station. Debra-Ann pondered *Helen's last words—My brother... orphan home—replaying them like an eerie chorus.* Never heard kindness or care in her *words. Thoughts of Helen always filled my thoughts of hell. Even Helen's voice had the cold chill of Hell; yet now, the tone and the words seemed to touch deeply, twisting and turning, awakening something within.*

Debra-Ann's gaze shifted to the cashier, who loomed imposingly behind the counter. In front of him, he lay four tickets, promising passage to far-off cities in the north and northeast, resting atop the scattered ashes. The cashier stared at his hand while hovering over the tickets, a wicked grin spreading sinisterly across his face. When they met the little black girl before him, his eyes sparkled with mischief.

"People play God every day! I reckon because they can," he declared. Laughter erupted deep within him as an older white man walked in with his wife and daughter. He yawned and appeared dismissive as he glanced at the cashier, then at the little colored girl standing at the counter. The cashier's smile gradually morphed into a full-bodied, shoulder-shaking laugh as he leaned over the counter, his frail frame extending outward, and his foul breath made its presence known to Debra-Ann's watering, profusely blinking eyes. "What's the difference between the white folks that swing niggers from trees down here," he roared, "and the ones that don't choose niggers for jobs up north in the big city?" Debra-Ann gazed at the family of three, her wide-open eyes searching for compassion as her body trembled. Yet, they stood silently, waiting for the cashier to finish his joke, which they appeared to have heard before. The little girl, nearly Debra-Ann's age, seemed familiar from their journeys to and from school. However, when their eyes met, the girl did not speak to Debra-Ann; she merely smiled while twirling the blonde hair resting on her shoulder. "The tree brings death a lot faster," the cashier rushed to reply, eager not to lose his audience's attention. Debra-Ann's focus shifted back to the cashier and the four tickets to four cities up north resting beneath the ashes, and now under his hand. He patted the tickets with his fingers, exhilarated by a sense of power and manipulation. Debra-Ann recognized the cashier's malevolent gaze as a reflection of her everyday life. In that moment, his malice from across the counter rendered her stiff. "I could sell you passage anywhere my country heart desires," he confessed. Debra-Ann knew her silence was her safety. She stood there, hand trembling uncontrollably, while the cashier dared words he knew would not be said. Eyes shut tight,

"Devil, get behind me," Debra-Ann mumbled in prayer. Her gentle words to the Lord calmed her racing heartbeat, though they also stirred her bundle, her son, from his slumber.

Michael, just two years old, named after his grandfather and great-grandfather—Grand Michael, her silent secret, no one in or around town knew about—looked determined as he burst from under his cover, startling the cashier and the white folks now standing behind Debra-Ann. The cashier's brows furrowed: *a bundle of clothes, maybe a loaf of bread,* until now. Michael's lunge for the ashes earned him tickets and a new life for them both. As tension in the cashier shifted from fear to rage and finally settled into a tense composure, his gaze darted across the room, taking in the reaction of the stunned white folks he was attempting to entertain. With a grin, he slammed his hand on the desk, causing ashes to swirl into the air again. "You get it," he said, a smirk appearing like a clown popping out of a jack-in-the-box, glancing at Debra-Ann, "no matter where you go, white folks are everywhere. We don't want to see you do better than the worst of us. See that smile, looking like you got money in your pocket, we gonna find a way to help you move on without it… one way or another." His words ignited a wave of laughter that rippled through the onlookers, but for Debra-Ann, the laughter was like a drumbeat in her chest, making her heart race wildly and her ears throb painfully. She took hesitant steps backward toward the bench from which she had risen, her calves trembling and urging her to sink back down onto the seat. Meanwhile, the cashier's gaze remained locked on Michael, a look of disbelief etched onto his face; then, as he rubbed the back of his neck, a flush of embarrassment crept up his cheeks as he realized a little pickaninny had managed to frighten him ghost white. Cheerfully, Michael clutched the tickets he had retrieved while diving for the ashes; he sensed that Debra-Ann desired this. His loud giggles persisted. Michael slowly returned to a dormant state once more when Debra-Ann softly hummed a church hymn.

Out the window, high above the doorway, Debra-Ann gazed at the sunrise as it transformed the sky into a breathtaking canvas of vibrant pink, oranges, and gold. A fleeting memory of Helen appeared. Her gaze shifted towards the boarding schedule for arriving and departing trains, while her mind swirled with questions in search of answers. She met the eyes of her little joy, "Michael, that will be our lesson on this road ahead; two things can be true at once: a bottle ain't the only way the Lord sends a message to you; and the devil will try to convince you that talkin` shit don't have the same stink as horseshit."

A train's whistle cut through the air, signaling its approach to this sleepy backwater small town nestled in Mississippi. Debra-Ann's heart raced as she watched a whirlwind of town folk—black and white—dash through the station's doors, a scene she had witnessed with wonder countless times before. But this time, she was one of them, ready for a change in her life that would last forever.

"A lot of niggers leaving," she overheard time and again, her pulse quickening with every word. Finally, a call for boarding repeated through the air, and for the first time, Debra-Ann glanced down at the ticket now clenched tightly in her hand. The destination of her new life had remained a mystery, still a dream until that moment.

"Philadelphia, Pennsylvania! And all points northeast of the Mississippi," the cashier bellowed, his gravelly voice laced with an urgency that pierced through the thrumming atmosphere. In an instant, Debra-Ann leaped to her feet, an exhilarating surge of energy coursing through her veins as she raced toward the door leading to the waiting train. She was among the first in the quickly forming line of colored folks searching for better. As she stepped through the threshold into the train's realm, it struck her that she was venturing deeper into the station than ever before, bringing her close to the great iron beast that would carry her toward her future. An enormous black-and-white sign loomed overhead, swaying slightly in the cool draft that swept through the station—a stark reminder to use only the side entrances in the last car designated for colored folks, a cruel emblem of their relegated status in this unforgiving world. Anxiety tinged the air with every step toward the train, amplifying the stakes. They all knew that any mistake could lead to being thrown off the train or, worse, being seen as an uppity nigger, a death sentence. Those who couldn't read felt the gentle touch of those who could, kind souls tapping shoulders and gesturing toward the appropriate entrances, ensuring everyone found their way. Now, it was Debra-Ann's turn to board, her heart pounding like a drum as her gaze followed the others, each eyeing the train with a mix of hope and fear.

A thunderous snore rumbled through the coach, rolling like thunder from beneath a wide-brimmed, Sunday-go-to-church hat adorned with a long-stem yellow flower perched high atop a lady's head that bobbed and danced with the swaying of the train. The portly woman's head, beneath the hat, stirred yet remained lulled as it rested heavily against the window, rocked by the rhythmic motion of the train, which had now stopped. Passengers hurried past. A sea of rushing bodies and shuffling feet; shoes bumped the backs of heels down the aisle in search of better seating. Left and right, curious eyes skimmed over the colored folks who were already comfortably settled. A silent message passed between them—*sorry, seat taken*—expressed in fleeting glances before heads turned away, retreating into their private worlds.

Meanwhile, the vibrant city dwellers, particularly the women with their painted cheeks and lips, sat beside the men who shared a love for bright clothing hues; selfishly, they claimed the seats and the air around them, casting unfriendly glares at anyone who dared to consider sharing their space. Debra-Ann's legs were tiring. Feeling an ache in her weary legs from her long walk through hell, she made her way deliberately to the seat next to the open-mouthed, snoring woman.

There was something oddly comforting about the rumbling sound, a reminder of the contented squeals and grunts of the hogs on her Grand Michael's farm. She smiled as she plopped beside the slumbering woman, sighing with relief. It wasn't until she settled in that she fully appreciated the substantial size of her companion, half-concealed beneath the floral hat or the uncomfortable position she might have put herself in. Still, Debra-Ann settled in. Her gaze fell to the lady's shoes, carelessly kicked off and resting haphazardly beneath the seat in front of them. Debra-Ann's brows knit together as she observed that the shoes had pointed toes with dirt rings circling the three-inch heels, resembling marks left after poking two sticks in the mud. She only saw fancy shoes like that on white women from the city, her heart pounding, and her eyes quickly darted to catch the portly lady's face under the hat. "I know why she sat alone," she thought, assuming she had sat next to some crazy white woman who had fallen asleep in the colored section. Debra-Ann sat, rocking her nerves to calm, her eyes fixed on the lady, only looking up to search for another seat until she saw her beautiful, bronze skin glistening under the hat.

The train's departure from the station was abrupt, causing some passengers to be nearly thrown from their seats. Yet, only cheers, sighs of relief, and tears of joy, especially from the first-time riders, could be heard. At the same time, the lady in the hat with the flower sitting next to Debra-Ann remained fast asleep. Her head jerked in a wild dance, bouncing like a rodeo cowboy holding on for dear life to a bucking bronco as the excitement of the journey unfolded around her. Inside, Debra-Ann felt a whirlwind of emotions, but to anyone watching, her face remained unfazed. Her heart weighed her down as if chained to the seat beneath her. She leaned forward, her lips pulled down at the corners, as a surge of pain welled up in her chest at the thought of her beloved Lancelot. Her gaze out the window had a calming effect until her sentiments gave way to a quivering bottom lip as the train passed the cornfield where she knew Lancelot had entered his final journey. The train gradually picked up speed, and with each chug, Debra-Ann arched her back, her eyes struggling to ignore the dancing yellow flower on the woman's hat beside her in favor of the endless cornfields that captivated her attention. Pressing her sky-blue straw hat firmly to her head, she searched the vast expanse of golden corn,

Maybe I see Lancelot parading like a pup, tackling that scarecrow right off its pole.

Debra-Ann's head turned as far as it could as the train picked up speed, her heart heavy with concern for Lancelot alone in the field. A deep sigh escaped her lips. Lancelot's fate seemed all but inevitable. Sadness began to darken her responsiveness, and her eyelids fluttered closed momentarily. Suddenly, she gasped as she shook back to awareness, her senses sharpening instantly. Could it be? "Straw Hat!" Debra-Ann shouted; her voice filled with hope. In an impulsive burst of joy, she leaped from her seat, tears of happiness streaming down her cheeks, as her face and hand pressed eagerly against the window, and her other hand held her brother close to her bosom. "Straw Hat!" she cried, her heart soaring with delight.

It was daybreak, and open fields flanked the road. Straw Hat traveled onward, painfully enduring the dredging of the deep scars of his life, a cornfield. A gray cloud loomed above, a lost friend now drifting away again. Yet, the air was thick with the refreshing scent of morning dew, filling him with a calming resolve as he exhaled deeply. Suddenly, a long, piercing blast from a train's horn erupted, slicing through the stillness and grabbing Straw Hat's attention as it thundered, gaining speed and urgency. His brows knitted together in focus.

The last straw stained with my blood, the crown of Debra-Ann's sky-blue straw hat... northeast to Philadelphia. He smiled.

Straw Hat pressed forward, drawn like a magnet to the wailing horn, until his feet met something unyielding. There lay the old bloodhound, Lancelot, as still as stone. A surge of hope flooded his spirit, assuring him life opened windows when it closed doors, and he'd see his great-niece on that train. Amidst it all, a pole, once meant to hold a scarecrow, stood temptingly bare. Straw Hat grabbed it, climbed to the top, and raised his hat. At that moment, lightning struck—the sky-blue straw hat he crafted for her shimmered in the sunlight, and their eyes locked across the distance. Straw Hat smiled as Debra-Ann wiped away tears and smiled back at him.

CHAPTER SEVEN
MOVED BY THE SPIRIT?

HEAVY BREATHING MADE the air stale; nurtured fear gripped the hearts of passengers, young and old, pounding at a marathon pace as reality began to sink in while the train rattled along its winding track. And now, overshadowed by the gnawing grip of hunger and the chilling threat of the unknown outside the dusty windows, their awe-struck gazes faded like the lush, tree-covered mountains receding into the distance. Although Debra-Ann's eyelids grew heavy, her spirit remained high; she hummed a tune to the playful dance of the yellow flower bobbing on the nearby hat. The smell of bread Debra-Ann tore for herself and her brother from the loaves filling most of the sack she used as luggage roused the lady from her slumber. The portly woman beside her, draped in a black shawl, finally lifted her head from beneath her hat, not due to the train's shake and clatter as it sped across the countryside but because of the enticing aroma of fresh bread. *That lady looked hungry*; it was the first thing Debra-Ann thought when their eyes met. Her stomach growled so loudly that Debra-Ann reached into her bag and handed her a loaf of bread before they were introduced.

"Thank you kindly, child, my name is Ms. Virginia," the lady said, tearing a piece off the loaf and reaching to pass the rest back with a smile. My gut growls all the time, telling all my business: fat, hungry, wit child ... lie to, I ain't wit child, least not for a long time now," she chuckled. Debra-Ann smiled; however, she quickly noticed the man sitting across from Ms. Virginia, his gaunt figure revealing a deep yearning. His eyes, hungry yet hesitant, followed the bread as if it were a mirage of a full-course meal just beyond his reach. With an encouraging nod, Debra-Ann urged Ms. Virginia to share the remainder of the loaf with him. Initially, Ms. Virginia shook her head—a subtle, almost protective refusal marked by a flicker of concern.

"My name is Debra-Ann; this youngin' right here be my brother Michael. He named after my...*our* father, and our grandfather Michael," she said softly, her gaze drifting to the bobbing yellow flower that swayed gently as if it were expressing its own emotions. A warmth spread through her heart, fueled by Ms. Virginia's concern; it reminded her of the fond memories of the gentle love that once surrounded her by her dad and Grand Michael. The man tipped his hat and thanked both ladies. Initially drawn tight, Debra-Ann's lips softened into a gentle smile as she caught the concerned expression of the woman beside her. Ms. Virginia's eyes darted from left to right, scanning the nearby passengers. When her gaze returned to Debra-Ann, her lips pressed thinly before gently giving way to a frown, reflecting her understanding of the moment's weight. There were more eyes and hunger, and Debra-Ann's heart raced; a deep yearning snapped through her. As the yellow flower finally quieted, Debra-Ann relaxed an unfamiliar stirring inside her. She could feel something on her; maybe it was in her… She didn't need to look around because her heart told her so. With her eyes closed, she exhaled sharply, letting the scent of bread mix with the musty train air, and she whispered her heartfelt, steadfast faith into the breeze, seeking to understand the plans for the journey ahead and the stirrings of her spirit.

"The Spirit Himself testifies with our spirit that we are God's children." (Romans 8:16)

"I am speaking the truth in Christ; I am not lying, my conscience also bearing me witness in the Holy Spirit." (Romans 9:1)

Ms. Virginia gazed out the window at the sunset, her eyes darting back into the train car, marveling as Debra-Ann held Michael inches from her face. "I promise you," she assured him, "I will make a life for us, little brother," before rubbing noses with the little bundle and receiving a full-body-shaking smile. A troubling experience from Ms. Virginia's past forced a pained grin as Michael grabbed Debra-Ann's nose. Ms. Virginia sighed, and her heart fluttered as she observed Debra-Ann's eyes darting like a hawk's, inspecting the crowd for signs of disbelief in the faces around her. Ms. Virginia frowned; Debra-Ann was in the zone, confidently practicing the phrase 'little brother,' with each word flowing from her like a perfectly executed performance.

"Debra," Michael mumbled, smiling at his big sister. A

big grin pulled at Debra-Ann's mouth as she hugged little Michael and softly whispered in his ear, "It's working cause you look like a big ole baby, maybe three, maybe four." Then, facing each other again, Michael giggled and called her Debra again, this time louder and more clearly. Debra-Ann caught Ms. Virginia's gaze, holding it just a bit too long.

Ms. Virginia's eyes locked onto Debra-Ann's; the connection was charged with unspoken tension. "I thought to myself, hmm, you all sure dress y'all scarecrows proper," she quickly exclaimed, a mischievous grin lighting up her face as if she were a cat that swallowed the canary. Debra-Ann frowned. "I saw that scarecrow waving," Ms. Virginia continued, her laughter trying to shatter the veil of awkwardness between them. I said, 'self,' you still asleep... until you nudged me awake when you rushed to the window. The plump woman's gaze drifted to the left, charmed by something beyond the nearby horizon. "What foolishness y'all up to down here?"

Ms. Virginia asked, tossing her head back with a flourish, the bright flower atop her wide-brimmed hat bobbing amusingly in rhythm. Debra-Ann nearly forgot her weariness as her heart began to race. At the same time, she unraveled stories from the past—tales of her father, Grand Michael, the loyal bloodhound Lancelot, the charming Straw Hat waving his farewell from the scarecrow's wooden post, and the kind-hearted Ms. Emma and Ms. Mary. Each person held a cherished spot in Debra-Ann's heart. Others lifted her spirits in times of despair: the spirited Pastor James, who brought joy with his sermons, and the wise Mrs. Evie, who not only advised her on being a proper lady but also patiently taught her the art of braiding hair. Also, Mrs. Evie's sister, Ms. Ledonia, a kind old lady, had a childlike joy that filled the kitchen with laughter as she cooked up delicious Creole dishes passed down from mother to daughter. Ms. Virginia listened with a smile, her eyes twinkling with warmth as she recalled these memories. Yet, amidst the tales of love and guidance, she couldn't help but notice the silence surrounding Debra-Ann's mother, with no mention of her, neither in life nor in passing.

In warm contrast to the wails of infants and the energetic commotion of restless children, Michael, a beacon of joy and innocence amid the morning chaos, had already reached for and comfortably nestled in Ms. Virginia's lap. His small frame bounced gently in her soft embrace. Debra-Ann watched them with a glowing smile, her heart swelling as she noticed the delight painted across Michael's face—a smile that had eluded him while being held by his grandmother, Helen, whose touch he always seemed eager to escape. With both arms freed, the weary Debra-Ann pushed herself up from her seat and moseyed down the aisle, generously distributing every loaf of bread remaining in her bag, keeping just one for little Michael. Ms. Virginia's gaze, tinged with disappointment, tracked Debra-Ann as she made her way up the aisle, her footsteps slowing as her eyes dropped to the grit and grime on the train's floor below her. But instantly, her gaze lifted to meet Ms. Virginia's broad, warm smile, which was just inches away.

"You can move mountains with what you carry inside you, child. You moved me, and I ain't no feather," Ms. Virginia joked, affectionately patting the seat beside her as Michael playfully swatted at the vibrant flower swaying atop her hat.

"Stop that, Michael! I thought you'd be happy to get away from me for a spell," Debra-Ann scolded, dropping back into her seat with a soft huff. She distractedly rubbed at a tic above her eyebrow, sighing as the moment's weight settled over her. "Don't know you, but somehow, it matters what you think of me, Ms. Virginia," she murmured, her gaze drifting to Michael. "My brother..." Debra-Ann stuttered, her voice trailing off as Ms. Virginia gently patted her lap, leaning in to speak, lost in her feelings and struggling to approach the moment.

"My sister is a teacher in Philadelphia... she's having my third grandchild," Ms. Virginia softly unburdened herself. Her head nodded slowly and deliberately; her eyes were warm as she took a moment to connect. Ms. Virginia waited patiently, giving Debra-Ann time to absorb her words. Suddenly overwhelmed, Debra-Ann scratched her head, frowned, tilted her head to the side, and was filled with deep emotion. At a loss for words, she looked down at her hands. When her eyes met Ms. Virginia's, they connected, forming a bond rooted in understanding and empathy for women's burdens before they become women. With a gentle, knowing nod, Ms. Virginia softly said, "That's right, child," she moved to the same city. "I see charted in brown around the brim of your beautiful sky-blue straw hat." As Debra-Ann furrowed her brows in thought, a flicker of doubt appeared. I learned to read a map as a child, Ms. Virginia smiled reassuringly. Hesitantly, Debra-Ann reached up and lifted her hat. It was now a symbol of the few beautiful things she had left, so she carefully placed it in her lap as if it were fragile. She looked at it more closely, her fingers tracing the fine lines and darker marks, as if each held a secret waiting to be discovered. Turning to Ms. Virginia, Debra-Ann broke the silence with a timid question.

"Train tracks?" Her finger paused at a particularly dark

mark, her heart fluttered as she looked up, whispering, "Washington, DC?"

Ms. Virginia responded with an encouraging nod, her eyes shimmering with understanding, creating a bridge of unspoken emotions between them. Debra-Ann continued exploring the map etched on the crown of her straw hat. "Baltimore, Maryland," she said confidently, before her eyes rose to a huge smile spread across Ms. Virginia's face as their eyes connected. And just as quickly, Ms. Virginia's eyes dimmed. "We were each other's everything, my joy until she moved hundreds of miles away," she conceded, her pain and sorrow heavy in the air. Debra-Ann looked longingly into her eyes. "Your daughter," she whispered. Her eyes fell to her feet as she shared Ms. Virginia's grief.

In the delicate pause that followed, little Michael clapped his hands with innocent joy, a bright smile lighting up his adorable face—a gentle reminder of the happiness still lingering amid the weight of their conversation. Ms. Virginia sighed, "Life will continue to press on with no never mind what you going through," her thoughts seeping out from the gloomy corners of her mind, masking her pain with throat clearing. Her eyes lingered sadly on a stain on the seat opposite her, causing Michael to kiss her cheek and warmly embrace her. Unaware, Debra-Ann shared a loving smile with Ms. Virginia and Michael, and the bond between the three seemed to weave a thread of comfort. "He be your child, or he be your brother," Ms. Virginia murmured with a thoughtful frown, patting Debra-Ann's lap as if to anchor their connection. She closed her eyes briefly; her bottom lip trembled as she took a deep breath, fighting back the tide of memories that threatened to spill over.

"Tell the world what you need, but Michael must love one and not yearn for the other. I tell ya, child, I *know* what I talkin' about." A resigned sigh escaped Ms. Virginia's lips, her gaze dropping to her feet as frustrations with life hissed like a tire's slow, relentless leak. Debra-Ann's eyes darted to the corners of her vision, listening intently as Ms. Virginia's story slowly unfurled before her like a cobweb catching the light.

"Can't confuse this here, child... Like I did wit my daughter." Ms. Virginia's chest swelled, her breath hitching as she prepared to reveal a long-held wound, but anguish soon gripped her heart, squeezing tightly. "Ain't called her my daughter in thirty years; even then, it was just a whisper in her ear as I cleaned her in a wash tub," she choked out, struggling to continue as the weight of regret hung heavily in the air. "Told my daughter... 'she mine, out of me,' too late. Now, I long to hear 'mom,' 'grandmom'...but..." Ms. Virginia glanced toward the window, her expression clouded with longing, unwilling to let her tears betray her. Debra-Ann gently reached for Ms. Virginia's hand as a quiet understanding bloomed within the surreal moment, urging her to relax her shoulders and let empathy wash over her like a summer breeze. She stayed in that position, her expression softening, her gaze unfocused as it drifted aimlessly before her. Listening to Ms. Virginia's pained voice—heavy with the weight of years—and battling the heaviness of her eyelids, Debra-Ann instinctively leaned her head, without hesitation or invitation, to rest tenderly on Ms. Virginia's shoulder, seeking solace in their shared moment of vulnerability.

"My daughter... we love each other, not the way I want. Not like my daughter wants. Just too many years missing out on who we could have been, who we should have been. *It's kind of like the toll that slavery takes:* Only I, the master of our fate, did her wrong."

She knows me; she knows my secret. Maybe Ms. Virginia has a Charlie who hurt her, too.

Debra-Ann's eyelids fluttered softly, heavy with fatigue, as Ms. Virginia began to hum a gentle church hymn. Nestled against Ms. Virginia's shoulder, she sensed warmth and safety wrapping around her like her Grand Michael's comforting bear hugs. Michael's uncontrollable giggle of delight at the flower's teasing reach fluttered throughout the train as he joyfully bounced in Ms. Virginia's arms. The setting sun filtered through the window, casting a reddish-orange glow around them while Debra-Ann took a peaceful moment to rest, savoring the sound of their happiness.

Ms. Virginia smiled warmly as she watched the little girl snuggle against her, mirroring her every movement with a cuddly response. "Debra," Ms. Virginia called softly, then raised her voice melodically, "Deb-bra." Debra-Ann's eyes slowly took focus, her vision leisurely settling on Ms. Virginia's, and her inviting face. A soft yawn escaped her lips, which she excused while covering her mouth. She hesitated to lift her head from Ms. Virginia's shoulder, the warmth surrounding her with a warmth she wished from a mother. Debra-Ann reached up with a small grunt and groan, arms spread wide as if anticipating something special, ready for a big reveal.

"I like that," she said gleefully, her face lighting up before another yawn overcame her. "Just Debra from now on. Debra-Ann's country, real country," she admitted. Ms. Virginia nodded her support with a smile as Debra reached for her brother.

As the hours drifted into the night, Ms. Virginia filled the time with a mix of what-ifs, reflected on her journey since she first arrived in the busy city, and the lessons she wanted to share with Debra. While Debra remained lost in thought, gazing into the darkness outside the window, Ms. Virginia quickly reached into her purse for a pencil and paper. Adjusting her bifocals, she began jotting down her thoughts. Suddenly, her pencil paused mid-sentence.

"Tomorrow is just around the corner, my dear child," she said softly without raising chin or brow, still focused on her notes. Cold silence drew Ms. Virginia's gaze, drifting briefly to Michael before settling warmly on Debra. "You can read, can't you, child?" Debra beamed with confidence, nodding eagerly.

"Oh, yes, ma'am! I read all the time! I even learned math up to eighth grade, and I just turned fifteen," she exclaimed, her eyes sparkling with pride and excitement.

Debra peered down at the note being written in Ms. Virginia's hand, turning it around with her eyes, her heart racing with concern. Quickly, she looked to face her, disbelief flickering in her wide eyes, and she instinctively raised her hand to cover her mouth, overwhelmed by a wave of anxiety. "Oh no!" she whispered, her voice trembling with emotion. "But… I thought you said Philadelphia is your stop." Without looking up, Ms. Virginia paused her writing, her pen resting on the period after the last word she had penned, 'love.' The silence, where Debra's words should have been, caught Ms. Virginia's attention. She looked up, mouth agape and speechless, as their eyes locked. Realizing something, she placed a hand on Debra's lap. Debra quickly lowered her chin to her chest and gazed down at her shoes, eyes shining.

"Oh no, dear child," Ms. Virginia said softly. Her smile is a platter she hopes to serve soothing words. I live in Baltimore, Maryland." Assuring Debra that there is no abandonment, she quickly turns the half-written note around. See, my address, right there," she points to the neatly written address on the page and explains warmly, "You have me as a friend. Once my little sister gets to know you, you and Michael will have two, see, there's her address in Philadelphia. If you need anything."

Ms. Virginia remained calm; her words were gentle in delivery. Still, Debra stared blankly. She swallowed hard as her heart raced, nodding in acceptance and concession. Ms. Virginia's shoulders slumped, a tear silently tracing a path down Debra's cheek tugged at her heart, a glimmer of vulnerability amidst her confusion. "By the time you reach Philadelphia," Ms. Virginia added, her voice cheerful and bubbly, "My little sister will have heard so much about you, she will be happy to help you get settled."

Debra's politeness overshadowed her pain in front of her new friend. "Thank you kindly, Ms. Virginia," Debra said, then forced a strained smile, her voice soft and her tone wavering slightly. Michael bounced on her lap as she gazed out the window, her broken heart heavy with pain and gratitude. The tall buildings blurred past as the train rattled toward the station through downtown Washington, D.C. The energy inside the train car was electric; though most didn't know where to go or what lay ahead, they felt it was better than where they had come from, with colored folks dancing in the aisle as they joyfully prepared to leave. Ms. Virginia, a dignified presence in her vintage attire, waited patiently as the train began to slow. A gentle smile suggested she had pleasant thoughts to share as she scanned the faces around her. The train, now creeping into the station, had departing passengers rush to their feet, gathering their belongings from the rack above their seats to beat the stampede for the door. Ms. Virginia quickly rose, then stood on her chair as the train stopped. She aggressively cleared her throat to gain attention before loudly roaring, commanding with her unwavering gaze. "Excuse me, good people!" she shouted. Debra and Michael sat amazed as she continued. This pretty little girl sitting in her lovely powder blue dress, holding her brother, shared her last with many of you. "Now, I'm gonna pass my hat around, and I want you all to think about what you will remember about yourself when you think about this moment," she said as she stepped down from the chair. The hat circulated among the group. Ms. Virginia brushed off her chair before sitting back down, smiling at Debra-Ann just seconds before suddenly jumping to her feet, playfully shouting, "Don't nobody take my flower!"

As it passed from hand to hand, some passengers added generously, some placed what they had, and some contributed nothing. Ms. Virginia lost sight of the hat when the little black conductor with his baritone voice and funny hat marched in.

"Next stop: Washington, DC," he bellowed. "When the train doors open, be ready! The strong help the weak; the young aid the old; and the men support the women. Do the same in the city... Go with God," he preached.

The conductor hurried down the aisle, squeezing past passengers and over abandoned luggage, through the doors just as quickly as he had entered. Most passengers connected with the conductor's words, helping those in need without expecting anything in return, still received a thank you and a smile. Ms.

Virginia grunted softly in her throat, abandoning her search for her hat, angrily shoving her hand under her arms. The nearly empty train car that once packed travelers like sardines now felt hollow, with remaining departing passengers moving down the aisle, mostly showing guilt or shame, along with old folks in no rush to be rushed. Leaning forward, Ms. Virginia rose to her feet and watched closely. Among them was a striking bronze-skinned man eager for the glitz and glamour of the big city, dressed in a flamboyant bright red suit with a matching hat and feather that danced in rhythm with his movements. He hunched slightly to navigate the crowded space, yet his feather trailed behind him, making an audacious statement as it brushed against the ceiling of the train car.

Behind him, an elderly lady, feather-light and seemingly disappearing every time she passed the train's seat backrests, steadfast and poised with a cane, crept forward. Her tiny two-inch heels clacked against the floor, like the ticks of a metronome marking the passage of time. The man cast sharp, almost accusatory glances at Ms. Virginia, then flicked his gaze back to the old lady behind him. His expression was a complex tapestry of emotions—traces of guilt mingled with indignation painted across his face, he a canvas ready for an assortment of masks. Ms. Virginia's gaze stayed fixed on him; her brow creased as she tried to read his face. His long strides, a foot race toward the train's door, creating greater distance between him and the old woman, urgency etched into his demeanor.

"My hat gone," she murmured, gently rubbing her hand across Debra's back to offer a measure of comfort amid the swirling emotions of departure.

"It's fine, Ms. Virginia. Lord knows, I measured for nothing, and I got nothing," Debra said reassuringly. Ms. Virginia's previously stern demeanor softened. "I believed my hat and flower gone," she exclaimed as she stood, relief radiating like a warm afterglow as she directed Debra's eyes. The old lady walking up the aisle quickened her pace at the words, "Last call to exit from the Conductor," but not toward the door. She stopped in front of Ms. Virginia and Debra-Ann, hat in hand, head shaking in disgust as she glanced at the man in the red suit rushing through the exit. "Fox always be himself," lowering her voice, her wrinkled lips curling inward as if sharing a delicious secret; they didn't just observe for themselves but for the details, adding a sense of intrigue to the moment.

"Do you see that tall red rooster strutting about?" She said, pointing behind her. "I swung my cane and cracked that cheeky bird muthafucka right across his head! If my legs were as spry as they used to be, I would've kicked him straight in the crack of his ass beak," the old lady declared with a mischievous twinkle in her eye before taking a moment to introduce herself. "Pardon, I go by Dot, short for Dorothy," she added, her smile brightening the atmosphere as the others shot disapproving glances at the man who had hurriedly jumped off the train unassisted. Debra and Ms. Virginia stifled their laughter, the sound bubbling just beneath the surface, as Michael gleefully repeated the delightful word that had tickled his ears.

"Ass Beak, ass beak" he chirped, his eyes wide with anticipation as he awaited the usual burst of laughter that never materialized.

"Excuse my language, ladies; I don't mean to corrupt the child," Dot inserted with a tilt of her head and a slight grin. Ms. Virginia interjected, her voice a mix of playful exasperation and genuine concern. "But," Dot continued, "shiftless niggas raise my dandruff somethin' fierce!" she continued, returning Ms. Virginia her hat. Ms. Virginia's previously stern demeanor softened, her lined face breaking into a warm smile as she grasped Debra's arm for support, a silent reassurance.

"My hat! Sure I'd seen the last of it!" she exclaimed.

"Damn near," Dot chuckled. She stepped closer, lowering her voice, Dot puckered her lips once more, curling them into a conspiratorial whisper—an instinctive gesture she used for even small infractions to share another tempting secret. She angrily continued, "Ya knows, he was gonna thieve that money you were tryna collect for this child, is why my cane met him without words," she said. Dot's head nodded continuously as she returned the hat filled with money, grinning. Debra and Ms. Virginia's brows creased as they glanced down at Dot's hand as she backed away, needing to leave before the train's departure. Dot giggled, feigning surprise as she looked at her hand, raising it to eye level.

"I was hoping..." she gazed at the flower, "telling my husband, Jesse, that a fella gave it to me, making him want to prove something," she added with a playful giggle. Dot's laughter was that of a kind-hearted old lady, mild-mannered with a switch, charming with a dash of mischievousness, handling what life throws her way with a smile. Ms. Virginia and Debra saw the image of a fierce warrior in Dot's petite frame, smiling at her lively personality as she stepped into the busy world beyond the door.

The mournful wail of the train's horn rattled the buildings as it slowly departed, marking the start of a new journey.

Debra held Michael as they edged to the far end of their

seat, foreheads pressed against the cool window. Their eyes darted left and right while they watched joyful reunions and tearful goodbyes. The circle of emotions overwhelmed Michael, who shared in the laughter and the tears. His hand slid across the window, waving hellos and goodbyes, reaching out to join the warm embraces celebrating joyful reunions and sorrowful farewells.

Debra couldn't help but giggle; she quickly covered her mouth when she spotted the elderly lady, Dot, and her imposing husband, Jesse, who looked every bit the caring preacher from Mississippi in his three-piece gray suit. Just before the couple disappeared from view, Ms. Virginia glanced up from her writing, her brows lifting in surprise, accompanied by a soft chuckle as Jesse's gaze fell lovingly on the flower Dot held, prompting her to respond with a shy smile.

"Huh. That old man is a tall glass of water for that little flower," she said, a playful grin spreading across her face. With a humorous shake of her head, she returned to her notes.

It wasn't long before a portly conductor, another man of color, filled the open doorway, his appearance marked by the familiar rumbling sound of the train's wheels sailing along the tracks. His eyes held a softness, reflecting a fatigue similar to that of a caged circus lion, yearning for the freedom to express itself but having long forgotten how to break the silence. Those seated for a while watched him with wonder, hoping for words of encouragement or inspiration, but were instead met with a gentle yet weary voice.

"Baltimore, Maryland, next stop!" he calls out. He steps forward in a hurry and feels the gentle sway of the train. His body is unsteady as he attempts to maintain his balance while in motion. Ms. Virginia's voice is anxious and filled with urgency as she rummages beneath her seat, her fingers frantically searching for her lost shoes, the soles of which have vanished into the shadows of the cramped space. Michael laughed as Ms. Virginia struggled to her feet, then sat back down. She pressed her hand firmly against Debra's shoulder.

"As soon as you get off this train, child, walk up the steps that lead to Market Street and deposit this money in the bank directly across the street."

"Yes, um," Debra replied with a nod. Cash and coins were counted carefully, and Ms. Virginia hurried to put them into her purse.

"Just let any bank teller know that Ms. Virginia sent you," she continued, "and keep your business your business. You understand me, child?" Her tone was stern and direct. Debra listened and nodded, her eyes widening as they met Ms. Virginia's gaze.

"Yes, ma'am," she repeated. After placing another note she had just finished writing in her purse, she said, "This is the address of an orphanage that will take you and your brother. Here's a dollar; take a cab after you leave the bank, give him the dollar and the note; there's enough change for a nice tip, so don't worry about anything." Debra's mouth opened to speak, but without the right words, it just snapped shut.

Debra turned away from Ms. Virginia, desperate to hide the tears welling in her eyes. She stared at her reflection's deception, revealing traces of every tear as she watched the train hiss, plumes of steam rising from underneath and clouding the windows. Lost in the moment, she gazed unfocused.

"Yes, child, my stop," Ms. Virginia said with a soothing smile that went unnoticed.

"Maybe," Debra replied hesitantly as Ms. Virginia gently placed her purse between Debra and Michael, who was now contentedly resting on her lap. Debra exhaled, releasing any thought of joining Ms. Virginia. She kissed both of them on the forehead before standing, as passengers began to exit the train, silencing this consideration. Ms. Virginia shot Debra a stern look as she backed away.

"The Lord dun put it on and in you, child... Strong enough, put faith in you, in me." Ms. Virginia turned away, wiping her tears as she approached the door. Then, she glanced back, her expression serious yet caring. "If you want to do right by Michael, get your education. My daughter would be pleased to help you, but remember to call her my little sister."

Not wanting to break in front of Michael, Debra continued to look out the window.

Before the train's departure, its hiss startled nearby horses into a frenzy, cats into giving up one of their lives, and made dogs stop chasing them. However, Ms. Virginia stood on the station platform, engulfed amid the train's thick steam long after the crowd had moved on. She sensed that Debra was still gazing out of the window, so she took a moment to gather her strength and prepared a reassuring smile as the train began to leave. Full of innocent, dancing joy, Michael clapped his tiny hands against the glass, calling out a cheerful goodbye. Behind him, Debra waved, fresh tears streaming down her cheeks, feeling the weight of their parting and the love shared in that fleeting moment. Debra looked to the heavens and mouthed, "Thank you," before pressing her hand against the windowpane and mouthing "Thank you" once more as she locked eyes with Ms. Virginia when the train passed her.

CHAPTER EIGHT
PROMISES AND PRAYERS

GABRIEL ERUPTED JUST beneath the dazzling threshold of Heaven and Earth, driven by an unyielding purpose that buzzed with electric energy. With his chin held high and his magnificent wings pulsating with vitality, he was poised to unleash a tempest of destiny. In that exhilarating, heart-swelling moment, his bronze skin buzzing to the irresistible pull—the courageous soul was being called home. Be it a fiery promise from long ago or the faith of a mustard seed prayer that sparked his unwavering spirit? Whichever, it detoured his climb back to Heaven, keeping him tied to the earthly mission that awaited. Questions whirled in his mind as he stood in the shadowy nook of Debra's bedroom, returning after more than sixty years had slipped away like fleeting whispers. Seeing her still, the little girl, holding on to faith and prayer.

The gymnasium, decorated with royal purple, lavender, and white by Sandy J. and her friends from nursing school, was transformed into a palace for princess Debra's fairy-tale wedding reception. Debra, remaining in a state of shock and awe, her body buzzing with energy, bounced on the balls of her feet in the middle of the dance floor, then gently swaying from side to side in her beautiful yet modest white wedding dress as the soulful sound of "Darling, I Love You" by B.B. King played, soothing everyone around her from the rump-shaking, foot-tapping started with the door's opening. Purple, lavender, and white balloons scattered across the floor bounced off her feet as she took off her high heels to feel more comfortable after dancing with Kevin down the early version of the 'Soul Train Line' for the tenth time. Balloons sent airborne by Debra's playful feet still hovered overhead, revealing the gym's center court where her reception was held; some even rested in the nets at each end of the gym. During a moment of rest, standing there and catching her breath, watching her husband, Kevin, and her little brother, Michael, find a table to sit and recharge, Debra, for the first time since rice had rained down on her at the church steps, took a moment to reflect. Her eyes wandered to some of the people she had met along her journey. Ms. Virginia, slightly frail but as feisty as Dot, the 'warrior granny,' sat at a table with her sister-daughter and her nieces-granddaughters. Their bond over shared bread, made on the train just hours after the country cashier had tried to crush her spirit and extinguish her hope, showed their close connection. Debra's gaze met Ms. Virginia's through her bifocals, a quiet thank you for the window when the door slammed shut. To the nursing school sisterhood gathered at a table, getting a little tipsy, Debra rolled her eyes at their ongoing teasing about her upcoming wedding night adventure, feeling once again that community of love she hadn't expected to find among Black women. From that group, Sandy J., her little sister—not by blood but by faith—became her true sister.

Debra's memories were interrupted by loud music once more, then by her brother. Dressed in his tiny tuxedo, Michael, the cutest little penguin, hurried through the crowd, crushing balloons in his path with his little patent leather shoes. Each balloon soared into the air, hovering like tiny rockets over the moon. Debra couldn't help but giggle. Michael waddled closer, Debra's face strained to understand, his eyes threatening to tear up just seconds before he leaped into her arms with all his strength. Out of breath, he cupped her confused face in his little hands to get her attention. As the music pulsed through the air, Debra leaned in, her heart pounding. "What's wrong?" she mouthed, but no sound emerged; she couldn't even hear her voice over the pounding rhythm. Her brows knitted in concern; the music felt deafening now—was it drowning out their moment? Once again, she pressed, frantic with urgency. Calmly amidst the chaos.

"Debra... wake up!"

Suddenly, Debra's eyes shot open, shimmering with the startled look of a deer caught in headlights. Her heart was racing with the frightened twitch of a hunted animal. Debra stirred. Her heart fluttered in her chest with the pitter-patter of a terrified child, and shock coursing through her like a lightning bolt, snatching her from a beautiful dream back to her pain-filled reality. She lay bathed in darkness, except for a nightlight plugged into the wall across from the bed. The candlelight fixture flickered, then went black, before shining as bright as car headlights, casting surreal shadows that danced briefly before returning to normal. Debra stirred, her eyelids fluttering as her body acknowledged its roadmap of pain and then drifted back to sleep. Suddenly, at the foot of her bed, an image appeared, before vanishing, a voice whispered, "Debra-Ann." It filled the space around her like the blast of an explosion, and she immediately opened her eyes wide like saucers. That name, Debra-Ann, given to her at birth and not heard for more than half a century, was a haunting return of the fear it had once produced.

Her heart raced wildly in her chest; a caged bird desperate for freedom. She inhaled deeply to steady her fraying nerves, filling her lungs with air, and slowly sat upright in bed. Slipping her feet into soft, worn slippers, she sighed and muttered, "Lord, have mercy," a daily prayer that had become a ritual since her life shattered her childhood innocence. With a deep exhale, Debra found herself adrift in her thoughts.

It feels like the morning has already begun without me, she mused. Perhaps it's merely my distorted perception of time...or was it just my time?

It was the latter of her reflection she conceded, as she glanced over at her closet where she had buried a cane inside an old, faded suitcase. She defiantly shook her head as if answering the cane's demands to use it, but then turned back to her task, determined to stand and walk about on her own. Her rise from her bed was slower and more challenging than most days. She rejected the excuses available, knowing that focusing on the pain was not an option; she pushed herself to take one step and then another, making the most of it. Her body unfolded with each step until the aches could be ignored and her stride became normal.

Debra ambled through the halls, stopping at each of the boys' bedrooms to reminisce about the memories they held. She grinned as her eyes caressed the notches on the closet doorframe, marking her children's heights, and the patchwork over the holes in the walls, still waiting for the truth in the stories that were told. Lancelot, the first Knight she saw each morning in the hall and the first to receive a pat on the head, was the one who left his position across from her bedroom door and trailed after her. He signaled to Galahad and Percival with a gentle bark.

Debra paused the longest at the threshold of the largest room—the baby's room—where all her children first slept in the crib; her eyes lingered on the spot by the window where she sat in a chair, holding, feeding each of them.

Every moment is a gift. Debra understood this; today, it held even greater meaning. Her children were a blessing from God, filling her heart with love, now shared with her grandchildren. Her brows furrowed when she caught a glimpse of the new small notches on the closet doorframe, the growth of mind and body in her grandchildren, she wished to experience; each one shining in her heart like a precious gem. With a bittersweet smile and perhaps a tear shed, Debra leaned her cheek against the cool, worn doorframe, a wave of gratitude washing over her for the memories lovingly created within these walls. Behind her, Lancelot, standing, his whimper, his worries to bring her back. A smile and strokes on the head were his reward before they made their way down the hall, passing Galahad.

Galahad jumped up and down with his ears pointed toward the ceiling, eagerly awaiting his head pat and food from his position on the top step. Always hungry and the first to bark in the morning, he announced it was time to eat. He knew to wait until Debra and Lancelot had passed before following. Percival, who always rushes to the bottom of the stairs to greet, whined once he saw Debra. He sat quietly in a shaded corner near the front door, head bowed like a prayer. Debra and Lancelot both stared without blinking, pausing their descent down the stairs. Hearing this, Galahad hurried to the front and stood beside Lancelot. As Debra reached for the banister, she gasped sharply, observing Lancelot and Galahad with their ears down and heads lowered as they moved from in front of her to join Percival. She looked down passively, signaling them to follow as she reached the last step. Debra turned, heading toward the kitchen without noticing the Knight's paws not thumping across the floor behind her— a sound she had taken for granted over the years. A missing sound that would have explained what was about to happen next.

At the kitchen threshold, Debra paused, glancing back— no knights had followed her. The room lay cloaked in shadow, except for the sliver of light dancing off the refrigerator and the gleaming chrome accents sparkling like stars in the darkness. On any other morning since she had torn down that forsaken house-for-sale sign, she would have flipped the lights on without a second thought. But today, her fingers trembled over the switch, caught in uncertainty. Sunlight dared to sneak through the curtains above the sink, but it felt different, almost unsettling. A chilling shiver raced down her spine—this was the first morning that the sun didn't warm the back of this spirited country girl. She couldn't pin this to an alarm clock—Debra had always preferred waking to the rhythm of nature. But there was no time to dwell on such thoughts; the excitement of preparing a glorious Christmas dinner awaited!

Lights on, Debra stepped just inside the kitchen, scanning the room from left to right. Her steps pause, a memory takes hold, like a smile you give after a little hand reaches for yours before crossing the street.

It has been many years since Debra last made breakfast before starting Christmas dinner for her 'boys to men,' yet she still pictures them looking up and questioning the breakfast menu — a moment she would gladly relive.

Moving directly to the cabinets over the mixer, she pressed her hand against them. Had the surrounding countertops prepared for her day of cooking, much like a general planning their attack. The room was filled with the rich aroma of cinnamon, nutmeg, and sage, from both the preparation and the early cooking done the night before. With the grace of a ballerina, Debra, eyes sparkling, darted from counter to stove to counter, with ingredients and utensils ready, repeating her movements again and again. Debra's pain, gone if not forgotten, sang the songs of Christmas, as the radio station played them all day, allowing her to dance a little two-step while reaching for a spoon to taste her late husband's recipe for brown gravy. "Almost there!" she exclaimed triumphantly, dipping a spoon to savor the rich, savory flavor. Suddenly, the room began to sway gently, much like waves on an open sea. The toaster appeared to be heading toward the floor. Debra looked at the mixer and a bag of flour to prove her eyes weren't lying. Now, the room was spinning. She reached for the counter with her left hand and pressed her right hand to her forehead, seeking clarity. With a staggering step backward, she stumbled until she felt the sturdy embrace of a chair beneath her. Gripping her trembling hands tightly, she pressed them against her chest, battling the tumultuous pounding of her heart drumming in her ears. With her eyes tightly shut, Debra loaded a prayer with Scripture and verse like one in the chamber, ready if the devil dared. Sitting quietly, the kitchen fell silent; as her breathing slowed, her hands steadied. Then, a soft and gentle touch caressed her face, from cheek to chin, liberating Debra's eyes to wide as saucers. Suddenly, serenity came with the sound of a familiar voice —the same soul-comforting voice that called to her from her grandfather's porch in Mississippi.

"It is time, my child. We must depart," the voice echoed. Debra looked toward the ceiling, where she believed the voice was coming from, only it seemed to be coming from within. Her breathing was faster and shallower; still, she found words in this moment of absolute calm.

"Angel…Spirit guide, when my pain was unbearable and many days after, I soundlessly asked for this. Why this day, when tears fall because of joy?" she asked. Without tenor or emotion, the voice replied, "A joyous day, this is to all believers. Your prayers have been answered, my child." Debra's chin fell to her chest,

"Can serenity be the last earthly reward before the storm, my family receives from me before my soul goes to rest?" she petitioned.

In that profound silence, she felt a stillness that whispered both possibilities and fears. What should have comforted her only brought more terror than the initial thunderous voice. Eyes shut, Debra's head met her chest, and her shoulders slumped as she stood awaiting her fate. The holiday music began to play once more. Seconds later, the dial spun out of control as if it were in a frantic search for another jingle. Debra's eyes opened quickly, darting to the counter where the radio played. She then glanced up at the ceiling, her gaze filled with childlike innocence as if silently asking a caring parent for guidance and reassurance in a moment of confusion.

The phone rang. Debra's head moved toward the sound, stopping only when her eyes landed on family pictures covering the refrigerator. Her eyes shifted from one photo to another. A grin appeared, like the pride an artist feels when they know they've created something special. Debra closed her eyes, her heart full, pressing tears from their corners. Her head gently bowed to her chest; she whispered the words of a prayer she knew would be her final farewell. The phone appeared to ring with fatigue as she noticed it. She looked toward the angelic voice for approval. Then, a gentle whisper floated in the air, saying, *"Prayer... answered."* The tension eased from her body as she closed her eyes.

"Hello?" Debra said, her voice trembling with anxiety and breathless tension. The air was thick with nervous energy. She felt unsettled by her recent brush with rapture in the kitchen, where the scent of baking mingled with her swirling thoughts.

"Hey girl," came Sandy J.'s cheerful reply, a bright note cutting through the heaviness. Her tone was light and playful, like a sunbeam piercing through a cloud. "I know you're almost done prepping everything. I just wanted to check if you could use an extra pair of hands—maybe for some taste testing and whatnot." Sandy J. questioned the silence between them, stretching like an unspoken query. Debra rubbed her forehead, feeling the weight of her visitor's request. *Rubbing a tic above her eyebrow eased the yoke of the question.* Debra giggled softly and awkwardly, casually trying to seem normal. A tear quietly traced the curve of her cheek, chasing memories of their wild, adventurous lives together. With her next breath uncertain, she found comfort in her best friend's voice.

"Well... yes," Debra's voice caught in her throat, the admission tinged with vulnerability.

"I am a bit worn out," she confessed, wincing at her raw honesty.

"I'll be right over, Sis!" Sandy J. exclaimed, her voice bubbling with infectious laughter that danced through the line. "Now, you get your big ass back upstairs and focus wrapping up that 'Putting Down the Hammer' wedding dream you always have around this time," she added. Debra held the phone away from her ear, jolted by Sandy J.'s joyful laughter and candid remark. Gradually, she returned the receiver to her ear as a hesitant chuckle escaped her lips.

"You are so silly, J," Debra giggled nervously, feeling her spirits lift with each shared moment of delight, the weight of her worries beginning to ease as her thoughts became clearer. "And no, it wasn't my dang wedding dream," she added with a playful roll of her eyes. "It was the dance with Michael, where I told him he was going home with you so I could have my *walls shaking,* 'putting down the hammer' wedding night!" Debra and Sandy J. shared a girlish giggle.

"Are you saying you need another hour, maybe two?" Sandy J. jokingly asked, her warm, comforting tone carrying her gentle laughter over the phone like an affectionate smile.

"Okay, Sis, see you in a minute! Sandy, I love you, and Merry Christmas," Debra said, a promise of minutes, let alone tomorrow, hanging in the air. Debra no longer felt the lingering spirit but paused to listen for the click, hesitating and struggling to hang up the phone, wanting to savor the moment's warmth just a little longer.

The Knights lounged by the front door when Debra approached from the kitchen. Instantly, their ears perked up in anticipation, and they showered her with high-spirited barks as she drew near. Debra knelt, reminiscent of her tender last moments with her beloved old hound dog, Lancelot, her first canine companion, she gently rubbed them, her gaze deep into their eyes, connecting with them, her gratitude for their love, loyalty, and friendship. Returning gentle nudges, loving leans, and soft whines were their bittersweet farewell, but perhaps it was her turn to journey deep into the cornfield for her final rest.

Just then, Sandy J. walked through the door, "Got some thick gray clouds out there, girl, and any body part you name is screaming snow!" She slowly stood up, towering, then quickly hugged her 'little sis' as if she were a loved one returning after a long absence. "Wow, you haven't hugged me like this in ages," Sandy J. said through her muffled voice, softly asking, "You okay, girl?" as they embraced and she gently stroked Debra's back. When Debra pulled away, a smile lit up her face, but Sandy J. couldn't help but acknowledge the tears soaking into her shoulder. The two women exchanged a knowing glance and another gentle and lasting smile as the Knights' soft whine pierced through the moment, drawing their attention.

"'Tis the season," Debra crooned as she turned to head upstairs. Her heart felt heavy, yet she was so grateful for the immense love around her. Sandy J. glanced at the knights in disbelief, *do you believe this bitch,* her tongue stifled. Sandy

J.'s mind was struggling to grasp the surreal sight before her. With furrowed brows etched deeply across her forehead, she watched Debra ascend the staircase with an effortless grace that sharply contrasted with the laborious struggles the stairs had posed lately. Each step Debra took seemed almost defiant, mocking the challenges that had become a daily ordeal.

"'*Tis* my ass... We discussing those tears tonight, once everyone's gone," she called up the stairs behind her. Sandy J. turned her gaze back to the knights. "What kind of shit was that? ... 'Tis *my* season, beating that ass, how about that. She must be out of her rabbit-ass mind if she thinks she can cry on my shoulder and not tell me what's wrong," she fussed while making her way into the kitchen. "Come, knights!" she commanded, "I'm going to feed you, bet not a single drop better hit the floor... or else you might find yourselves out back!

In the cozy warmth of the kitchen, cheerful holiday music floated gently through the air, soothing Sandy J.'s earlier fear-filled frustrations. Biting her lip, her fingers mimicked piano play on the countertop. *Okay, it's too cold for the backyard today,* she mused, her gaze drifting to the trio of dogs sitting, each of their heads shifting to the side, questioning the delay in dispensing the bag in her hand, with subtle whimpers and paw taps to her foot. She poured their kibble into their bowls with a soft chuckle, marveling at their uncanny ability. "Huh, you three ain't gonna make more work for me, *leap that fence and press the doorbell at the front!*" She laughed again, shaking her head in disbelief. Her hand raised to her waist as she swayed from side to side, her back straightening.

"And how are you dogs gonna have some attitude if we take too long to let you in!" The dogs' expressive eyes seemed to confirm her playful accusation, eager for their meal and ready to claim their moments of affection.

CHAPTER NINE
BLOODLINE DEFINED

As FAR AS the eye could see, the sky was unblemished except for the gray cloud racing toward Scott, a mid-level angel with mid-level wings, and the small, pillow-soft white cloud he traveled upon. Scott transported souls. He had one route: from Heaven to Earth and back to Heaven. It was a simple task for a simple angel. Recently, however, Scott's days had been devoid of celebration; he veered off his straightforward path and traversed the expanse of Earth for what felt like an eternity, at a height that allowed him to gaze out—something he often did—upon the magnificent view of Heaven's gate. So, when the crack of thunder called, he thought it a return to his humble route and its lowly existence, as he always did. But this thunder marked the moment Gabriel's gray cloud collided with Scott's.

Scott jolted awake as a crack of lightning surged beneath his feet, swirling energy igniting his senses. Thunder rumbled from within, like the heart of a beast circling its prey —a potent reminder of its herald: the arrival of a high-ranking angel. But which member of the celestial hierarchy might be visiting him? His mind raced with possibilities. Suddenly, the mist settled, and the archangel Gabriel slowly appeared from the storm—a radiant and commanding cherub, the lion with eagle's wings who delivered visions and messages from God himself. Scott and Gabriel were immersed in swirling murkiness, the atmosphere charged with anticipation. Scott's presence intensified, merging with the gray mist surrounding them. Scott's now larger and darker cloud moved with a grace he had never experienced; he questioned his wings' strength to navigate and whether this cloud was still his to command.

As the fog began to settle, Gabriel approached, moving with ethereal grace. A figure of awe and authority, he knelt beside his unnerved young protégé. The moment was electric, filled with energy that promised revelation and destiny.

Scott slowly began to rise, his gaze reflecting confusion as he noted the presence of someone like Gabriel, especially in light of the wounding words spoken of him by other angels.

He was, is, and likely always will be the angel humans over-look, choosing to dismiss rather than engage with him, remaining at a mid-level, wings and all. They claim that the music Scott cherishes holds him back from reaching his potential. Yet, instead of the celestial harmonies of Heaven's angels, Scott was captivated by the music created by the God-blessed souls of Earth. This wasn't restricted to just gospel or spiritual chants that celebrate God's greatness; it also included the soulful sounds that inspire deep reflection on the love that truly embodies God's spirit.

Regardless of the truth within him, which other angels

debated passionately, Scott stood respectfully, letting himself absorb Gabriel's message. "At ease, Scott," Gabriel gently commanded.

"There is a courageous soul down there, not seen since the Great Receiving, called home on this route," Gabriel reported with conviction. Scott's chin gradually lowered, his voice barely above a whisper.

"1968, Anno Domini, and the preceding years," he murmured. The overwhelming loss of courageous souls caused humanity to erase life changers from its world in those years - the sudden surge of emotions stunned the angels, causing them to pause their work. Why do we remember this, Scott questioned? Gabriel watched intently as Scott's lips formed his words. This mysterious communication hung between the two angels. Gabriel closed his eyes as their radiant wings shimmered with a kaleidoscope of colors, processing the overwhelming feelings that filled the air, and a profound stillness settled around them.

Scott buried his face in his hands, his head trembling with a mechanical rigidity that mirrored the disbelief coursing through him. "I awaited the moment this cloud drew nearest to Earth, allowing me to hear, faintly as it was, the music I cherished," he confessed, his voice filled with emotion. Scott gently withdrew his head from his hands, a mix of curiosity and concern washing over him as he looked down at them and then up into Gabriel's eyes. "Why do I speak with the mouth of mortals?" he rattled. "Why do I feel this deep sense of loss? My feet have not touched Earth, nor have I laid eyes on a human. Is today the day I am meant to fall?"

Gabriel gently placed his left hand on Scott's shoulder,

a sudden sense of brotherhood enclosing them both, even though they couldn't fully understand it. Urgently, he pressed his right hand to Scott's breastplate, speaking earnestly, "The memories I share will guide us, and those that have slipped away, well... You have asked many questions, and the answer to all... Meditate on the Word; it will be your sword in battle," the spiritual warrior declared. Scott's cheeks lifted in amazement as his gaze met Gabriel's eyes; his lips pressed flat before a smile appeared for the first time. He exhaled a breathy chuckle, his eyes crinkling with joy while his heart pounded. Yet, feeling brotherly love in that decisive moment, Gabriel briefly looked away, and the task at hand—its seriousness heightened by their deep connection.

"You entertained the courageous soul before embarking on the thrilling pursuit of this modest mid-level angel," Scott asked with growing enthusiasm. Gabriel let out a soft sigh, his gaze fixed on Scott. He awaited the moment of reflection that was about to wash over Scott, whose lip trembled, and eyes widened in disbelief.

"What is this? What strange sound was that... My face and mouth, Scott petitioned Gabriel's understanding." Scott's voice trembled with panic, a hint of desperation threading through his words. A heaviness saps their strength, but only Scott's legs are dragged by gravity to kneel.

Scott ran his hand through the thick murkiness before him, letting it slip between his fingers. "Earth?" he whispered.

Gabriel's wings fluttered, a celestial light danced off the feathers, dispersing the swirling fog as he extended his hand toward Scott, inviting him into a realm beyond comprehension.

"Yes, I traveled to Earth...I entertained the courageous

soul. And that strange sound you made with your mouth was laughter, Gabriel asserted, offering confession and counsel.

Scott looked into Gabriel's eyes, where the weight of countless adventures and the stories of humanity sparkled like distant stars. "We have a long journey ahead of us, Gabriel confessed, his tone filled with a sense of purpose that resonated in the cool, crisp air. One last prayer on the lips of our courageous soul was asked, and it has come at the very moment of elevation.

We now need to seek the origin of the prayers asked and answered from our courageous souls' past for guidance, Gabriel stated. "We must find the strength to pass through this increasingly destructive force, seeking the roots of that prayer.

Scott gently took Gabriel's hand. "Why does this worry the archangel, Gabriel? Surely, you have faced challenges like this before," he said, standing beside him.

"This courageous soul's story has been lived and written into history; like many others, it is her deeds when faced with oppression and reigns of terror," Gabriel said as he turned, walked to the edge of the cloud, and looked over the side. "The courageous soul will relive her story, the pain, the sorrow, and question whether it was a wonderful life," he confessed. "I believe I have a memory that I lost memory for a reason... this is something I have never encountered." The cloud darkened to a gray heather as it slowed, hovering over Mississippi. Scott noticed the changes around him, things he had only heard of before. Gabriel's wings collapsed behind him. "It was this day; I remember the moment," Gabriel murmured, his gaze at the land below haunting his thoughts. He turned from the edge of the cloud, seeking solace. Each step he took was deliberate and careful, as if treading on fragile glass. "I have failed the courageous soul," Gabriel confessed, his tone laden with regret. Scott noticed the sorrow reflected in the mighty warrior's gaze. He hurried to approach Gabriel, but it was too late; his head dropped to his chest, and he started to cry.

"No, Gabriel," Scott corrected, moving him and the dark cloud forward by the width of a single hair from an angel's head. "This is where you lifted the voice of humans with prayers on their lips for the courageous soul," Gabriel observed, scanning the cloud beneath his feet in every direction.

Suspended above a church, the cloud had become lighter with hope, though it remained gray. Scott recognized that his mid-level cloud's height offered a unique view of Heaven's gate, a marvel he could hardly comprehend, and he struggled to understand his own words and the achievement just completed. He stood still, awestruck by the beauty of his creation. Gabriel came back to life and greeted him with a warm, gentle smile. "There's no need to worry, young angel," he said in a soothing, deep voice. "Today's journey was made possible by a mortal, who was severely injured and bedridden, but still able to keep you, my young angel; entertained with songs that were mere thoughts as you stood by his side for four long days in 1973, witnessing the light of his spirit."

Stunned by the lack of memories, "Gabriel," Scott began, then bowed his head as he realized his place and stepped back. Gabriel smiled. Scott's steps paused. Gabriel flapped his wings once and stood before him, placing his hand on his shoulder, "I searched the expanse of the courageous soul's lifetime, and if not for a rainbow of ribbons in the sky, a melody from a human, I would not have been led to this mid-level cloud and you, Scott."

Scott's brows furrowed as he stared back at Gabriel. "I remember none of anything you speak," Scott said, raising his hands before his eyes. Laughing, Gabriel raised his right hand, placing it on Scott's shoulder. "Yet, still your hands move to pray. And I knew to touch your shoulder when I knew to touch your shoulder," Gabriel replied. Staring down at Scott's laced fingers, his grip tightening on the young angel's shoulder, "You will know when you know."

CHAPTER TEN

A FRESH START, A LOST ANGEL

ENERGIZED, GABRIEL STRODE boldly to the heart of the swirling cloud, where Scott stood mesmerized, gazing down at the vibrant, pulsating timelines that revealed the courageous soul's journey. The scenes before him flickered like the same rainbow of ribbons that had led him to Scott. Eager to claim a place and time that would keep Debra's mind focused, Gabriel rushed to kneel, but where? He swiftly sought the ideal place to offer his support. Gabriel gave a short, harsh gasp as a buried memory resurfaced, his chin quivered as he darted glances at Scott for what he believed had been his failure to provide comfort in the courageous soul's moment of need. It was 1947, in Philadelphia—a time that marked the beginning of Debra's brave new journey and the last moment she spoke of her past. Scott knelt beside Gabriel, his heart heavy as Gabriel reflected on the precious moments he shared with Debra, cherishing how she brought light to those around her. Scott pressed Gabriel's shoulder, his gaze gentle, drawing attention to the gap in the timeline—a missing piece in the story that connected them.

He was curious about Ms. Virginia, whom he sensed was a heartbroken and lonely middle-aged woman rapidly losing her connection with her surroundings, and Scott was right. It was only depression, not laziness, as the stigma of the shiftless nigger is placed on every closed eye and bowed head. Like many other colored folks, survival was crucial; Ms. Virginia's preferred escape was sleeping through the hours of each day rather than engaging with life until she met Debra and Michael. "Was she one of your vessels?" Scott asked, his tone laced with curiosity. Gabriel sighed with a gentle smile, feeling a weight settle on his shoulders as memories flickered through his mind.

"No… her actions moved by the Spirit within were entirely her own," Gabriel said softly. "I couldn't unshackle my feelings of guilt and connection to Debra-Ann… Debra. It left me weak and hesitant, unsure whether my sorrow or hers kept me from allowing myself to be entertained by Ms. Virginia." "However, Ms. Virginia's heart and soul were so pure that she brought a profound sense of hope to our courageous soul." Scott smiled at Gabriel as he linked with the following timeline. He closed his eyes and took a deep breath, holding it in as he turned to Gabriel.

"That smell?" Scott murmured, his brows creasing, "But what is it?" Frustration shading his voice. Gabriel's body froze in place, his eyes wide as headlights looking within himself, his brows raised in support, as he struggled to understand the confusion settling over him; was the task at hand too great for this warrior? Scott's eyes bulged, and his lips pressed into a thin line, mesmerized by the shimmering threads of another timeline. "We must dream her dreams before she dreams," he urged, his voice steady, confident, and authoritative. "The scent," Scott grinned, "our guide—faith." He locked eyes with Gabriel, his gaze piercing and unwavering, demanding the confidence that Gabriel struggled to muster. "Take hold," Scott insisted as the weight of their mission hung palpably in the air around them.

Cars drifted by, each slowly capturing the mouthwatering aromas wafting through the air. People from every corner of the city formed serpentine lines outside the Oak Tree Diner, eager for the outstanding comfort food that touches the soul, as promised. On this perfectly sunny Saturday afternoon, heads lifted to the sky, eyes shadowed with concern, at the sight of an ominous gray cloud hovering overhead, all but declaring rain. Yet no one budged, their hunger for a delicious dish swelling their chests with anticipation, as they drew in deep breaths filled with the promise of comfort food, even as they pressed onward against the faint drizzle. A lively discussion bubbled among the would-be diners, their voices mingling with the warm breeze, animatedly debating the merits of "crispy fried catfish served alongside creamy grits" versus the irresistible appeal of "succulent fried chicken, savory collard greens, and tongue-tantalizing macaroni and cheese." It was this culinary magic that had drawn Debra to work there part-time. While the food might not quite measure up to the celebrated meals created by her Grand Michael, it came tantalizingly close, sparking joy among the growing crowd that spilled out of the diner and wrapped around the side of the building like a living ribbon of impatience and hunger.

The line stretched before Debra and her brother Michael, winding behind them, while a restless ocean of eager patrons exchanged playful jabs and glanced impatiently at the slow clock. Layla, an attractive and bubbly waitress, returned from a cigarette break, sauntering alongside the long line as she took the last few drags before flicking her cigarette butt to the curb. With her chin held high and chest out, she moved confidently, causing the hem of her flared skirt to dance flirtatiously against her thighs, drawing admiring glances and momentarily quieting the lively conversations that resumed only after she passed. This was her routine to prepare for the dinner crowd and the high tippers she always identified and seated in her section. Layla spotted Debra and Michael in line, grasped Debra's arm, and led them past the waiting patrons. "Child, you work here, bring your behinds in here and have a seat in my section," she asserted as she rushed them along. Michael giggled at the speed of their steps, and Layla's vibrant hat perched jauntily on her fluffy afro, bobbing playfully like a piece of felt on a large black Q-tip. The air buzzed with envy and irritation; some familiar faces squinted, trying to place Debra without her waitress uniform, while others—primarily men—pretended to feign disinterest, their gazes lingering a fraction too long on her poised figure.

Layla artfully moved about the crowded space, while her confidence in her tight assets energized the room. Michael, hawkishly protective, stares daggers, each one a threat and a cause for the invisible barrier he formed around his sister. His jaw clenched and brow furrowed in frustration.

"We just left the shooting range.... *pop*, nigga, *pop!*" Little Michael's words, filled with venom in defense of his sister,

133

burst forth quickly from an untapped emotion; his vision was still clouded with swarms of dark red as they continued toward their table. Neither had he noticed the appreciative glances exchanged among the onlookers, fixated as he navigated the presumed hostile atmosphere. When they reached their table, she placed the menus down with a grand gesture. Her enthusiasm was infectious as she noticed Michael gently tucking Debra's chair in for her.

"Deb! I gotta tell you, girl, your brother is just so adorable!" she squealed, her eyes sparkling with delight as her smile stretched wide.

"*Nigga, what!*" Layla echoed Michael's tone. "I never heard *nigga* said like that before, and believe me, a *nigga* gets around!" she laughed, her voice ringing with genuine amusement as her head bounced her afro in every direction. The shared chuckles rippled through the seated patrons, many whispering, nigga, creating a warm wave of mirth sparked by the little protector's unexpected wit.

Oh, by the way, and Happy Birthday, my—Michael! Layla's eyes widened as her lips curled at the corners before pressing thin. "Pulled that one back in, pretty good, huh... You're six years old today, Michael, right?" she added, a bright twinkle in her eye as she connected with Debra's raised brows, then moved on. Michael beamed with pride, soaking in the excitement of being celebrated not just once, but twice on this day.

No one remembered his birthday during the first three years he spent at the orphanage until Debra reminded them, so Michael saw it as not counting.

"Thank you, legs!" Michael shouted enthusiastically

as Layla glided past their table. An elderly gentleman at a nearby table, dressed more stylishly than any Sunday best outfit Michael had ever seen, perked up from his meal. Leaning closer to the aisle, he glanced at the captivating legs, his eyes sparkling with intrigue. His lips pressed into a tight line as he nodded in agreement with Michael, then returned his focus to his meal with purpose. A stern gaze across the table waited for Michael; only he could feel the heavy eyes on him from his sister. So, he just sat with his head down, giggling. Still, Debra's piercing look made its point. Michael's side-eyed glance performed a quick check on the old man. He sensed that the old man was someone not to be messed with.

The old man's eyes jerked up from his plate once more, as if sensing something in the air. Michael's brows knitted together until they rested on him. The old man's pause was primal, reminiscent of a lion interrupted during its meal. His intense gaze lingered just briefly, enough to determine there was no danger. The old man's stare veered away from Michael, his back arched as if another predator was near; he scanned the diner completely, it was chilling, as much as it was powerful, and telling. Michael sensed he was about his business, and do not let the smooth taste fool you.

Suddenly, Debra's fingers drummed against the table, snapping Michael from his trance and reigniting the tension in the air. *What was about to unfold?*

"You only get to act that way to scare couples away from wanting to adopt you, Michael?" Debra angrily jabbed her finger, her voice steady. Michael's eyes widened, tears welling up and quickly transforming into fear as his sister's words hurt him more painfully than any lash from a leather belt used for discipline.

A twinge of self-pity shaded Michael, Debra thought. Regret-
tably, when his head fell to his chest this time, it stayed there.
Debra froze. She dented his armor, 'Teflon,' with words driven
by fear and guilt. Michael saw himself as a failure. His only wish
was to protect his sister, as she had always protected him. So, he
avoided eye contact, and in doing so, he avoided his tears. For
Debra, the moment recalled was the advice the portly lady on the
train, Ms. Virginia, had given her years ago. She remembered
that Michael must love one and not yearn for the other. Debra's
gaze at Michael lingered, her eyes tracing their years together. She
understood the weight of the lie that kept Ms. Virginia and her
daughter apart. Michael was her smile, her joy, her love. She could
not let the same thing happen to them.

Michael sighed deeply, tilting his chin down while his
frown deepened, burdened by his emotions. "Look, sis," he
began softly, "I'm never hungry because you give me your
last, and your smile brightens my sad days at the orphanage
long after you've gone. I know that acting out is the only way
to keep me from being adopted, but it's part of me now. I
can't believe in fairytales coming true, 'cause they don't." He
quickly wiped away a tear, swift as swatting a fly. Raising his
gaze to meet Debra's, he smiled. "You know, sis, sometimes
when you're getting on me for doing bad things, I see you
almost smile, like when you look at all those old sky-blue
items in that footlocker under your bed: the dress, the baby
cover, the ribbon, or that straw hat. It's like you're soaring
above your troubles, completely free." Michael shook his head
in confusion before a half-smile emerged. "So, if you can fall
asleep sad and hungry, I can take the leather and the paddle
from teachers, nuns, and even you."

"Hey, Mike," Debra spoke softly, her voice imbued with tenderness as a gentle, timid smile appeared on her lips. Michael wobbled in his chair before he snapped to attention, like bread being readied from a toaster. *The way she said his name was smooth, and his grin told of his approval. Instantly, he thought, the name moved smoothly and purposefully, like that old man sitting across from him.* Michael glanced at the old man to see if he heard his cool name and to soak up more of his smoothness.

However, Michael's heart sank at the unexpected sight: a young Black police officer appeared and sat across the table from the old man. The cheerful grin that had stretched across his face vanished in an instant. "*Sell-out to the man*", Michael fumed, turning towards Debra. He found her wiping away tears, teasing the corners of her eyes, with a shared understanding passing silently between them. His jaw dropped, recalling the conversation he thought they had moved past. "I love you" were her only words.

Debra locked eyes with Michael, feeling profound empathy for the burden she had imposed on him. That burden had once belonged solely to her, a remnant of her childhood. She recognized the heartache that came with her decisions; it was a struggle they both faced together.

Be a child of mischief and spite, but only when necessary for survival, like a light switch, only when needed. It's unfair for any child to know that fairytales can never be true, mainly because of their skin color.

"I like that name, Sis; call me Mike from now on, okay?" he said with a playful grin, his eyes sparkling enthusiastically. Debra's smile grew wider, as if reflecting his happiness. Her blissful smile covered him like a comforting hug, and Mike reassured himself that everything was fine.

Haunting, Sis—the name 'Mike' had chosen for her—felt like an irreversible reality. With a heavy heart, Debra let go of any lingering hopes of ever revealing her true identity as his mother. In that bittersweet realization, she yearned to be called "mother" by her beloved Michael, just as Ms. Virginia wished to be cherished by her daughter.

"Catfish and grits for the country girl and fluffy pancakes with sizzling sausages for the city slicker," Layla chimed cheerfully, sliding an array of steaming plates, fresh coffee, and chilled milk before them with a warm smile. As she returned to the table, her head bobbed with the thought of mentioning that the kind old man across from them had covered their meal. With a gentle turn, she flipped the receipt to show his handwritten note: "Eat and grow strong. Read and grow wise." Layla chimed in with a playful sparkle in her eye, "Lion cub today, lion that lions fear tomorrow, as your sister always says," before moving along her way. Debra exhaled softly before glancing at the old man, her mouth dry and her heartbeat pounding. She hurriedly pressed her hand to her forehead as her head lowered and shook in disbelief. *He knows our business.* Raising her head, she managed a clumsy but cheerful smile and mouthed Thank you. The old man flashed a grin. Clenching her jaws, Michael drew Debra's attention. He struggled and failed, irresistibly drawn to the black fishnet pantyhose Layla wore, her legs taking long strides again. Curiously, Debra felt drawn to the old man, whose eyes flicked away from Layla and then to hers. They exchanged a knowing stare, shaded with a touch of guilt. Despite her unease, Debra's annoyed exhale went unnoticed by Mike.

"Mike," Debra said, her voice trembling as her eyes closed in annoyance. Unintentionally bringing laughter to others seated nearby, Debra's jaws clenching as Mike, with emphasis, the 'I' in his name, rolled off her tongue. Mike's hand and eyes fumbled their way back to his plate, but not before exchanging glances with the old man. The air was filled with anticipation, and a flicker of wonder stirred inside him.

Mike, a curious kid, pinched his chin with his thumb and index finger and frowned. "Hmmm, do you think that old man's going to jail?" he excitedly questioned. Debra had closely observed the handsome Black police officer from the moment he entered the diner. She watched as he paused briefly, thumbs hooked casually on his police duty belt, exuding relaxed confidence without looming over his holstered weapon. Her eyes followed the young officer as he scanned the room, finally resting on the elderly man at a corner table across from her and Mike. As the officer moved through the diner, women, young and old, took note as men frowned at his tall, muscular build. He was captivating in some way to everyone, including Debra. Whose heart raced, and admiration grew; his well-groomed afro, she thought, had been freshly picked after he took off his hat, emphasizing his chiseled features. When the officer and the elderly man shared knowing glances, Debra noticed the warmth in their exchange—a slow smile blossomed before the officer sat across from the old man. The whole scene exuded a sense of intimacy, deepening Debra's intrigue.

"Deb... check out that old man! He's dressed in those fine threads; he even paid for our meal—I'm telling you; he must be a bank robber or something...! What do you think, Deb? ...Deb?"

That's one fine-looking man.

Debra furrowed her brows as she refocused her attention. Her eyes briefly sparkled at the officer before he turned his attention to the elderly man. Although they were both intrigued by each other, pressing matters required their focus. "Yes, Mike," Debra responded, a vacant grin spreading across her face as she turned her gaze back to their table. Her top priority was seated there, grinning with a milk mustache dripping from his upper lip, still, there was wonder.

"He's a bank robber, how cool," Mike whispered, "easy money, easy life," as he stuffed pancakes into his mouth.

"No, Mike!... huh? That's his dad—definitely family," Debra asserted firmly, her brows knitted together. "Mind your own business, boy."

Layla, the waitress, quickly arrived at the police officer's table to take his order. She turned to Debra and shared her enthusiastic admiration for him, which made Debra giggle with delight.

The cop and the old man sprang up from their seats with sudden intensity, resembling two gunfighters ready for a standoff in the dusty streets of the Old West. An electric stillness filled the diner as they locked eyes, with palpable tension in the air. Around them, some diners froze, while others, fascinated, took in the drama, much like dinner theater in the hood, watching between bites and sips from their table, ready to move out of the way, plate in hand, if fists began to fly. Mike's plate of food, now a second thought, was moved to the side as he leaned forward, heart racing, eager for the story to unfold. "I got a nickel on the old dude!" he called out. Receiving a chuckle from the table behind him, Mike turned around and smiled. A confident grin spread across his face as he slammed the coin down and pushed it across the table. His drama drew an irritated glare from his sister. Yet Debra composed quickly, returning her gaze to the cop's rugged features.

Debra didn't perceive anger or worry from either, not a single wrinkle between their eyebrows that might spark conflict; only a sly smirk that needed no words yet screamed something deeper—admiration, love, and possibly a bittersweet farewell between these two strong, silent figures. Time stood still for Debra as she shared an experience filled with history. Quietly, in her mind, she hoped to see the love she knew her father had for her grandfather, her Grand Michael. One of the possible farewells between father and son, the cruel South robbed them of. *A quiet understanding that many could relate to if they allowed themselves to feel and remember.* It left everyone enchanted by this remarkable bond laid bare before them, culminating in a hug.

"Ugh!" Mike groaned, narrowing his small eyes as he watched the two men embrace tightly. Curiosity gnawed at him while he saw the old man lean in, whispering something into the cop's ear, tension thick in the air.

The cop shifted, sliding down in his chair while adjusting the grip of the holstered gun by his side. He cast a quick, intrigued glance at Debra before relaxing again. Mike furrowed his brow at the unfolding scene, his attention caught by Debra as she deftly slid the shiny nickel off the table and into her pocket. Unable to sit still, Mike folded his arms, watching the cop's every move, looking for anything he could criticize—the way he walked, stood, and spoke. Nothing stood out; big knots formed in his stomach. Mike wanted to cry, the cop was cool, had a subtle swagger—a blend of street smarts and bravado. As he continued to observe the officer, a pang of concern crept in, but he didn't have a reason for his stress, only that it was somehow concerning his sister's affections. Stinging just beneath the surface like a hidden wound, jealousy, Mike didn't have a name for it, but it had his number. He needed to scare this cop off, but how could he do it?

"Hey, cop, you've got Similac on your chin," Mike exclaimed. "You're not a cop, you Tom!" It was mean, Mike knew it, knew he would be in big trouble. He didn't care, not until he looked at his sister. Debra glanced around at her surroundings, making eye contact with everyone, except Mike, her face stoic, as if to convey that the things said by this child were not funny, not right. Staring down at her plate, Debra took a deep breath and held it, squelching a humiliated giggle. Disbelief swayed her head from side to side,

"Mike, *pinball*," she insisted. With a cautious hand, Mike sifted through the scattered coins on the table, his fingers grazing the cold metal while he wished to see his sister's face. Mike's eyes darted to the cop as he stood.

"Sorry," Mike whispered as he brushed by the cop. Glancing back once, wanting to see his sister's eyes, only her head was still bowed.

The young cop shifted nervously, a tight grin on his face, his hat tucked securely under his arm. As the little boy darted past him, the officer moved aside like a matador, weaving his red cape from the rushing bull's horns before focusing on the young lady seated before him. Debra shook off her embarrassment, her confidence rooted in childhood independence and bordering on cockiness; however, in the presence of this intriguing man, her lips pressed into a thin line that barely masked her shyness, which even she had not known until this moment.

"Kevin... Kevin Hunter," he said, reclaiming his composure. A gentle smile and calming voice eased the tension in the room and between them. His voice draws Debra's gaze from his extended hand, palm up, receiving nothing but empty air in front of her, to his eyes, where they linger. She swallowed hard, gathering her courage.

"Debra—uh, just Debra," she managed to stammer, a breathless smile breaking through her initial nervousness.

Kevin's gaze drifted momentarily to the now-vacant chair across from Debra, the faint warmth of her smile pulling him back to the moment. She offered a subtle nod, encouraging him to settle into the space. "I'm sorry about that... my brother..." Debra exhaled deeply, her brows knitting together in annoyance and concern. "You know how it is around here; the cops can be relentless in their harassment of us colored folks; whites in blue, coloreds in blue... You boys in blue treat us people of color the same." Her eyes fluttered toward Mike, utterly absorbed in the disharmony of lights and sounds emanating from the pinball machine.

Each button press seemed to mirror his inner turmoil.

"My brother faces this reality daily; he sees cops pressing for no reason and knows his day is coming," she surmised. "The day the police finally perceive him as a threat, his age won't matter; that's when his true struggles begin. I can see he carries justified anger."

He glances behind him at Mike angrily attacking the buttons of the pinball machine and chuckles as his head shakes. Mike stared at each silver ball as it bounced seemingly from pillar to post, willing it to stay in the fight; it was less about the game itself and more about the battle he faced every moment. Debra's expression, filled with worry, confirmed the concern threaded through her voice: *My brother is not focused on trying to win that game; he's just trying to survive it.*

Kevin felt his breath catch in his throat as he turned his gaze back to Debra. "My father already likes your brother better than me, and now I say why; they're identical, piercing words and a powerful punch." Kevin couldn't help but smile as he reflected on his past. He let out a soft chuckle, recalling when he would meet his untimely death. It had once filled him with dread, yet now it felt almost surreal, like a scene from a distant memory.

"I stood at my father's front door two years ago in this uniform. He opened the door, took one look, and dropped me with one punch. He sat on the top step; I could feel his intense glare long before I came around. And when I finally did, he loomed over me, blocking out the sun. He looked down and said, 'Before you get up,' the clean version was, 'Why did you decide to join the enemy?'" Kevin chuckled at the thought., "I lay there, blood pooling in my mouth, staring at a bat resting heavily in my father's hand while his other hand, balled into a fist, was clenched so tightly that his knuckles turned white. Kevin let out a resigned sigh, a sound thick with unspoken worry. I took a deep, shaky breath and locked eyes with my father.

"In my mind, I had carefully crafted my speech, each word infused with the significance of everything I needed to convey to him. ...: all that came out was, 'Plant seeds and cut down trees.' When he unclenched his fist, I looked into his eyes, then

I noticed each finger relax; I thought, nah, he's just tightening his grip on that bat… but he helped me to my feet."

Among the nosy ears, a gentle, soft-spoken old woman sat at a weathered table across from her husband, her eyes shining with the concern of a paused soap opera as she leaned forward, hanging on every word as the police officer spoke.

The sun's rays burst through the window without remorse, casting a gentle light around them. Suddenly, her brow furrowed with curiosity, fear, and worry as she interrupted Kevin, her voice trembling slightly. "Why did your daddy hit you, son?" she asked, her gaze searching for reassurance. Her husband blinked words he wished to scream as he let out a low grunt from deep in his throat, his eyes briefly drifting to the ceiling as if looking for answers in the cracks above. The spoon clattered from his hand, splashing into the steaming grit bowl with a soft thud. He quickly replied, a hint of frustration creeping into his voice,

"Sally Mae! Mind your own business, please! The police have been doing wrong long before we even came of age. That boy's father would rather see him dead by his hand than some cracker in blue. I see his father around town; I know he'd get things done when it counted." The old man's brows shot up at the certainty of it all. "Listen closely," he said to anyone who found it their concern. "I could tell you for sure: fuck with that Hunter, and find out! There would be such a ruckus in these streets that every crooked cop, from Prohibition to now, would find themselves marched from the grave straight to jail to keep the rest of them crackers and boot-licking *Tom's* safe from that gentleman." The moment the old man nodded in agreement; he accepted the pain from his past. His reflection faded with a deep breath and a long exhale, only to be replaced by the familiar annoyance of his wife.

"Dammit, Sally Mae! You've got my heart pounding in my chest over things that happened before these young folks were even born, butting in and stirring the pot like some old hen. My food ain't gonna get cold listening to you, nosy!" he exclaimed, munching on a piece of bacon, his voice tinged with playful frustration as Kevin watched the couple bicker good-naturedly.

The old man struggled with a spoonful of hot grits that burned his lip, while Sally Mae giggled at his mistake.

Kevin chuckled, casting a knowing smile at Debra. "My father said he ain't raise no fool, told me at least introduce myself to that young lady over there."

To Kevin's surprise, Debra's determined expression showed she would not yield to any pressure. "That was smooth," Debra declared before her grin appeared and disappeared just as quickly. Her eyes gestured to where Mike played, "My brother will have lost all six of his pinballs in about five minutes." Debra leaned forward, glancing at her watch as she claimed the space, her head swaying gently to an internal rhythm, her eyes sparkling with both mischief and genuine concern. The corners of her brows lifted, her lips curved into a knowing smile as she fixed her gaze on him, with the light catching the accents of her expression.

"So, Mr. Kevin Hunter," glancing up at the ceiling, she began, her tone playful, "do yourself a favor and *not* sit down; it's already taken." The harsh tongue thrashing made Kevin grimace as he shut his eyes. When he opened them, a playful grin broke through.

"That was quicker than the right hook my father caught me with. You're blowing ice-cold wind my way, Ms. Debra, but it's too late. I've seen the sun – it's beautiful, it's radiant, and I have no fear of getting close to it." His brows lifted as if to reflect the challenge in his words, accompanied by a deep exhale. "My dad has a knack for spotting good people; the only blind spot was my mother, and that dragon burned us both, and it still burns me," he chuckled, and I don't have pickup lines ready for beautiful women; my truth stands before me — you see it for what it is or you don't." As the women nearby swooned over his words, Layla, enchanted, fanned herself with the menu, a glimmer of tickling amusement in her eyes.

"Well, alrighty then," Layla chimed, glancing down at the group of female customers she had just seated. Debra felt a wave of humiliation and regret wash over her as she followed the arc of his expression. When their gazes met this time, it was charged with authenticity; she sensed an unexpected gentleness in this man, but time was slipping away, and she had no room for distractions.

"Goodbye, Mr. Hunter," Debra said firmly, her body stiffening, her voice clear and unwavering. Neighboring tables, once filled with the laughter and chatter of diners enjoying their meals, now debate like a panel of judges in shocked conversation about what went wrong in what seemed to be a budding romance. "Too much 'man,' not enough 'bad boy,'" from a colorfully dressed woman eating alone, was grumbled to silence, but not before the loudest laughter among them. A man at the table nearest the window, who unsettlingly and annoyingly licked sauce from his fingers before he spoke,

"Boy ain't lying! He got no game at all," he snickered while sitting across from a pregnant woman as she rubbed her belly. The woman paused mid-belly rub, staring down at her bare ring finger.

Clenching her jaws, she blurted out in frustration, "No, this is what happens when you got game," her voice slicing through the diner, igniting a new round of engaging conversation. "Next thing you know, you're sitting across the table from a man-child, still living with his momma, lying about telling her he's gonna be a daddy." The man sank into his chair as her widening eyes struck a tinge of fear as she continued her hormonal rant. Kevin joined the unrelenting laughter with a slight grin breaking through the tension as he locked eyes with random strangers who seemed equally captivated by his unfolding drama and that of the mama's boy seated nearby. When his eye returned to Debra's, the outside noise surrounding him was silenced by her alluring brown eyes and beautiful smile, and he was left almost speechless. "Well, five minutes isn't the kind of time I can work with," Kevin confessed, his tone light yet tinged with amusement as he adjusted his hat. The atmosphere danced with anticipation, a blend of disbelief and reluctant curiosity.

Debra watched him, her lips curving into an amused smirk, fully engaged in the spectacle before her. "So, until I have the chance to hear that long story, Ms. Debra—uh ... Debra, I'll be having breakfast, lunch, and dinner here every weekend," he added with a charming smile." Debra lifted her cup in helpless awe as Kevin strolled away, her mind filled with wonder.

Kevin counted his strides until he was just a few steps from Mike, then stopped; he could feel Debra watching him. His shadow cast a faint glow over the pinball machine, making Mike turn in annoyance. He shot Kevin a fierce glare before quickly glancing at his sister, uncertainty flickering in his eyes. Kevin leaned in to share a quick secret before heading out, just like his dad did with him after leaving some cash on the table to cover their meal.

Sally Mae, the curious elderly woman, sat there, her inner troublemaker nagging at her peaceful mind until it surfaced, much to her husband's chagrin. She stared intently as Kevin strolled by; her eyes confirmed, along with her darting finger, beckoning for attention. "Man walking!" she exclaimed; her voice filled with intrigue. Her husband looked up from his plate,

"Easy, Mae, I'm right here," he confirmed as her finger hovered toward Kevin, tracing the space from where he stood to his exit. The noise of Sally Mae shifting in her chair pulled her husband's attention once more, his stare, his warning. He watched as her gaze shifted, clearing his throat as her lips pressed thin; they curled in disapproval, landing squarely on the table where a young lady, round with pregnancy, sat. Her finger jabbed the air like a hot stove poker, ready to deliver a searing truth.

"More child than man right there," Sally declared irritably, her tone dripping with disdain, as if revealing an uncomfortable secret to the world. "I'm too old to be fighting out here, Mae. I still got my one-two, but if that doesn't take him out, he's gonna get me with the three-four," he chuckled.

"I may not know him from Adam, but one thing's for sure: he's destined to live with his momma for the rest of her life!

Sally Mae arched her back, and her head swayed from

side to side as she continued, "Don't nobody want that, not after the 'games played,' not after seeing what they're getting. Just wait until you see that young cop in action! He's ready to impress, and trust me, you won't be the only one noticing his talent. Hear what I'm telling you, young lady, I had to beat down many hoes when I was young, them seeing what I saw in this man right here." Sally Mae smiled warmly, her heart full of affection as she looked across the table at her husband, patiently waiting for his attention so she could deliver a devilish wink. *A smile teased at the corners of his mouth as he resisted her gaze.* "With all the incredible qualities I recognized in him, it was tough not to be enchanted by his presence!".

The old man's eyebrows lifted slightly before he looked up from his plate. "Was that a sparkle in your eyes I just saw?" Sally Mae bashfully asked. He chuckled,

"Just one eye, one sparkle, Mae, you know what happens the next day when I put this hammer on you, girl," he teased with a sly smile. Sally Mae's laughter burst out before she quickly covered her mouth. "I end up making breakfast the next day," he continued. Sally Mae chuckled.

"Exactly… so who's zooming who?" she wisecracked, raising her eyebrows. Her husband nodded, chuckling again—this time longer and louder—while he wiped his mouth with his napkin.

"My breakfast is done. When you finish, I'm going to pay this check, then cash the check you just wrote," he said after sitting back in his chair.

Mike's steps away from the pinball machine were slow and defeated. "It's going to be okay, chin up," and other words of encouragement, along with pats on the back, urged him on.

Still, less than six minutes had passed when Mike reappeared before his sister. His heart was pounding as his eyes locked with hers. His mind scrambled for the right words. Laughter from the elderly couple at the nearby table caused a slight frown to form on his forehead, but he welcomed the pause. Debra's eyes sparkled before her smile slowly spread across her face. Mike rushed to Debra, arms open wide, and whispered "Sorry," as she pulled him into a hug.

An old lion and a young cub shared a profound understanding of each other's hopes and dreams; both knew the paths they needed to take to achieve them. Was the deception justified?

Mike knew his sister had questions for him; she watched his every step and everyone around him at all times. "You want to know what both of them said?" Mike grinned.

"Huh," Debra replied. Mike burst out laughing at her, pretending not to hear or understand what he said. The standoff raised eyebrows like a duel, neither blinking. Seconds later, both tilted their heads and laughed. Debra relented. Coins fell onto the table like those from a slot machine to feed the pinball machine. Slowly, he slid each coin into his awaiting palm. Mike giggled.

"Well, the old man told me not to fear the dragon, whatever that means," Mike said casually, a mischievous glint in his eye. Debra fought to suppress a smile, amused by his adorably clumsy attempt at bravado, until he suddenly pivoted to walk away.

"Mike!" Debra exclaimed, urgency lacing her tone. The lightness in the air vanished as his shoulders slumped, and he turned to face her, a subtle weight of sibling tension lingering between them. He kept up an exaggerated look of fatigue, his eyes wildly rolling side to side as his eyelids blinked excessively.

"Yeeees, Debra," he replied, feigning annoyance. His sigh was drawn out until his body fell limp. Mike's brows furrowed as he playfully looked up at the ceiling, joking about the words the cop had whispered in his ear. *This was the toy he teased his sister with?* "Hmm… let me see," Mike said, tapping his chin. Oh… I think he said something like… "Beauty bows to you." Stunned, Debra swallowed hard. Her loss for words made Mike smile. He looked into his sister's eyes and said, "It's true." His words were gentle and sincere.

It wasn't the first time she had encountered that clichéd pickup line, but today, it felt different, almost as if it were the first time it truly resonated with her.

Debra's eyes lit up, as if she didn't realize she was attractive. Has she never looked in the mirror? Mike saw it in his sister's eyes; she needed to hear that. He felt the weight of her lonely life, the moment's significance pressing on him as he turned and ambled back toward the flashing pinball machines. Sally Mae traced the little boy's steps until he was out of earshot. She struggled with her wooden chair, pushing with her legs, it creaking in resistance as it scraped across the floor. Slouching when the back of her chair met the back of Debra's chair, she relaxed. Sally Mae's husband rolled his eyes in disbelief at the sight, crossing his arms and resting them against his chest, exhausted by her enthusiasm.

"Lord, have mercy, he mumbled, his eyes closing and his chin falling to his chest.

"Darlin," Sally Mae whispered, your plate will always be full of something, you have to make way, make room for dessert," she stressed, her eyes sparkling with a knowing, playful smile.

CHAPTER ELEVEN
CAN'T BREATHE

THE OMINOUS GRAY cloud loomed heavier, its edges darkening while low thunder grumbled in the distance like a restless giant awakening. Scott pressed forward, his body pushed against the fierce winds that howled around him, thick mist swirling like a living entity and obscuring his path. Scott's face slackened. "This cloud has never darkened as much—tears and sorrow, yes, but this, never," Scott said as he studied its heavily shaded corners. Gabriel sank to one knee, looked around, then down at the swirling mass of cloud he gathered in his right hand.

"No, these are concerns of the courageous soul that has turned into fear," he sighed… She's on the move right through the shadowy fears of her past, Gabriel declared," urgency punctuating his voice.

"A brief respite from my daily quest," Scott mused until now. Gabriel grinned the same grin before every battle,

This journey takes us through darkness and peril, much

like the courageous soul who continues onward, guided by faith. "As do we," he responded.

Below, Debra stood with her brows furrowed, then quickly accompanied by a sly smirk as she gazed upward, the shifting skies today feeling so appropriate. Around her, the trees were alive, Birds filled the trees singing songs of summer instead of gathering for their long flight south. Squirrels frolic in the park, chasing each other and the occasional jogger, instead of preparing for winter's arrival.

The bus driver's head tilted to one side, and his eyes narrowed into slits as he lifted his chin to stare down at Debra with an icy glare. She stepped onto the crowded bus and handed over her fare, then crept up the aisle, her eyes fixed on the eerie old castle that had been converted into an orphanage through the foggy window. The fading image of her brother's pleading eyes stayed with her long after the bus pulled out of view. Debra passed empty seats as she made her way, with no blaring signs; however, the stench of 'white only' loomed over every one of them. She felt the piercing stares of the white passengers upon her, their gazes sharp and unwelcoming, like the prickly thorns of long-stem roses. But as she reached the rear of the bus, her eyes were met with a burst of color and life—an eclectic mix of smiling faces: Black, Puerto Rican, Asian, Indian, and White, all radiating a sense of community that warmed her spirit amidst the tension. "That's right, child, come on back here; they think just because we have the right to sit beside their stank ass and stank attitude, we want to? Wrong!" an older lady in the crowd seated in the back of the bus shouted.

The bus driver's eyes shot up, hard and scrutinizing as

he glared into the rearview mirror, scanning for anyone who dared to pay too much attention. After a brief moment, he turned his gaze back to the newspaper's front page, clutched by the woman seated in the first row by the door. He read aloud with a tone meant to draw her attention: "The Pricket School of Nursing has officially desegregated. I notice a crowd gathered outside that school, holding signs during my first trip through the city." As the woman lowered the newspaper, Debra settled into a seat sandwiched between two elderly ladies dressed in crisp maid uniforms, the fabric slightly worn from years of service. A wave of distraction washed over her as she glanced down at a photograph resting in her palm—a candid shot of her brother Michael and his beautiful smile. But her mind replayed the memory of their last encounter, his face etched with sorrow and streaked with tears, his desperate plea repeating: "Please don't leave me, Deb."

With a heavy heart yet a fragile smile, she raised her gaze to respond to the curious group surrounding her warmly. Most inquiries required nothing more than a simple nod or shake of her head, "Yes or no, ma'am," but the effort of keeping up appearances felt like a weight on her shoulders.

"Look at all those *demon*strators; they've brought their southern ideas about negros with them in their northern migration," a little old black lady seated next to Debra chuckled, leaning forward to make her comment heard by her co-workers nearby. Debra's grip tightened on the rail as she looked out the window behind her. She rushed to her feet, her eyes fixed on the school and the protesters as the bus began pulling away from the stop. She yanked hard on the cord without hesitation, prompting the bus driver to slam on the brakes. He shot an angry look through the rearview mirror, clearly frustrated by her sudden decision.

"Dumb-ass niggers!" a frustrated white man seated near the driver yelled before he even looked to see who pulled the cord. Livid passengers scrambled to retrieve their scattered belongings from the floor, with the remnants of their disrupted journey strewn about them. Meanwhile, a chorus of anger and discontent reverberated from the front of the bus, amplifying the tension in the cramped space.

"Stupid black bitch," a woman sitting three rows behind him shouted. Her children, two young boys recently out of diapers and in desperate need of baths, suddenly joined the conversation by screaming, dirty nigger as they turned in their seats to watch Debra gather her belongings and head toward the back door. "If we never brought niggers into this country, it would be a fantastic place to live!" another shouted, and the crowd chimed in agreement, shouting "Amen!" as if he were responding to a fiery sermon at a Klan church picnic. Debra clung to the pole beside the rear door. She caught the bus driver's gaze, still on her in the rearview mirror—silently, she pleaded for him to open the door and let her escape. Debra's foot tapped nervously as she clenched her worn-out suitcase. Her heart sank quietly, as if she were drowning in the muddy Mississippi River. Suddenly, a grey-bearded older Black man in a worn winter coat appeared, his bloodshot eyes reflecting long days and nights. He seemed like an outsider long before age took its toll on his youth. He danced the Bop with an imaginary partner, causing traffic around the bus to halt.

His lively dance was undoubtedly fueled by the false

prophet in the brown paper bag he carried, promising happy days and warm nights.

"Merry Christmas," the drunken old man, already celebrating the season of giving, yelled as he wobbled in front of cars like a performer on a tightrope. Drivers shouted out their windows, leaning on their horns in an attempt to get the old man to move along. Debra's eyebrows raised as she watched the old man through the side window do a little shuffle step, then tip his hat towards the cars after he was safely across the street. He clumsily approached the bus's windshield, tapping with urgency to catch the driver's attention.

"Fuck all y'all crackers, let him on and let this child off," a woman's voice shouted from a seat behind Debra. "If he ain't got it, I got him!" Debra raises her eyebrows immediately; the woman's slow Southern drawl was clearly from Mississippi. Curious, Debra glanced to her right and saw a plump, elderly lady dressed in a black and white maid's uniform. Her silver hair framed a face marked with the gentle creases of time, and her bright eyes sparkled with understanding and compassion. They shared a warm smile, then Debra turned to look out the rear door's window, grinning from ear to ear. "Just two years," she sighed softly, her heart swelling with hope as she rested her head on the pole she held tightly. "I can finally take my brother out of that orphanage in two years."

"Don't be afraid, as the good Lord says, and everything will be alright," the same kind old lady gently encouraged, her voice infused with a comforting warmth wrapped around her words, reminiscent of young Pastor James's sermons. As the front and rear doors swung open, the elderly Black woman greeted the visibly intoxicated, staggering old man with a gentle, encouraging smile that radiated warmth. "Wishing you all the best, Mississippi, I may be old, but I ain't deaf," she said, then let out a small chuckle. Debra, smiling brightly, quickly turned and grinned, but the elderly woman's focus had already shifted to her silent colleagues.

"You bitches wouldn't be so quiet if you knew your fuckin` history," the old lady shouted loud enough for the white folks in the front of the bus to hear. "Whenever we stop at a traffic light: Garrett A. Morgan? Black man! They're quiet up there because they know!"

"Quiet back there! Or I'll kick all of you off my bus," the bus driver yelled as he glared into his rearview mirror. The wide-eyed coworkers nervously watched the old lady, their expressions a blend of surprise and apprehension as she leaned forward, her frail frame extending deep into the narrow aisle to catch the bus driver's attention.

"Who's going to drive the bus?" she replied, her head gently swaying from side to side like a pendulum. The old lady's eyebrows raised; she glanced at her coworkers in disbelief, then looked back at the front of the bus. She let out a little chuckle. 'Cause I'm gonna kick your ass if I'm late for work.' The bus driver briefly looked up at the rearview mirror, eyes on the old lady, before deciding to pull away from the curb. Glancing at her coworkers, her brows raised as if to say, *'Do you believe this muthafucka?'*

The acrid stench of body odor and the pungent scent of cheap liquor stung the bus driver's eyes as a gray-bearded man shuffled his way up the steps, humming an off-key tune. Grabbing hold of the farebox tightly, he steadied himself from the imaginary shifting of the bus. Looking at his audience of stunned faces, the old man chuckled, "Y'all feel that?" he asked, before breaking into a silly snicker. Offering the old lady in the back a reassuring smile, he fumbled through his heavy coat for loose change. "I got this, Ma'am," he said.

With a playful giggle, he turned back to the bus driver and, adopting a deep, dramatic baritone voice, broke into song, "Someone's gonna get their ass kicked." The bus driver shot a brief, annoyed glance at the old lady, who seemed undeterred. She glared over at Sheila, a long-time bus-riding friend, "Learn the history they want to hide and ignore, girl! You're half Navajo. If it weren't for your people's help, the Code Talkers, those fuckers up there would be 'Sieg mother fuckin Heil.' to 'mother fuckin Hitler!' right now!" The bus driver's eyes flicked to the review mirror, checking on the old lady and her co-worker as he stopped at the traffic light, while her words lingered in the air like a rallying cry, blending pride and urgency perfectly. Debra stood on a strip of brittle grass just beyond the curb as the bus pulled off behind her, its engine fading into the distance. Before her, the hate-filled white men and women walking back and forth symbolized the concealed machine that operated the city, an unsettling reflection of a system that thrived on division. It was easy to discern that they were mid-level and low-level managers in the industry, their polished shoes and crisp suits concealing the venomous ambitions that fueled their march. They embodied the slow, insidious death the toothless old cashier at the train station in Mississippi had once humorously lamented, a grim reality now taking shape before Debra's eyes. She hoisted her suitcase high above her head, using it as a makeshift shield against the onslaught of hawk spittle, jagged stones, and other debris hurled at her and the other women of color marching resolutely ahead. Debra murmured, "Fear not," repeating the gentle yet firm words of the elderly woman from the bus, who had offered the mantra in the face of imminent danger. Squinting against the chaos around her, Debra's eyes stayed fixed on one sign as she walked through the mob: 'Niggers not wanted,' a haunting sight from her past. With her gaze cast downward, she caught a fleeting glimpse of polished shoes— glinting in the harsh light of hatred—as they approached. Looking up, she saw the laughing police officers wearing them; their presence was meant to protect her. As they shouted death threats and hawk spit on each colored woman walking in front of her, it left her feeling more vulnerable than safe.

Debra was greeted by the incredible, indifferent smiles of administrators and office staff as she walked through the bustling school corridor. Yet, despite the friendly faces, a heavy sense of unease lingered in the air. She and the other women of color stood together, yet apart from the vibrant tapestry of their peers—some with glossy blonde hair, others with rich, brunette locks—an actual rainbow of diversity. The tension remained intense; no one spoke about the outside world or commented on the recent assault's aftermath. The blood and bruises narrated a familiar story, but the women endured silently. Debra sensed resentful eyes watching her in every classroom. A spectrum of hair colors—blonde, bleach-blonde, brunette—created a visual rainbow that challenged the façade of normalcy. Most days, she found strength in this animosity; after all, being despised had woven itself into the fabric of her existence.

These white city folk were kept on a leash, unable to express the full extent of their hate, at least during daylight, most of the time.

Debra quickly discovered solace in the company of five remarkable women of color, each bringing their strength and stories to the group. In return, they found a sense of comfort in her youthful presence. At just seventeen, Debra, an intelligent, outgoing, and naturally beautiful woman, stood among the many new nursing students, a tall, five-foot-ten-inch woman; her body had the maturity, height, and build of a model; still, she was the youngest in the entire nursing school, colored or otherwise, regardless of her race. The smell of country innocence followed her like a road-kill on a hot summer's day…it made the target on her back even broader.

Yet, the captivating smile and piercing gaze of one who roamed the halls with an air of authority made Debra's heart race with fear. From that fateful first day, those eyes—dark, brooding, and laced with an unsettling intensity—met young Debra's gaze, lingering on her in a deeply uncomfortable way. They belonged to Dr. Dunlap, a towering figure who stood at six feet three inches, with dark, tousled hair that framed his chiseled features and deep brown eyes that held untold dark secrets. Respected at hospitals throughout the tri-state area, he cunningly positioned himself among the most influential people at the city, state, and government levels, yet something about his presence blurred the lines between admiration and unease.

For months, his relentless scrutiny would evoke in Debra the sensation of being a fly ensnared in a spider's web, while thoughts of Charlie, her mother's husband, back in Mississippi, sent her heart racing and made her breath labor. Debra couldn't hide in the woods behind her grandfather's shack, so she met his gaze defiantly every time their eyes locked. The doctor relished seeing the uncertainty and fear in her eyes, concealing his sinister intentions, treating her like a mythical unicorn he hoped to ride one day.

Due to his arrogance, Dr. Dunlap failed to notice the subtle change in his unicorn; the shift from an innocent country girl to a city-slicker was just the beginning. Debra was nearing her eighteenth birthday, a young woman nurtured by five wise, city-savvy Black women who had protected her since they all marched through the crowd of protesters and into nursing school. Yet, there was something more within this young lady—a fearlessness reminiscent of the strong, opinionated women of color she had met on her journey so far, from Ms. Mary, the demure, timid by day and assassin by night, to the one she only recognized during her quiet moments of solitude at this school, Ms. Emma, the tall and aggressive 'bull in a China shop.' To this day, Debra wasn't sure why her Grand Michael had secretly told her many years ago that she was her grandmother. Perhaps it was to prevent her from being surprised by what might emerge within her, or maybe to help her someday embrace her—along with all the strong women she has descended from—tempered only by the task ahead.

The quiet and coldness in the first-floor corridor pulsed with anticipation and anxiety as Dr. Dunlap strolled through the halls, his set of keys jingling rhythmically against his thigh as he walked, like an ominous toll of bells searching out the fate of his next victim. The unnerving sound sent ripples of unease through the first-year nursing students and their instructors, who paused mid-conversation, casting wary glances toward the source of the noise. When the chiming finally ceased, he stood poised at the threshold behind a cracked-open door of the classroom he had chosen to invade. With a deliberate air of authority, Dr. Dunlap pushed open the door, and a hush fell over the room. The teacher, having many years of experience with this behavior from the doctor, instinctively gathered her belongings without care or thought, exchanging nervous, silent glances with the class before slipping away into the safety of the hallway without uttering a single word.

Once comfortably inside, behind the desk, Dr. Dunlap fixed his gaze on the blackboard, its surface cluttered with hastily scribbled notes and diagrams of human anatomy. Without breaking his focus, he addressed a student in the second row, fifth seat from the back, as if her presence and position had been etched into his mind. That day, students were addressed by row and chair number rather than by eye contact or name. This unusual tactic by Dr. Dunlap aimed to isolate the weak and vulnerable from the herd. His voice, cold and direct, said, "Now, student… explain how you would prioritize care for a patient with multiple needs." The bluntness of his question, like a sniper's shot, carried with it shame, embarrassment, and the intent to bring her down, thick with expectation of failure. Dr. Dunlap barked three more questions, each aimed squarely at the student in the second row, the fifth seat from the back—each more challenging than the last, and each answered precisely. The rest of the classroom felt the weight of his tone, tangled in a mix of helplessness and guilt, but ultimately relieved it was her and not themselves. Debra's confidence surged with each correct answer while the doctor's eyes dilated, a clear signal she would never forget.

Dr. Dunlap began to leave the room, his sharp, penetrating gaze locked onto Debra with an almost tangible intensity. It was as if his gaze could pierce through her very being, sending an involuntary shiver racing down her spine. A chill of anxiety enveloped the air around them, thickening the silence.

In those moments, Debra silently mouthed, "*The Lord is against those who do evil,*" *from* 1 Peter 3:12, *a passage from the* Bible. Dr. Dunlap saw this as an uncivilized voodoo chant every time she looked into his soulless eyes, and it made him want her even more, showing his contempt for her faith and the lustful thoughts consuming him. With effort, she forced a polite smile, carefully hiding her fear while feeling his scrutiny grow heavier with each second. The relentless barrage of precise, selective questions, meant for second-year and graduate students, that he directed at Debra, and sometimes at the other women of color, had transformed her late nights in the colored section of the school library into almost a sacred ritual. There, gathered at a table with her fellow women of color, ranging from caramel to dark chocolate, their eyes fixed on books, yearning for answers to the most challenging questions they believed Dr. Dunlap hadn't yet considered asking. They joked about enjoying the challenge of knowing more than their formal education required, exploring topics well beyond the classroom boundaries.

Meanwhile, shadows flickered behind them, serving as a haunting, teasing reminder to keep pushing forward and never pause. Deep into the night, their teasing of each other fueled their tired minds and bodies. "We're a little long in the tooth for that ol` devil, Dr. Dunlap," one of the women joked, her laughter ringing out like a bell through the quiet space, as she looked at Debra. Debra laughed and smiled at the joke and the camaraderie around her. Still, deep inside, the weight of her youth and the unknown burden of her tragically lost innocence felt heavier than ever, pressing down on her heart as she navigated the complexities of her reality.

Debra treasured the limited hours each Saturday she spent with her brother, thanks to the time granted by the orphanage. Unfortunately, her exhausting weekend shifts at the diner often meant she only glanced at Mike from afar, smiling if their eyes met while he sat at a table in her section. The burden of her demanding study schedule brought sympathy from those who adored them both. "How is my future husband?" the long-legged waitress, Layla, teased as she rushed to the front of the diner, playfully grabbing Mike's hand and guiding him to a table adorned with crayons and drawing paper. At the same time, Debra sprinted to punch the clock and changed into her skimpy uniform to begin her shift. Mike seemed to lose his usual spark, settling into his chair and removing his jacket. This routine was tiresome. Mike's arms hung at his side, his body slouched, and he let out a heavy sigh.

"I wish we could go to the range, rent some guns, and have fun, watch Deb show those hillbillies how it's done," Mike sighed, absentmindedly pushing the box of crayons away, resisting the urge to throw something. Layla gently lifted his chin and smiled. She caught a glimpse of his eyes, and at that moment, her heart ached for him, recognizing the sadness lurking beneath his playful façade as he smiled back at her.

With each break her shift provided, Debra settled into a chair at the small, scarred table that had witnessed countless conversations and shared secrets between her and her brother in the past ten months. She welcomed the chair, only to sink into it, like reuniting with an old friend, the muscle tension in her body dissipating. Debra mumbled a thank you for the moment and the chair that welcomed her tired body. Mike looked up from his drawing, his gaze a witness to the exhaustion in his sister's face. Shifting in his chair, his crayon tapping rapidly against his drawing. "I hate it there, Deb…" His eye lit up with a thought that crossed his mind many times; only now have they escaped. "Deb! Let's just run away," he exclaimed, urgency seeping into his tone. She managed a tired, soft smile, her eyes crinkling at the corners as she studied the seriousness of her brother's face, so much like her father's, yet tinged with the innocence of a troubled heart.

"I don't remember my… *our* father as clearly as I do our Grand Michael, but you carry pieces of both of them that grow inside you," she said, her voice steady despite the storm of emotions swirling within. "If we gave up and ran away, you wouldn't enjoy it for long, and soon I wouldn't either, for giving up. And, Mike, I wouldn't like myself." Mike's lips pressed into a thin line, his gaze drifting away from his sister as he fought to suppress his disappointment. His open palm rested on the table, fingers lightly tapping against the worn wood; a subconscious gesture of frustration caused his hand to move to the center of the table, pushing aside the open box of crayons.

"Pinball machine, please," tipping his head down and frowning, Mike asked, his tone shifting beyond defeat. Kevin, seated at his usual small, intimate table for two in Debra's weekend serving section, kept his watchful gaze fixed on Debra and Mike as their conversation ended with severe tension before Mike's quick escape. The ambient noise of the arcade faded around him. Kevin's gentle voice cut through the chatter like a soft breeze,

"Perhaps if Mike had a target for his frustration or maybe someone to share tips on how to beat those arcade machines over there, the choice being his, of course," Kevin suggested, his voice calm, warm, yet still able to cut through the noise of Debra's thoughts. "Not sure if you realized it yet, but we've had dinner a few times now; I consider us almost friends." Startled, she turned to him, her expression softening as a curious, warm smile began to form. Something genuine about his demeanor sparked her interest beyond the enthusiastic praise from the older woman, Sally Mae, encouraging her to seek a more profound connection amid the lively chaos of the arcade surrounding them.

"Three meals a day, every Saturday and Sunday? We're talking five months. Mr. Kevin Hunter, this food here is good, ...?" Debra asked, raising her eyebrows and staring unblinkingly. Kevin scratched his chin and chuckled softly, the warm sound blending with the surrounding noise of diners and the faint ping of arcade machines. "Hmmm. See, if I had more than five minutes," Kevin flirtatiously responded. He gestured toward the pinball machine, smiling as Mike fiercely pounded on the buttons, with the colorful flashing lights and sounds sporadically reacting. Debra's eyes darted around anxiously before she glanced at her brother, then back to Kevin, noticing his badge—maybe his gun, too; perhaps she'd ask for both. Her demeanor shifted as she absorbed his kind words, her heart repeatedly telling her he was a good man. Still, she casually demanded, "Driver's license." A flash of surprise crossed his face. Kevin, taken aback, rolled his eyes upward and fidgeted with the silver badge clipped to his belt. He searched for his license, which was curled at the edges. With a slight grin, he placed it on the table. Debra's curiosity, a complex part of her frustrating personality, leaned in closer, staring intently. "21. Huh? This picture is giving me Similac vibes." Debra nodded with mock seriousness as she slid the license into the pocket of her waitress uniform for safekeeping. Kevin staggered backward, staring with his mouth gaping as Debra stepped away with his ID.

Mike, giving a sideways glance at the sound of footsteps, narrowed his eyes as Kevin approached. "What, Tom?" he said with a grunt of annoyance. Kevin stopped just a game away from where Mike played, a smirk slowly spreading across his face. "Nothing... nothing, I thought we were past 'Tom,' that's cool," Kevin nodded confidently, his frown turning downward as he fed the machine a nickel. Kevin's silver ball danced around like a spinning ballerina, scoring easily, loud sounds from his game filling the space between them. Mike allowed his ball to roll into the gutter, amazed at Kevin's gameplay. The sparkling light is much like exploding bottle rockets on Independence Day.

Mike's breath hitched in his throat when he looked at Kevin, "Not bad... for a cop!" he exclaimed.

For a moment, it seemed like Mike was about to hit Kevin with more sharp words, but instead, they exchanged a quick, mischievous glance, and both burst into laughter.

Kevin's gaze was fixed on Mike's struggles with the pinball machine as the silver ball zipped across the playfield, bouncing from jet bumper to pop bumper, then slowly rolling toward his flippers. "Hit those buttons now!" Kevin's excitement is evident. The silver ball crashed and careened wildly around the machine, accompanied by a flurry of high-score celebrating sounds and lights. Mike's eyes sparkled as he pumped his fist in the air. A sense of weightlessness struck Debra as she witnessed the joy in Mike's eyes. Still, Debra walked past confidently, holding a tray of empty plates as the bells continued to chime wildly on Mike's pinball machine.

"How are you making out with this cop, Mike?" she asked assertively. He frowned at his sister.

"His name is Kevin, Deb, be nice," Mike scolded, his voice filled with uncompromising seriousness. Kevin acknowledged Debra's sacrifice of her ego for a bonding moment with a nod, but Kevin, with a playful grin, stuck out his tongue, relishing the opportunity. Debra spun around, a smile barely contained, her shoulders rising, elbows tucked in, and she shot Mike a big, silly grin.

Just then, a fight broke out outside the diner's picturesque front window. The sound of fists hitting and angry shouting drew the attention of Mike, Debra, the other waitstaff, and nearby diners, all of whom froze in shock and awe. The two men fought fiercely, exchanging blows over a parking spot. Kevin, quick to react, hurried outside to break up the fight; however, they turned their aggression toward him once they saw his shining police badge on a belt clip inside his waistband. The larger of the two, backhanded Kevin across his face, then laughed, calling him a little bitch! Kevin reacted instinctively, quick and fierce, with a three-punch combo that buckled the man's knees while the other man circled behind him. Kevin pleaded, "You don't want to do this, Man." Kevin heard the man's rushing footsteps behind him. Kneeling, he flipped over Kevin's shoulder and into the side of a parked car. "That nigga can fight!" Mike yelled, trying to be heard over the chaos.

Debra shot him a disapproving look and nudged him, her tone becoming urgent.

"Mike, watch your language!" Mike stared at his sister with his mouth open,

"I mean, nigga good, not nigga bad, Deb," he said, shaking his head in disbelief. Mouth quivering, Debra's mind searched for calming words as her lips moved silently. Then, before she spoke, "Sorry, Deb, but that's one bad nig," he began to say, as the unfolding scene pulled him away. "Seriously, how did I miss it?" Mike asked, his eyes wide as saucers. A man seated nearby exclaimed, "He dropped those big guys on their ass!" "I bet his dad taught him that," Mike added, a confident grin spreading across his face as he looked at Debra, excitement brightening his expression. Mike wasn't going to miss another scene; he didn't take his eyes off the happenings outside the window, like a magnet to metal, his curiosity pulling him in. "What?" Mike frowned.

Kevin, instead of hauling the men off to jail, offers them a handshake before sending them on their way.

Mike scratches his head while edging closer to the window, eager to hear the exchange of words between Kevin and the men, hoping to uncover the mystery behind this unexpected act of kindness.

Mike glanced at his sister for an explanation.

"Hey, sis, why is he letting those two dudes go? They were gonna whip his ass, and think nothing of it!" Debra went straight to biting her upper lip and clenched her fist.

"Mike!" she replied angrily, her voice plowing through the lighthearted banter of the diners and her co-workers like a bulldozer. "Say another bad word, just one, and the tooth fairy will go broke paying you back!" "Remember when you couldn't whistle, that 'missing fronts,' stage!" Her threat clouded the air, playful yet serious. Mike whistled, then casually let out a deep sigh, his shoulders slumping at the thought, as he waited for an answer to his question.

Debra's gaze drifted outside, admiring Kevin as he slid into his car, the sun shimmering off its polished surface. She stared until his brake lights disappeared from view, swallowed by the winding street. Turning back to the group and then down to Mike, she said thoughtfully, "Ask him Saturday, you know where he's gonna sit." Mike sighed as his chin fell to his chest... "But, I figure, he knew those brothers had problems, not hard, we all have problems, and missing work on Monday would make life tough for them." Mike looked up at his sister, his brows furrowing with concern as she continued, "Kevin has enough respect for the struggle to do something about it."

"Damn," he exclaimed, quickly covering his mouth. "Sorry, sis," he murmured, eyes wide with realization. "Did you get all that from just watching?" Mike continued, moving past his slip-up. Debra smiled gently, her fingers tracing the edges of Kevin's forgotten license, which she had just retrieved from her pocket.

"Well, both of those men wear wedding rings—whatever happens to them affects their families," she responded softly. Mike looked back at his sister, his eyes filled with admiration and empathy. "He sure ain't no Tom!" he shouted.

Back at school on that lackluster Monday, Debra radiated newfound energy, her eyes sparkling with excitement and a bright smile lighting up her face. Her thoughts were of Kevin, her step, light, and free-flowing; she smiled brightly as she and the other women of color exited the segregated shower, chatting happily. Wrapped in towels, their slippers slipped across the floor in rhythm. One of the women called Debra's name, but she didn't respond. Looking at Debra's face, they exchanged knowing glances, playfully calling her name again and again, this time like giggling young schoolgirls. They all recognized the look—the beaming smile, her distant gaze— her mind was elsewhere. "She got a man on her mind!" one of the women shouted. Debra furrowed her brows in confusion,

"No," she said defiantly. The women surrounded her as she shook her head no, just in case they hadn't heard her. They enjoyed her innocent confusion, but they knew what they knew. The questions came from all sides,

"What's his name?" "Is he cute?" "Is he tall compared to her?" Sandy, a petite girl who arrived just two weeks ago, spoke up from behind Debra.

"He has to be tall, look at her, she's a giant." The ladies laughed, and Debra relented. Debra took a deep breath and exhaled very slowly.

"His name is Kevin, yes, he's tall, but he's a friend… my brothers' mainly," she reassured.

"A friend put a smile on my face like you showing, give me his name, address, phone number, and the best time to call," the oldest woman said as she leaned in with a hand clap. Debra hand-clapped the lady but kept hold of her hand. Debra's eyebrows raised.

"Ain't, you married?" Debra said. The lady nodded. "Yes, this is my third one, and they all were just friends," she said before bursting into laughter. Debra's feelings for Kevin were already a mix of budding friendship and tempered desires. Suddenly, her mind was a jumbled mess of mixed feelings as she quietly stepped away and into her room. She could hear them continue chatting through her closed door. Debra hurried to her closet, remembering Kevin's driver's license, which she had pocketed days earlier. His driver's license was, at that moment, a golden ticket to a world of possibilities. Debra marveled at the small piece of plastic, tracing her fingers over the image of Kevin Hunter smiling back at her, before she realized it had expired some time ago. She giggled at his cleverness.

The ominous influence of Dr. Dunlap became more apparent during the first year, creating a deep divide among the school staff—those who accepted and tolerated desegregation and those who hated it, putting them at odds. Still, everyone remained silent as he manipulated Debra's academic success out of fear of losing their jobs and community standing. Beneath a friendly smile, Dr. Dunlap carried out his sinister deeds openly, turning her excellent grades into demoralizing failures and reveling in the chaos he caused in her school life. Throughout it all, Debra kept going. With all his influence, she knew that State board certification was something Dr. Dunlap couldn't control. Her teachers gradually discovered that the failing grades fabricated by Dr. Dunlap bore their signatures, implying their compliance and, if uncovered, their great hatred, not Debra's extraordinary abilities, but rather the flaws in their teaching methods, which were at fault. In a counter move, they secretly united—not to support Debra, but to protect themselves, restoring her grades if they were called to account for their supposed misconduct.

[In this tale, both scorpions sting each other, and the frog survives.]

The Jersey Shore. The gentle breeze coming off the Ocean

cools the hot sand under their feet as they walk. Debra's wide-brimmed, floppy straw hat shades her lovely features as they search for the perfect spot. It's the bouncing brim of her hat that catches her attention first, lighting up her eyes with disappointment when compared to her long-lost family friend, Straw Hat. Her wonder-filled smile shifts to her brother's lively eyes. Mike hurried to scoop up the sand, letting it run through his fingers. "Wow," he said in awe. Debra did the same, but she contained hers. "I wonder how it tastes," Mike quickly asked, his daring gaze locking onto his sister's. Debra raised her eyebrows, returning his daring gaze,

"You should make sure the tooth fairy has enough cash on hand to fill your pockets," she casually replied. Mike paraded a cheeky smile before covering his open mouth with his lips over his top and bottom front teeth. Kevin, carrying an ice chest, two large umbrellas, and beach towels, chuckled at the thought and quickly apologized to Mike.

"Sorry, buddy, but that was funny," he justified.

His friendship with Debra and Mike was still new, and this was the first outing Debra had committed to with her brother during this turbulent phase of her nursing career. His connection grew stronger over many meals and pinball games each weekend, sometimes with his father tagging along, to Mike's delight, who looked forward to tales of his amazing adventures. Mike was not quite sure they were all true, but still mind-blown. Each cup of coffee was accompanied by shared laughs between the two; their bond, rooted in faith and family, deepened, strengthening their friendship and creating a lifeline amid the chaos surrounding them. Kevin found himself warmly invited to their table before long, a gesture that solidified three lives and three struggles, proving to be an invaluable support system for all during such a challenging period in their lives.

Debra's long nights in the segregated section of the school library echoed with loneliness. Although she had persuaded the other women of color to distance themselves, they now wrestled with their conscience as the pressure on them eased, and she stared at empty chairs. Dr. Dunlap's frustrated focus had vanished, and she became his sole primary focus. No longer desiring the forbidden, it became primal—predator and prey—especially as time dwindled and his deviant teeth were bare. The quiet, dim space Debra filled with stacks of books that delved into the realm of the doctor's field of practice was a place that made his heart race. He pushed open the door, the scent of medical school now a possibility, lying at Debra's feet, and he knew it was him. Dr. Dunlap saw this and instantly regretted it. Now, the potential future of this young Black woman becoming a peer torments him.

This late-night ritual was not unnoticed by Ms. Stevenson, the school librarian. With her silver hair neatly styled and a demeanor shaped by forty-five years of nursing experience, Ms. Stevenson exuded authority. The thin chain holding her reading glasses grew taut as she raised them to her eyes, a habit she had introduced to separate herself from her country pass whenever she spoke to anyone. Hailing from kinfolk deeply rooted in country hill traditions, Ms. Stevenson was a hard-nosed advocate of the racial divisions that permeated the school's atmosphere. When their gazes first met, Debra's and Ms. Stevenson's eyes locked in a sharp exchange, silently acknowledging their deep Southern roots and the unspoken history of oppressor and oppressed that defined their existence.

Moving to a quiet corner of the library, Ms. Stevenson's breath caught in her throat, and she felt a surge of emotional turmoil. Ms. Stevenson's urgent concern, an unwelcome disdain, festered within her, mainly aimed at some entitled white women whose casual mockery of her profession cut deeply. Their actions—lifting their skirts and provocatively revealing a hint of ass cheek—were a blatant display for easy praise, exposing a troubling ignorance and alarming disregard for the seriousness and dedication that nursing requires. Her beloved alma mater had transformed from a place of learning into a breeding ground for ignorance, with its singular goal seeming to focus on securing a doctor to lead a life of unearned leisure instead of embracing the serious responsibilities entrusted to those in the healthcare field.

Amidst this internal conflict, these thorns in her side softened her judgments of Debra, seeing beyond her skin color to a dedication to learning the nursing profession that resembled her own in her younger days. Despite maintaining her reserved exterior, this evolving perspective turned the librarian into a silent sympathizer of Debra. The flickering lights signaling closing time, meant to alert everyone and encourage those lollygagging—particularly those gossiping about their day's drama—to leave, were not meant for Debra. A subtle, almost conspiratorial eye contact between Debra and Ms. Stevenson, along with a note, appeared as a sign of favor and was no longer the same piercing stare she once directed at the colored students.

This invitation allowed Debra to linger, even as the cleaning ladies began their rounds, further emphasizing the unique bond quietly blossoming in that tranquil, dimly lit sanctuary of knowledge.

From that night on, their eye contact shifted from intense to something warmer and more welcoming. At first, there were moments of mutual respect for their shared commitment to learning, with quiet acknowledgments passing between them. Soon, a connection formed through revealing conversations and sharing coffee at the same table. Ms. Stevenson lowered her cup from her lips, smiling softly at Debra. Her eyebrows lifted; she was pretty sure this was the first time she had seen Debra's smile. Ms. Stevenson nodded slowly. "You have a kind and beautiful smile," she confirmed. Debra smiled politely again, then nodded in agreement. "Is there some trust-building between us?" the old white lady wondered. Debra took another sip of her coffee, trying to quiet her tongue, but it only made her more cautious. The country girl, with lion's blood running through her veins, bared her fangs.

"Forgive my boldness, Ms. Stevenson. I respect you deeply, earning you a place in this man's world, but... trust gets me hung in the South we come from. Ain't much different for me here," Debra continued, acknowledging the hint of Southern drawl still in Ms. Stevenson's voice, then sipping her coffee again.

"Yes," Ms. Stevenson replied admiringly. "There's some trust here, child, we sipped coffee," her Southern drawl now softly filled every word she spoke. Debra laughed, her head nodding in response to the humor swirling in her mind. "Yes, we did... You sipped first," Debra said with a smile. Pursed lips, Ms. Stevenson's brows creased. Her nod was slow at first, then quicker as her mind replayed the moment. "You taught right," she said, bursting into laughter, her brows raised. "Let's change that," she added before taking another sip of coffee.

Debra's Grand-Michael had taught her never to smile at any white folks to make them comfortable in your presence if they weren't willing to do the same for you.

Ms. Stevenson and Debra's chuckles were a Southern comfort to both, the sound light and airy, filling the cozy atmosphere between them.

In the final weeks before graduation, Debra desperately clung to hope as she prayed fervently each day, longing to walk across the stage while resolutely ignoring the harsh realities around her, the influential figure within the school who seemed determined to block her path to becoming a Registered Nurse. She relentlessly continued her studies, night after night, with heavy textbooks open before her, undeterred by all the signs that the most powerful person in the school was determined to see her fail. For more than a few nights, Debra sat in the library, almost broken, her weary eyes lifting only from her books when her muffled screams for justice became audible, fracturing her concentration and causing tears to stream down her face. Sadly, this toll also became evident during the times Debra set aside for her brother and their friend Kevin. Weekend outings approved by the orphanage were now limited to just a few hours—long enough for lunch, a walk in the park, and possibly a visit to the zoo. These trips always started and ended with Kevin and a concerned Mike exchanging glances in the car's rearview mirror, as Debra often dozed off in the passenger seat, pressed against Kevin's shoulder from exhaustion.

As they drove home, Mike couldn't help but notice the

concern in Kevin's eyes reflected in the rearview mirror. Debra's serene demeanor masked the fatigue that burdened her. Mike, unable to overlook the despair hidden in his sister's smile, had stopped his harmful, antisocial actions when adoptive parents expressed interest in him. He transformed into a charming little boy, eager to participate in the adoption process to free his sister from her commitment to him.

On the day that Debra shattered, she stood poised at the entrance of the library, her short, shallow breaths creating delicate fog patterns on the cold pane-glass window. Tears streamed down her cheeks. One hand frozen on the brass doorknob, the other holding an open letter from the orphanage. Debra's head came to rest on the endlessly repainted wooden door as her hand fell to her side, releasing the letter. With a heavy heart soaked in sorrow and despair, her head turned to join where her eyes had just cut to, down the far end of the emptying hallway to Dr. Dunlap's office door, where her fate awaited.

As the last few nursing students trickled into their classroom, Debra stood firmly at the door, her presence almost magnetic. The remaining students couldn't help but notice her hurried strides—each step radiated urgency, nearly as if she were sprinting through an invisible obstacle course. The last nurse to see Debra noticed the look of determination on her face, perhaps tinged with a hint of rage; she wasn't entirely sure. While it resembled an everyday look that women sometimes share when they are at their wits' end with men, life, or both, it was the final straw. Debra was a woman of color, and her stoic expression was deeply ingrained in her. This face of exasperation—an internal struggle dating back to before the era of slavery—had rarely been seen by the white world; it seemed almost otherworldly, as if driven by the rhythm of African drums.

The casual whispers circulating among the students about this "tall colored girl" carried an undercurrent of jealousy, a wild beast on the loose, instantly igniting the air with tension. Chairs screeched against the floor as students rushed to the door, spilling into the hallway in a flurry of chatter and excitement.

Debra didn't knock or even test the lock—she yanked the door open with a forceful determination that sent ripples through the hanging American flag, causing it to flutter like the one raised by the Marines over Iwo Jima nearly seven years earlier. The door slammed shut behind her with a resolute thud, securing her inside the sanctuary. As she passed beneath the flag, now settling back into place, her eyes, previously aflame with resentment, softened into something fragile yet hopeful when she spotted the new, pint-sized colored student. At that moment, her burdens seemed to lift, if only slightly, as she felt an unexpected bond spark between them.

Sandy Jefferson, a gentle young girl with warm bronze skin and a bright, inviting smile, stood quivering, her shirt loosely undone. Just months prior, she had been warmly embraced along with four other women of color and wittily informed about a little blonde-haired, blue-eyed girl named Sandy, whose first name would certainly not be prefixed by "white." Debra resolutely stated, *"We'll call you 'Sandy J.' before those little heifers start with their jokes."* Sandy graciously accepted the name and treasured the friendship that blossomed between her and Debra during the long study sessions in the library; they were consistently the last to leave.

Dr. Dunlap, the predator Debra had warned her about, loomed ominously before her. The wooden floors creaked eerily as Debra moved forward. Dr. Dunlap froze briefly, his attention shifting to the noise, then slowly turned his head to the side at the sound of more footsteps. Whimpering softly, Sandy J clutched her shirt, desperately trying to cover herself as she leaned slightly to see if it was help or more horror coming her way. When Dr. Dunlap turned to face Debra, a clear intensity filled his gaze, revealing the unspoken desires he had harbored for too long, spilling forth like venom. In a frantic effort for safety, Sandy J pressed her back against the cold wall, inching away from the corner until she finally slipped beyond his reach, her heart pounding in her chest.

Thinking herself unnoticed, Dr. Dunlap cast a furtive glance at Sandy J. as he nodded, "Thought myself a snack, but with you here, my little unicorn." The playful term lingered in the air, thick with an unsettling atmosphere. Keenly aware of the dynamics at play, Debra head-gestured for Sandy J. to leave as she assumed a boxer's stance, ready to engage. Dr. Dunlap moved closer to Debra, his legs shoulder-width apart, his hands resting on his waist to make his large frame appear more intimidating. Meanwhile, Sandy J. watched the two with a mix of trepidation and defiance, gradually backing away. She stopped beside Debra, her body language protective, as Dr. Dunlap moved closer to Debra.

"This school ain't worth the blood of a sister on my hands," Sandy J. declared, her voice full of contempt for the man standing before her and the system he ran. She glared fiercely at Dr. Dunlap while she moved to stand beside Debra as if to share the looming threat. Dr. Dunlap's dismissive laughter rang out, a rich sound that masked his fear of being challenged, as he observed the two women standing resolutely beside each other. A hearty laugh at the sight,

"Niggers united? That's rich!" His stare aimed to mock. With a quick sidelong glance, Debra met Sandy J.'s gaze; their unspoken alliance strengthened, a bond brokered.

"This white trash makes a little money, calling us niggers. I'm offended he didn't add *dirty*," Sandy J. joked, shaking her head. Tickled, Debra's mind relaxed,

"In Mississippi, when a mule kicks you, you know what happens," Debra challenged. Sandy J. raised an eyebrow, her eyes dancing with intrigue. Delivering a sharp kick without hesitation, hitting Dr. Dunlap squarely in the groin, he fell to his knees, clutching himself. Debra snapped,

"The same thing that happens everywhere: Ya fall!"

Chairs tumbled and tables overturned as Dr. Dunlap fell, while Debra and Sand J. quickly pounced, stomping and kicking. He swept the legs from under both women, sending them to the ground like a house of cards caught in a gentle breeze. With his legs barely under him, he wobbled to his feet in front of the women. Dr. Dunlap swung wildly, keeping the two at bay, and managed to compose himself after the kick enough to fight back. With his glasses knocked to the floor and broken, his vision was blurred. A series of wild, desperate swings landed with a satisfying thud, depleting his strength and sending both women across the room, disoriented and reeling from the unexpected counterattack. Debra and Sandy J. stumbled to their feet, their breaths hitching in their throats as they struggled to regain their balance, but the exhilaration on their faces was unmistakable—a wide grin spreading from ear to ear, the doctor saw clearly.

"You hit like a little bitch," Sandy J. shouted back at his furious glare. It elicited a humorous chuckle from Debra and provoked the doctor to charge at them, only to run into a barrage of punches. He fell again. This time, he stayed down.

Debra and Sandy J., exhausted and injured, leaned against the solitary feature in the room—Dr. Dunlap's polished oak desk was as esteemed as it was dreaded. Debra, battered and feeling like tenderized meat from the pounding on her body, contrasted with Sandy J., who grimaced, a pirate's eye patch and scarred arms told tales of a fierce fight—marks on their bodies serving as badges of honor after facing a brutal adversary. As they gasped for air, the atmosphere was thick with tension and the sharp smell of the large Cuban cigars he smoked, the ember glowing dangerously close to where he puffed. They watched the doctor... his breathing steady, unchanged beneath them. Still, when he rose, his authority, cloaked in an aura of wealth and privilege, would hover above them. The report of abuse, tainted by the glaring disparity in their statuses—two women of color against the word of any white person of modest means, let alone the head doctor of one of the most prestigious nursing schools in the country— felt like a distant explosion, powerless against the realities their skin color granted them.

The women heaved for their next breath, seated cross-legged in a Native American style on his desk, Sandy J. lighting a joint; their breathing was more labored but with purpose. Sand J. took a long drag on the joint, filling her lungs and trying to explain how to smoke it properly. Debra grasped the thin, twig-like joint, a sad representation of the country cousins she freely grew and rolled on her Grand Michael's land. She held it at eye level, inspecting its sad, slender form before taking a drag that lit the joint like glowing embers from a campfire. "Girl, I used these as matchsticks to light joints as thick as your fingers," Debra chuckled. Sandy J. laughed, admitting her ignorance as she playfully leaned against Debra, who had a dismissive look on her face. This made puff, puff, pass slow and methodical. The ritual was hampered by pain as smoke curled into the stale air, offering a brief respite from their brutality. The swirling smoke and rings represented their silent screams for justice served.

As Debra and Sandy J. stared at Dr. Dunlap, sprawled awkwardly across the floor, it became evident that raccoon eyes would haunt him—those darkened circles from the impact, gazing back at him from any reflective surface for months to come. The doctor lay crumpled like a discarded puzzle, limbs twisted like a pretzel, seemingly dead on the cold, hard floor. Suddenly, his foot twitched, followed by his finger lifting and pointing directly at them. Debra and Sandy J.'s brows slowly raised as they observed the scene. Quickly exchanged glances, their eyebrows furrowing together in surprise at the sight of the seemingly lifeless doctor stirring. With a sudden jolt, as if shocked back to life, Dr. Dunlap suddenly regained consciousness and sat up. Debra and Sandy struggled to their feet, each supporting the other as best they could. The air in the room crackled with tension as he glared at the ladies; they scowled back at him. Sandy J. moved frantically, pushing chairs out of her way before unlocking and opening the door, while Debra watched the doctor's every twitch and movement, anticipating what might happen next.

As the raucous uproar from the classroom surged into the hallway like a tidal wave, a sea of weary faces dressed in crisp white nursing uniforms met the sight of two battered women. The crowd instinctively raised their hands to cover their mouths, their eyes wide with shock and horror as they watched the unsteady figures of Debra and Sandy J. stagger into the now-congested corridor. Wincing in pain as she hobbled, Debra pressed her left arm across her midsection to stabilize her bruised ribs beneath her student nurse uniform. Meanwhile, her finger interlocked with Sandy J., Faint, desperate cries for help drew many onlookers to the open door where chaos had erupted. Dr. Dunlap stumbled into the hallway, disheveled and gasping, his belt loose, pants falling to his ankles, forcing him to his knees.

"Call the police! Those black women assaulted me!" the battered old man shouted.

Sandy J and Debra supported each other as they shuffled down the corridor, limping. Disgusted, students and teachers who witnessed the aftermath of the confrontation stared at Dr. Dunlap in silence. Gradually, their gazes shifted and followed the two girls as they entered the crowd, effectively dismissing his claims. Then, quite unexpectedly, applause erupted from the heart of the student body, swelling like a mighty tsunami and sweeping through the hallways—a surge of support for Debra and Sandy J. At last, they reached Debra's room, a cozy sanctuary where they could privately care for each other's injuries. Debra had cleverly kept several cola bottles balanced precariously on the windowsill, the fizzy liquid inside chilled to perfection. They took turns sipping from the bottles while sharing distracting, lighthearted banter. Sandy J., nursing a swollen black eye, admired the tingling taste from the bottle after each sip, occasionally pressing it gently against her bruised flesh to relieve the ache.

"I know this black eye will eventually fade; it's not the first and probably won't be the last," she said with a bittersweet grin, raising the cold bottle as if toasting their endurance. Sandy J. focused intently on it with her good eye as if it held all the world's remedies. "But cold cola…! Not going to see one of these for a long while," she said, laughter bubbling between them as they shared the moment, the sweetness of the drink, and their camaraderie soothing their wounds.

Dark imaginings haunted Debra and Sandy as they nervously listened to every sound, both consumed by deep anxiety and a sharp awareness of their bleak, looming fate. Their conversation stumbled repeatedly; each pause was punctuated by the thin, tense atmosphere around them, as shadows flickered unsettlingly beneath the door. Both women braced themselves, expecting at any moment the thundering boots of the police or the fury of a lynch mob to burst in and seize them. Surprisingly, as the hours dragged on, the only sound was Sandy J.'s voice telling her life story in an eerie calm, while holding a now-empty bottle of cola pressed to her eye, which now served more as a makeshift lens to her past than for its original purpose. Debra nodded and smiled at all the right moments; her mind was only half-engaged with Sandy's tale; her focus was mainly on the window. Through the window, she observed the optimistic, 'the world is my oyster' look of white people walking just beyond the school's walls, each wearing expressions of hopeful determination and endless possibilities. She knew white folks had bad days; she'd heard them talk about the dreadful things happening to them. However, Debra wondered if they ever considered how much worse the daily chaos would be if they were colored.

"Yes, girl, that's why they smile as they go about their day. Bad day? Hang a nigger. It doesn't have to be from a tree; they can mess with you at your job, in school, or even while you're just walking down the street, minding your own fuckin business. Don't know you from Adam, but steal or cheat you out of your money just because you colored—nothing else." Debra's brows furrowed as she turned away from the window.

"How?" Debra cried out. Her voice almost pleaded for understanding of a question that had never been asked. Sandy J.'s amusement was tempered by her pain; she grimaced as she reached for the cola bottle to press against her eye.

Debra rubbed slightly above her eyebrow, sighing for the tenth time. Her thoughts drifted to her brother, remembering him as a thick-legged infant and the wild mustang he's becoming—she felt the weight of his sacrifice pressing down on her chest like a heavy stone, her lips trembling. The warnings, him quietly coloring on paper instead of playing the pinball machine, not trying to look at Layla's legs, so many things overlooked during her spells of exhaustion now flashing before her, as stark and undeniable as her destiny.

Mike's choice had encompassed both of them, and though it had been a painful decision, she now believed it was the right one.

With a solemn air, Debra lowered her chin to her chest, a gesture filled with resignation. She struggled to breathe. Once again at the hands of an evil man, her thoughts to question

God became a moment of confession. "My brother is my son," she revealed, barely above the screams reduced to whispers for help that her mother ignored, before turning to meet Sandy J.'s wide eyes. Her mind muddled, her voice silenced by shock, as disbelief surged through her. "No one knows this outside of Heaven, except for a sweet old lady named Ms. Virginia, I met on a train coming to Philadelphia, ... and Helen," she held a pause, her voice trembling slightly as the memories resurfaced. "...And Charlie, he raped me, I was 13," Debra continued. Sandy J. stood, lacing fingers taunt until her knuckles turned white.

"You were *thirteen*!" she exclaimed, still trapped in the haze of Debra's agonizing memories, Sandy J's eyes brimming with tears of pain and sorrow as she sprang to her feet.

"Forget them cops coming for us; W-We need to find this man," she stammered, rubbing the back of her neck. "If he ain't dead, we need to dead him," she insisted fervently, nearly hyperventilating as she started pacing the small room, the tension thick around them. "Who is this woman, Helen? Is she with Charlie?" Debra's head rose slowly, and her gaze locked onto Sandy J.'s with an intensity that betrayed her turmoil. "Charlie's wife... my mother," Debra finally replied, the words hanging heavy in the air between them. Sandy J. rushed to the edge of the bed, the urgency in her demeanor commanding.

"You know that *bitch* gotta go?" Sandy J. seethed, standing up before Debra, her body trembling, and her fingers curling into tight fists; Debra stared down at Sandy J.'s clenched fist, trying to decide what to do next.

"Ms. Emma," Debra said confidently. "There was this woman back in Mississippi, Ms. Emma." She repeated, smiling gently through her sorrow, her eyes crinkling as she chuckled softly.

"You're a bit shorter, but you share the same 'ornery spirit' that, as my Grand Michael would say, gets you hung in the South." Debra sighed as she let go of Sandy J., the brief warmth of their embrace contrasting with their difficult surroundings and somber talk. "I hadn't thought about it in years, but I believe they passed shortly after I boarded that train to Philadelphia." Sandy J. shrugged, looking into Debra's eyes for more clues, her curiosity sparking then fading.

"Shortly after? What are we talking about, Hours? Days…? Ms. Emma?" she cautiously inquired. "Might she be a witch? Did she put one of those, ruts… no roots on them?"

Debra sighed.

Time and reflection cleared some of the uncertainty *about why her Grand Michael never spoke of Ms. Emma as her grandmother; she just smirked at Sandy J.*

Sandy J., overwhelmed by her emotions and dizziness that heightened her senses, winced as she pressed a cold cola bottle against her swollen black eye, trying to alleviate the pain. Meanwhile, her suppressed trauma from years ago flickered in her subconscious beneath her composed exterior. "Say what? I'm not some wicked witch of the east, bitch," she said, her tone playful yet protesting. Debra nodded, understanding evident in her expression as Sandy J. spoke, with a hint of doubt flashing in her eyes as she leaned in, showing interest. Sandy J., her cheeks slightly flushed with emotion, apologized profusely, a warm smile spreading across her face as she playfully raised her hands to shield herself from any potential backlash. "Look, sis," she smiled with deliberate calm, "I've been called a 'bitch' so often, I didn't answer to anything else but bitch until I was ten, so I barked every time my mom called me that, you know, whatever it takes to smile another day in these streets," she joked. Debra shook her head, closing her eyes and relaxing as she took in Sandy J.'s quirky personality. "Deb, I thought my ass was beat for sure, girl. You hold your hands like a man and stay calm under pressure—talking about mules, then kicking the shit out of that man... I mean, I smell something. Best you embrace the bitch inside you, gonna hear it a lot in this city, trust me," Sandy J. playfully admits, her hand quickly covering her open mouth. "Oh, I called you Deb—is that okay?" she asks with a smile. Debra giggles happily, her laughter soft and cheerful, as she reaches out her hand. That gesture brought them closer, creating a shared moment of friendship.

"You can call me 'bitch,' *bitch,* as long as it fits the occasion," Debra warmly replied as Sandy J. reached for her hand. They both relaxed, with Sandy J. sitting on the bed and Debra in the chair by the window. "I'm here wanting to feel angry at something or someone, but the crazy thing is, this shit is just normal for me," Debra calmly admitted, her head slowly swaying from side to side. Sandy J. nodded in understanding.

"Me too, my shit was so fucked up; ... My mom told me I don't have many choices in life." She chuckled. 'Sandy, she said, your options are limited.' Choose a path before you get old." Sandy J. laughed. "My top two options were to become a nurse ...or a hooker. And I can't take dick every day, so..." Debra muffled a cackling laugh as Sandy J. joined her.

"Girl, you still high, 'cause these some new stories you telling?" Debra giggled.

"Yeah, but it's true," Sandy J. replied. "My mom died a few

months before I came here; her pimp stuck a knife through her heart." Debra sensed that the right time to tell Sandy J. about shooting off Charlie's dick had slipped away, so she shared tales of her old hound dog, Lancelot, until silence filled the room.

Shadows whisked across the floor behind the closed door like discarded paper in a gentle breeze, catching their attention and interrupting their conversation each time. Until a shadow hovered like cloud cover ominously, before whooshing into anonymity. Debra exhaled and held her breath to ease the pain from her bruised ribs as she rose from the creaky chair. As she moved toward the door, Sandy J., filled with concern, rose quickly from Debra's bed to help, but was promptly waved off with a raised hand. Sandy J. remained standing in the center of the room; her wide eyes fixated on Debra. There, she threw open the door to an empty hallway, her chest heaving from a racing heart. Not trusting her eyes, she quickly turned left, her gaze darting down the hall. Debra's eyes remained fixed on one door, then another, and another—waiting for the police to come out of one of the closed doors. Her frustration with the police's absence somehow grew. Sandy J. cemented in the center of the room, eyes wide and unblinking; her chest rose and fell rapidly as if she had just sprinted sixty yards, and her foot tapped quickly. "What do you see?" she asked cautiously, her voice barely above a whisper as she gingerly edged closer. "Deb?" Debra stepped fully into the hall, scanning her surroundings with squinted eyes. At the far end, a figure slowly came into focus—a person standing like a sentinel in the distance.

"Hey!" Debra yelled, her voice surfing off the sterile walls as she rushed to close the distance between them. The figure stopped, turning to face her just as Sandy J., now leaning out of the doorway, signaled for Debra's attention. Ms. Stevenson was the one who came into focus. Debra kept moving toward her.

"Debra… look!" Sandy J. called out, her body vibrating with anticipation. Debra turned. Sandy J. pointed at two letters taped to her door, one of which was already open. Debra moved toward Sandy J., then looked down the hall at Ms. Stevenson, but she had already turned and walked away, fading from view. "Debra!" Sandy J.'s voice begged her to stop staring down the hall and focus on the envelopes. The sealed letter looked official and bore the school's letterhead. "Just open it," Sand J. urged. Debra noticed, then flinched at the black eye on Sand J., looking back at her before glancing down at the envelope in her hand, worry etched on her face as she was being passed it. With trembling fingers, Debra swiftly tore open the letter, and they leaned closer, their bodies tilting together as they processed the news. "What does it say, girl? I can't even get past 'Dear' with one eye working," Sandy J. shouted, pressing a now-warm, empty Coke bottle to her swollen eye for relief. They moved their lips in unison as they read the letter dated two weeks ago.

"Valedictorian!" Debra exclaimed, her mouth fell open as she staggered backwards. Cheering and squealing, Sandy J. bounced on her toes as Debra reread the letter, slower, if questioning the truth her eyes just revealed. Nervous laughter seeped from her as the letter floated from her hand.

Their injuries be damned, they grimaced through a painful embrace that symbolized freedom, victory, a form of justice, and a renewed sense of hope amid their struggles. Debra, filled with an energy her exhausted body could barely contain, raced back into the room as if she had been reborn, with Sandy J. closely following her.

"Where are you going?" Sandy J. asked, her voice a mix of confusion and excitement. "We just stood up to a white man who dangled our futures like throwaway toys and won; we gotta celebrate!"

"Mike believes he is completely alone, thinking we'll never see each other again. Debra's eyes dart anxiously around the room, as if the right words to soothe him are hidden somewhere under the bed or in a dark corner. I have to reassure him that everything is okay," Debra said, moving around the room, grabbing her hat and coat, her painful injuries seemingly ignored or forgotten. Her breathing grew quick and shallow, tears welled up in her eyes and streamed down her cheeks as she struggled with her thoughts, which played out like movies showing how badly Mike was dealing with his grief. Sandy J.'s eyebrows knit together as she caught Debra's gaze, gently stroking her arm while softly speaking to calm her, "No, no, no, girl, we won." Sandy J. whispered urgently, almost pleading. Debra lifted the letter she had received from the orphanage earlier that day and held it out for Sandy J. to read.

"They found adoptive parents for Mike; he likes them, and they like him," Debra emphasized, her voice breaking as the weight of the situation sank in. Sandy J. took the letter from Debra's shaking hands, set it decisively on the desk, and cradled Debra's face with her hands, her gaze unyielding.

"Just hours ago, you rescued a stranger from a life filled with nightmares. So, Victory now, breathe later," Sandy J. declared fiercely, her words forging a promise and a connection. "You have a true friend in me for the next hundred years,"

193

she added, smiling as she placed Debra's hat on her head and stepped back to hand her the coat. "Put this on, now." Sandy J. tapped her foot impatiently; my arm throbbed from holding it up. "Go tell that boy he's coming home with you—whether we have to snatch him back from the ends of the earth or not, he will have a home with you..."

As their smiles and lingering gazes gradually faded into the background, a heavy sigh from Sandy J. pierced the serene moment like a quiet revelation. *It was a poignant reminder that their challenges had settled into an unsettling rhythm, casting a persistent shadow of eerie normalcy over their lives. Living in this country meant the struggle would never cease; however, with genuine friends and true family, we always have a chance to reclaim what was taken.* Debra moved hesitantly toward the door, as if something kept her back. She turned to meet the gaze of her urban friend, catching a glimpse of her southern, resilient self beneath the polished surface; their embrace was instant, drawing them together like opposing poles of a magnet.

Debra sat quietly on a bus, nestled in a seat located midway between the front and back doors. The engine's hum filled the air as she glanced toward the rear, where a lively and colorful group of schoolgirls erupted in fits of giggles, their laughter ringing like cheerful bells, each of their joyful tones reflecting their diverse backgrounds and radiating pure joy. Debra couldn't help but wonder whether her perspective or theirs brought warmth to her heart. However, their loud and exuberant departure—a whirlwind of energy as they bounded off the bus—suddenly extinguished her smile, leaving a still void in its wake. Debra's eyes kept glancing at her wristwatch; each look carried a quiet plea, as minutes and hours seemed to slip away with the seconds hand racing around the dial, and she wished to slow down time itself. The urgency of seeing her brother weighed heavily on her; every time she looked out the window at a stop, her restlessness turned into an uncontrollable foot-tapping frenzy. The bus filled and emptied of passengers several times during the long ride, only to overflow as she approached the orphanage.

Her mind raced with thoughts of Mike, praying he would linger by their special window, where they waved at each other after she dropped him off or after dinner in the orphanage's mess hall, eager to see his sister show the long-awaited sign of good news—the promise she had sworn to keep. Debra rose from her seat on the crowded H-bus. "Ugh," escaped her mouth as a nostril-invasive, hazy, briny, pungent odor assaulted her. Instantly, Debra's lips curled upward into a sneer. Her nose wrinkled as she encountered each offender while squeezing past and out the back door, a block away from the orphanage. Debra glanced at her watch. Gates locked and dinner over, she scurried down the street as fast as her pain tolerance allowed. Half a block remaining, Debra could see children cheerfully parading past the windows that lined the hall; the sight deepened her anxiety, and she prayed she wasn't too late to see her brother pass by. Stopping feet away from the locked gate, Debra had positioned herself in plain sight of any of the windows Mike would look out of. Only now did the foot traffic past the windows decrease to the point of being almost nonexistent, each passing moment punctuated by the growing quiet that suffocated her like hands tightening around her throat. Debra gazed at the windows, her hand slowly rising to cover her mouth. "He gave up on us… On *me*," Debra sobbed, tears spilling down her cheeks.

Exhaustion swirled within her, a potent blend of fatigue and guilt, clouding her mind and dulling her awareness of the fading light, mirroring the dimming spark in Mike's eyes. Ignoring the agony coursing through her body—perhaps choosing to forget for a moment—Debra gripped the gate tightly, shaking the bars as if she could somehow reach through the barriers that separated them. All she wanted was to hold her lonely baby brother again, to bridge the gap that time and space had created between them.

Defeated, she released her grip on the bars and turned away in sorrow. Her weary feet shuffled listlessly until she realized she had returned to her starting point. Shoulders drooping, Debra looked down at her worn shoes. She wiped the tears that continued streaming from her eyes and exhaled. *By faith,* Debra whispered with resolve, then turned around confidently, guided by that faith. She inspected each window with renewed hope before finally finding her brother and making eye contact. Both arms waved… only… Mike just stared blankly, as if she weren't there, then raised his hand calmly, signaling goodbye. Debra's wave faltered, her spirit sinking; her arms drooped, and Mike's hand fell limply at his side. He waited in agonizing stillness for her to depart, and when she took a tentative step away, she felt an ache unfurl in her chest.

However, Debra quickly straightened; she refused to let her brother feel abandoned, even though she planned to return the next day.

Determined, Debra unbuttoned her coat and laid it gently

on the damp ground, her hat carefully placed on top of it. A smile broke through her deep sorrow as she closed her eyes briefly, letting herself recall the joyful, whimsical dances Mike used to perform to chase away her frowns when she dropped him off at the orphanage. With a burst of energy, Debra jumped up to spin around and face Mike with a smile on her face, despite the pain she was experiencing. She whimpered softly and grunted with each hard landing on her feet, every movement reaching for her brother's heart, while a cheerful expression told Mike a different story. His unwavering gaze kept his sister at a distance, shutting his heart and refusing to accept what his eyes revealed. It felt like forever, but Mike ultimately trusted his heart and burst out laughing, surrounded by his friends, who joined in. Mike's eyes sparkled, and he grinned as he waved to his sister, blowing kisses and making big hearts with his arms above his head. Shoulders relaxing as she mumbled a prayer of thanks, Debra sniffed and wiped away tears while waving and blowing the biggest air kisses back at Mike, he had ever seen. Then she hurried to grab her hat and coat as the rain shifted from drops to drizzle. Debra waved one last celebration of love and hope, before rushing as the rain started to fall steadily.

Debra's eyes sparkled with delight as the sky unleashed an unexpected cloudburst. The sudden, torrential downpour became an exhilarating adventure as Debra took shelter, while others around her scattered frantically, scurrying from storefront awning to storefront awning like players in a high-stakes game of hopscotch. Water-driven trash clogged all the drains. The street quickly turned into a chaotic sea of jumbled, stalled cars trapped in a swirling mess. Frantically waving while eyeing the few empty passing cabs that cruised into the storm, she watched as they seemed to vanish, ignoring her hopeful gestures as they sped away. Her arm fell from pain, frustration, and exhaustion. At the same time, overcrowded buses rumbled past, their windows fogged with heat and frantic expressions of commuters. Debra thought it was the same stench that had turned her stomach earlier. Her search for transportation halted after she caught her reflection in one of the storefront's windows—a wet mop, she mused. Unbothered by worries of getting wet, she now walked in the rain, uncomfortable but carefree.

Debra, embodying her country girl spirit, walked through the rain, relishing the moment with a sense of adventure. She looked up at the street sign, a thrill running through her as rain poured from a soaked newspaper she held over her head like a shield. Within seconds, a tingling sensation spread through her body; she was only a few blocks from Kevin's apartment. Her mind filled with snippets of overheard stories—some amusing gossip about friends' escapades, others more sensual and passionate, causing a flutter in her chest. Feeling renewed, she stepped with more bounce, her pain replaced by unexpected thoughts. Despite her inexperience, she felt curious and a little excited. For the first time, Debra began to explore her wants and desires.

As she arrived at Kevin's apartment building, Debra climbed two flights of stairs and stood outside his door, pacing back and forth as the cool rain dripped from her hair and clothes onto the hallway carpet. The rain soaked her through and through, leaving small puddles at her feet each time she paused. Although she heard voices inside drifting through the door, she could only make out the television and muffled sounds of Kevin's laughter, creating an inviting atmosphere that heightened her anticipation. Still, she would enter his apartment without a chaperone. Debra's nervous foot tapping splashed the puddles and stirred an ocean of uncertainty.

Inspired by Sandy J's words, 'Victory now, breath later,' like a soothing mantra, she decided to knock on the door. Debra gathered her courage and stepped forward. She clenched her fist, ready to knock, but hesitated just inches away from making contact. Her hands dropped to her hips, and her head drooped toward her chest, filled with uncertainty. A deep sigh escaped as she rubbed the back of her neck, standing indecisively. Debra's head turned away from the door, deciding not to go in after all, expecting her feet to follow. Frozen in place, her feet, and now her smile as she looked down at them in disbelief, *she experienced a brief internal struggle.* Her head lifted quickly with a surge of resolve, and she knocked with more urgency. Shifting her weight from one foot to the other, she waited, counting what felt like an eternity. Just as she was about to leave, the lock clicked open with a creak on its hinges, and the door seemed to open by itself. To her surprise, no one was there, leaving her standing there with her heart pounding.

In front of her, fresh from the shower, Kevin was wrapped from the waist down with a towel. One hand on the doorknob for balance, he was crouched down with a finger on the trigger of his service revolver, which rested on his lap. Standing tall before him, Debra, her hair damp and shining, was left speechless. She didn't see the gun, even though it was visible. Kevin's physique was beyond anything she had ever imagined—a chiseled chest, bulging biceps, and defined washboard abs were much more impressive than she had imagined. The shadow of his spread legs under the bath towel demanded her attention. The air between them instantly thickened with tension; Debra whispered, wondering what this feeling was, her tongue unexpectedly gliding flirtatiously over her now pulsating lips in a way she had never experienced before. Her body radiated an overwhelming and intoxicating heat she couldn't understand as Kevin quickly stood up, apologetically. Debra's eyes hesitated to meet his. "Fine," she whispered, the only word she allowed to leave her mouth, as they begged the towel to loosen its grip, to reveal what lay beneath.

Both smiled as Kevin gently led Debra into his cozy apartment, the rain pouring outside and casting a soft gray hue against the windows. He noticed the distress in her stride—her shoulders slightly hunched and her gaze averted—but decided to wait for her to speak first. "Hi," Debra said, her voice light and lilting, quickly followed by a nervous giggle. Inside, her mind felt like a barren desert; words and thoughts were as elusive as the sun on a day like this. She stood motionless. The room was all-encompassing, like a warm chair by the fireplace. Everything was now wet, her womanly told her.

"Uh, I graduate next week… Valedictorian! I have to give a speech," Debra stammered, her voice a lively mix of excitement and shyness.

"Valedictorian! Wow, that is amazing, Debra," Kevin shouted. At first hesitant, he hugged her briefly before pulling away. Debra grinned.

"Would you like to come?" she shyly asked, batting her lashes, her gaze flickering aside, waiting for his reply. This modest woman, whom he didn't recognize at the moment, left him speechless. "Yes, I would love to," he finally said, his voice filled with eagerness as Debra's eyes lit up and her smile blossomed into a bright beam, while she stared into his eyes and smiled.

He joked, "You swam over here to invite me?" while softly chuckling and observing the dreary scene outside, with rain steadily pounding on the window.

"No, Kevin," Debra quickly replied, her voice returning to its confident tone, now tinged with a shy sweetness that made it all the more endearing. Every gesture Kevin made caused his muscles to flex, and each breath was steady, engaging his abs. Debra's gaze slowly danced all over Kevin's body, swallowing hard, "That was loud, wasn't it?" Debra guessed, her brow furrowing and her voice trembling slightly, revealing her mix of regained confidence and frayed nerves. "Isn't that kind of—oh, I don't know—bold to think?" she said, before a broad grin spread across her face. Hiding her face in her hands, she slowly looked up. She added, "I'm sorry, I was being difficult...I got caught in that downpour coming back from seeing my brother," her gaze flickering to the floor as Kevin rushed throughout the cramped apartment, quickly bagging clothes. She watched him pick up clothes that had been scattered around for days, tossed carelessly into corners, and noticed the slight furrow in his brow as he hurried to clean up. "Kevin, you don't have to straighten up for me; I just...," she began, her words trailing off, but he cut her off, determined to hide his flustered state. Stopping in front of a chair, he grabbed his neatly ironed uniform, the crisp fabric contrasting with the casual chaos of his space. He glanced at

Debra, who stood frozen, a small puddle forming at her feet from the moisture of her soaked clothes.

"How about I order some takeout, and we celebrate? I was planning to do a little overtime, but seeing how the rain treated you… I'm not going out there," he suggested, a grin breaking across his face. Laughter bubbled in the room, providing a light relief from the dreary weather outside. Debra shrugged off her coat, revealing the soaked nursing uniform that clung to her figure like wet satin.

"Dinner? …A date?" she nodded, flashing a cheeky, playful grin before strolling toward the bathroom. Kevin studied each graceful step of her long legs, like the eyes on a statuesque fashion model walking down the runway. The soaked uniform clung and released against every curve of her figure, making her seem both vulnerable and enchanting as she paused at the bathroom archway.

"First date?" Kevin chuckled, his voice teasing as he picked up a torn, bloodstained uniform shirt from the floor. Debra frowned at the sight before Kevin glanced at it and said, "Gang fight, not my blood."

"Anyway," he continued, "I've been *courting* you ever since I first gazed into those big, beautiful, brown eyes of yours." he grinned. Debra blushed, speechless, her heart racing as her body thrummed with energy. She slipped into the bathroom, and the door shut behind her. Kevin moved closer to the bathroom door, his ear pressed against it as he yelled over the sound of the rushing shower water, his voice blending with the soothing cascade of water. "You can hang up those wet clothes and tell me all about your day when you get out, you know, on 'your' first date!" he joked.

Kevin tried to maintain his composure, but the excitement bubbling inside him was nearly impossible to contain, leaving a flutter in his chest as anticipation filled the air.

Vivid images of Debra's vulnerability emerged in his thoughts, igniting hope and desire that distracted him. As the shower ended, Kevin's eyes remained glued to the bathroom door, completely mesmerized. When Debra stepped out just into the archway of the bathroom, Kevin's breath caught in his throat. In the background, just over her shoulder, in the steamy mist, Debra's undergarments swayed gently on a clothes hanger; the thought of how this day would unfold was enough to make Kevin's heart race. He stood stunned, like a statue, the towel wrapped around him, his fig leaf. "Chinese okay with you? They're the only restaurant brave enough to deliver in this weather," he asked, his voice slightly hesitating as he moved the phone's receiver away from his ear. Kevin's mouth dropped open, and his eyes widened, taken aback by her natural beauty. Debra tilted her head to the side, eyebrows raised playfully,

"Not even a pair of drawls," she playfully teased, as she gestured with her hand for Kevin to keep talking. Kevin smiled as her gaze wandered over his body, lingering briefly at each detail.

"Well, ahh…" Kevin stammered, searching for a proper response as his cheeks flushed, his gaze dropping to the towel snugly tied around his waist. Slowly, he began to feel a stirring below, awareness washing over him like a tidal wave. "I ordered Chinese," Kevin quickly added, attempting to divert her gaze from his 'pitched tent.' Debra's head jerked back, her curious eyes widening in surprise. Kevin's gaze flew back to hers, his jaw dropping in fake astonishment while he tried to get Debra to ignore the fulfillment happening below. She arched her right eyebrow, extending her hand with a sultry smile that beckoned him closer. In that electric moment, they drifted toward each other, Kevin's breath came faster, and Debra's heart danced.

Suddenly noticing the bruises on Debra's arms and knuckles, Kevin's brows creased with concern. Debra's head slowly shook 'no' as she kept moving closer, pressing her index finger against Kevin's lips. "Later," she whispered, her eyes pleading for this moment to occur. Debra's heart was telling her, if only for this one night, Kevin loved her, and if her heart wasn't deceiving her, she loved him too. Debra, trembling with emotion, reached out her hand, her eyes conveying a longing that transcended the moment. She softly guided Kevin to his bedroom, gently pulled him closer, and tenderly stroked his face before sharing her first kiss. His mind told him a powerful punch struck him, and it weakened his knees. The space around him slowly faded.

He retreated until the back of his legs met the bed, which absorbed his weight with a soft, barely perceptible creak. As he staggered back, Debra felt entranced by the graceful way his muscles flexed and shifted beneath his skin, a visual symphony of strength and vulnerability that left her breathless. Still in pursuit, Debra pressed Kevin until his broad shoulders knocked into the headboard. Debra straddled Kevin, releasing the tension while holding her towel in place. It draped her back and then fell, sliding down behind her across his lower legs. With her right palm pressed gently against his chest, she felt the rapid thud of his heart—a rhythmic beat that seemed to echo their shared energy. Their eyes locked in an enchanting gaze, pulling them closer and immersing them in a moment that made the world around them fade away.

He was on the verge of describing her breasts as voluptuous when more bruises on her body came into focus. Debra moaned, licking her lips again as she took hold of his pulsating manhood with her left hand. It brought him back to the present moment directly. Her head tilted back, as did his. As she gently began to place Kevin inside her, his hands came to rest on Debra's waist, grazing a bandage; it paused his pleasure, but he stayed silent. Debra moaned softly for a long time. She held his head in the palms of her hands and thrust it against her breast. Her hips rolled slowly from side to side and back and forth as she lifted herself up and down, gently at first. Then, with a force that flexed his thighs under her. Kevin's toes spread wide as if they had found a reason to celebrate. Debra's confident grin in the mirror across from the bed revealed she was in control. However, Kevin's body is ready to release. His mind pleaded for a distraction from the self-indulgent thoughts that raced through him after over a year of neglect. Kevin gently traced Debra's curves with the tips of his fingers, moving slowly and tenderly, along the crease from her shoulders to the small of her back. She wiggled and giggled as if touched by a soft feather. Somehow, Debra knew it was coming, and when it did, it felt even more intense. His hand froze after reaching her soft buttocks. Kevin's fingertips pressed firmly, gliding smoothly in that moment, creating a rhythm that resonated with fluidity and grace.

As Kevin's chest rose and fell, he envisioned himself as a mighty bass player, deep in the groove of a smooth jazz band, where every note was rich and resonant, and the air was filled with the sultry harmonies of the night.

Refocused, he calmed himself and released a slow sigh as his eyes closed while caressing, then palming Debra's well-rounded, cotton-soft bottom. He paused the rhythm of Debra's hips and spun her, laying her on her back. There, gazing desirously into her eyes, Kevin slowly and gently lifted her left leg, placing it over his shoulder and right over the other shoulder. Debra, swept away in a tide of pleasure, her gaze locked onto Kevin's eyes, which sparkled with joy until she only saw the top of his head. Her breath is first caught in her throat and then escapes her mouth in tiny pants as Kevin's tongue dips between the seams of her lower lips. Breaching Debra's unexplored demanded squirming twists and turns of ecstasy before his lips and teasing tongue leisurely returned to gentle sucking and soft touches. Her fingers gripped, playfully getting lost in the soft mist of his afro as they lovingly rested on his head, guiding him to fulfill her desires with every delicate touch.

CHAPTER TWELVE

FEARS AND FAITH OF THE FIRST

IN GABRIEL'S EMBRACE rested the first child of a courageous soul, a being so pure that innocence radiated from them, casting a gentle glow over the moment as though the very essence of their heritage was intricately woven into their fragile form. "I touched the child's chest... a lion roared," Gabriel whispered, his voice laced with amazement as he gazed upon the reverie. "The courageous soul has gone beyond our reach, quickly working to soothe this child's fears and strengthen his faith," Gabriel assured Scott. The air around them shimmered with possibility, a reverie that danced like sunlight through the leaves, connecting the realms of faith and dreams, her destination and now theirs.

"Gabriel...how, that's not...," Scott began, gesturing toward the reverie. Gabriel's smile interrupted Scott's thought as he glanced at the reverie, which started to waver.

"Faith moves mountains, so why do you question this?" Gabriel asked as the image of the child in his hands vanished.

∼

Mike and Lancelot stood at the mountain's base, some hundred yards from his weathered cabin. A blistering wind whipped through the trees, swirling dried leaves around them like a chaotic ballet. It seemed to have taken Mike, who slung his sniper's rifle across his back, and Lancelot just minutes to scale the rugged mountainside to a clearing near the top with a breathtaking view. They paused, inhaling deeply, their lungs filling with the crisp, invigorating air; each exhale was marked by the mist rising like smoke from a chimney, as they surveyed the sprawling landscape surrounding them. An early frost had covered the sparkling tapestry of fallen autumn leaves. Still, the frost-bitten leaves rose and danced in the wake of Mike and Lancelot's tracks as they ripped across the mountain terrain. Their pace quickened, and their breath expelled into the bitter cold, resembling the forced smoke from the copper-rimmed chimney of a Great Western locomotive, hinting at the chill that bit through Mike's jacket. Their pursuit was aimed at neutralization; an operative was at least "six-four" in height by the tracks ahead of them across the unforgiving terrain. It wasn't long before a crack of thunder echoed around them, spurring Mike and Lancelot on more. Their speed doubled by adrenaline and determination until Mike found new tracks. His abrupt slowing caught Lancelot off guard, causing him to spin around like riders in a teacup at a carnival. Mike's brows furrowed as his eyes darted across the rugged landscape, a cunning female tracker pursuing the same target. The footprints came out of nowhere. This tracker is good, playing cat and mouse. The pause allowed sweat to pour and steam to rise from Mike as he crouched to study the tracks in the brisk cold. Lancelot uncovered a scent, instantly shifting from curious to alert. His gaze was on the wooded areas as he paced the surrounding expanse, whining and barking an urgency to Mike before tearing off into the dense thicket of nearby woods. Mike followed.

The flawless motion had Debra spinning around, drawing a sleek handgun from her waistband, and firing two shots with breathtaking speed aimed at the ominous rustling of leaves and snapping branches under a heavy foot that betrayed the approach of the unseen figure. Much like the elegance of a ballerina, her flow felled the towering operative just moments before he unleashed his deadly intent. The deafening gunfire reverberated through the trees, a thunderclap that startled Mike and Lancelot only moments earlier.

But as Debra collapsed onto the forest floor, her body was still and silent. She realized the operative still clung to life, a desperate flicker of defiance in his eyes as he labored to get his legs under him. His camouflage melded seamlessly with the surrounding tapestry of the autumn foliage. Debra squinted. Still, through blurred vision, she could see him struggling to his knees. He stared at her intensely and whispered, "Double-tapped by 'Grandma Dynamite,'". The large man grimaced in pain, his wild gaze now challenging the calm and eeriness of the soft tune he hummed while fumbling to patch the two holes in his chest with the fingers of his left hand as his right hand combed through the carpet of leaves, searching for his gun.

As he contemplated the choice of his boot knife, a heavy, shaky breath escaped his lips, mirroring the tension that hung thick in the air. In an explosive moment, he lunged forward with an inhuman urgency. Quick huffs and a deep, menacing growl reverberated around him, sending a jolting wave of primal fear through the operative and causing his eyes to widen in terror. Turning instinctively toward the source of the sound, he lifted his gaze. What he saw next froze him in place—a glint of sharp, formidable canines poised to strike, reflecting the light with a menacing gleam that would be his last sight.

A low growl reverberated through the air, followed by the sickening gurgle of a blood-filled last attempt to exhale from the operative, which awakened Debra from her stunned state. Paralyzed by the sounds, her eyeballs darted to the shadowy corners of her left, then to the right, searching for salvation. Debra's weapon was lost in the chaos of her fall. Still, her fingers instinctively found life, reaching out to brush against the rough texture of the forest floor for her weapon, until the sounds of scattered leaves moved in her direction. So, steadying her breath, she closed her eyes, awaiting her demise—a wolf, maybe a bear.

Debra winced as the sniffs and prodding nudges drew closer to her throat. Her eyes flew open wide, resembling the startled expression of someone who had just witnessed an explosion. A loud snarl escaped her lips as she bared her canines, the only weapon she had in response. Lancelot's tail wagged when he saw her eyes open; his tongue swooped in, giving a long, warm lick that traveled from her chin to the top of her head. Debra's relief flooded over her instantly; her tears were the sidecar of a happy smile as Lancelot barked with excitement, letting Mike know where he was. Her gentle strokes moved softly through Lancelot's fur, as faint as her voice, and stopped after a few touches while he stood watch over her.

Debra chuckled along with a fading smile, "Friend for life; kinda figured you walking into that cornfield wouldn't be the last time you'd come to my rescue." After a few exhausted breaths, she placed her hand on his back, feeling the comforting warmth as he stood vigilantly, ever loyal. She pictured a bright smile crossing that old hound's face, showing the strength of their bond—a connection so deep that even time cannot diminish its shine.

Lancelot's deep bark reverberated through the rugged mountain terrain, altering Mike's course and propelling him into a frantic run. Striding high through the dense, tangled undergrowth stirred memories of his time in the jungles of Vietnam, yet even those memories felt distant as fatigue began to grip the older man. The thin, crisp air seared his lungs with each breath while the biting wind lashed against his face, heightening his senses.

Pushing himself up the next incline, he burst into the more expansive woodland, where the trees towered like sentinels around him. With urgency fueling his every step, he emerged from the thick forest cover into a vast clearing. The pestering stillness caught his eye; every death he had encountered began with this stark contrast to the vibrant life surrounding it. His heart pounded in his chest. From afar, Mike saw the stillness, the blood, the dead operative. Fear-stricken, it was a nightmare come true as he, a scared little boy, sprinted to Debra's side. Kneeling, "No, no, no," the only words to tumble softly from his lips as he hovered over his sister in silent prayer. Lancelot whined; *maybe it was the same prayer. His muzzle stained with the operative's blood; he looked the part of a sad carnival clown.* When Lancelot turned to Mike, gazing up at him as if he understood, his paws danced in place, and his eyes pleaded for help. He sensed the moment's weight in the air, *perhaps seeing a reflection of Mike's fears.*

Mike's fist clenched to halt its tremor before he gently touched Debra's neck for a pulse. With a deep sigh, he hurriedly pressed down on the entrance and exit wounds on Debra's right side. She flinched at the pain, then smiled softly as her eyes lifted to his. Debra gradually reached out to touch his hand but missed, falling into his lap. His left hand, burdened with gauze, moved with frantic urgency, packing the gaping gunshot wound to stop the gushing blood flow that stained her shirt—the fabric soaking up the life force that threatened to slip away. "Pressure; I need you to apply as much pressure as you can," Mike urged, his voice quivering as he replaced his hand with hers. Tears, welling in his eyes, evaded his cheeks and cascaded down the bridge of his nose, gathering before splattering onto Debra's shirt just above her heart. Mike gazed at his sister, mustering a brave smile that belied his rising panic. "You're going to be just fine, sis," he reassured. Debra's cheeks lifted as she tried to smile at Mike, understanding the deception; she had told the same lie many times herself.

"Is that rain? I guess it's raining," Debra teased, sharing a smile as Mike's cheeks squeezed more tears from his eyes. The banter was often exchanged between them during both good and challenging times. Suddenly, everything changed; her breathing grew shallow, her eyes became glazed and rolled back before closing.

"Mom," Mike cried out as he embraced Debra, sharing his heartbeat with her. In his massive arms, he held his mother's fading life close to his body as she once held him in that Hush Mississippi train station, humming the same church hymn that soothed his soul. Nearby, Lancelot nervously paced, his whimper and cry revealing his distress. To Mike, God was more like a friend, listening when he sensed his death approaching. So, when he closed his eyes, it was not for himself he prayed. Lowering his head, reverent prayer from a simple man with simple beliefs came forth with a desperate prayer of supplication. The calm in the air causes Lancelot to stop. He approaches Debra's feet, where he lies down. Mike sensed his mother drifting away, but he refused to let her go. With his head lifted to the Heavens and voice loud, pouring every ounce of his being into the plea, he pleaded, "God, please," until despair took over.

A world without his mother was unimaginable, leaving him to stare into nothingness.

Mike's heartbeat slowed, syncing with his mother's faint rhythm. Gently rocking her, he fought his fear of losing his anchor until a child's confession brought clarity. "Hey, sis, do you remember that preacher and his wife who nearly adopted me?" Mike said with a smile. He paused, chuckled, then added, "I think I was five or six." He chuckled again before becoming more serious. "That was the only time I ever felt like giving up on us. I thought I was going to lose you," Mike admitted softly. "Needless to say, they didn't go for the 'possessed child' act like I told you... hell, what was I thinking? I guess I'm lucky I wasn't drowned in holy water, huh? Both turned to the backseat of their old Buick at a traffic light, laughing as if I had just told the funniest and nastiest Redd Fox joke," Mike exhaled.

There I was, thrashing and flapping in that old Buick like a fish out of water, desperately trying to maintain a wild-eyed, frantic look. They let me wriggle from one side of that large back seat to the other; I hardly had the strength not to slide off the leather. Eventually, their disbelief caused their lips to curl as they kept looking down at me. The preacher raised one brow, half amused and half concerned, and it wasn't about the devil; they just burst into laughter. Mike paused to laugh—his brows furrowed in thought. "He said, "Son, the devil ain't got time to possess no negro child; it just ain't no fun.'"

"In that instant, a heavy weight settled in my chest as the reality of his words hit me—I realized he was right. And Sis, let me tell you, my world came to a standstill as if time itself had halted for what felt like an eternity. Just like it is now," Mike said, his voice heavy with emotion as he glanced down at her, the burden of his memories pressing down on him. Tears welled up, mirroring the flood of feelings from that moment. With a soft nod, Mike recalled what happened next—his brows knitted together in thought, his eyes wide as they flickered with the past.

"They pulled over to the curb, and we sat on an empty bench at the bus stop, drinking soda pop as buses passed by— people getting off, people getting on. We just smiled at the bus drivers. We talked for hours. Do you believe that? They kept throwing some scriptures at me, but they were cool. Mike's head fell to his chest. Looking at his sister's face, that's when I cracked."

That was the moment I finally unveiled my truth: I revealed to them that you were my mother, and the orphanage believed you were my sister. I explained how we needed a little more time for you to graduate from nursing school and officially adopt me so we could finally be together as a family." Mike's face broke into a warm smile, the corners of his lips curling up before he let out a soft chuckle. "That was the first and only time I dared to voice what I held a prisoner in my heart."

Softly, thump...thump...thump. Mike felt the rhythm of Debra's heartbeat intertwining with his, their worries gently melting away as her eyes slowly fluttered open. A radiant smile bloomed on her face when she met his gaze. "Mom... I've had dreams of hearing you say that simple word, and I've even wished to hear it jokingly or by a slip of the tongue." Debra beamed. Mike smiled back as she continued, "Anytime you fall or have a bad dream, and call for your sister or sis, Mike... my heart aches; I measured 'sis' as the closest to Mom I would ever get—just a whisper away from the embrace of calling me Mom." Mike returned the smile as he gazed down at the woman who had loved and protected him his whole life.

"I've always known you were my mother," he replied, his grin piercing through the emotions swirling in the moment. "At first, I thought it was just a game—one of those wild pranks we loved pulling at the orphanage. I was all in, you know that! I reveled in the roles of brother, brother-in-law, and uncle. However, over time, it evolved into something more profound. It seemed you hoped I'd see you as my sister; yet, each 'Sis' felt like a small step closer to being able to call you Mom —even if just in my heart. 'Sis' has three letters, like 'Mom'. Crazy kid stuff...I know," he laughed. "It felt right, it felt real." Mike's eyes, shining a light on his pain and trembling with unshed tears, glistened. They spilled over, reflecting the silent, deep emotions between them. Behind that smile, a quiet prayer hovered in Mike's heart. Debra reached up to gently touch Mike's cheek. His eyes followed her, noticing a slight tremor in her fingers, but he said nothing, simply tilting his head slightly to accept her touch. Debra smiled back; her raised cheeks shed tears from the corners of her eyes, leaving a path back to her ears. Debra sensed her child's fear in the air, having formed a bond that transcended any words they longed to hear.

"I know prayer has never been easy for you, but I thank God you found a way to do it," Debra said softly, her warm smile lighting up her features as she gazed at him. Her eyes sparkled with fierce determination, one brow arching playfully as if to challenge him to embrace this shared connection fully. "We're not done yet," Debra declared. Mike's quiet laughter shed tears down Debra's forehead. Her body fought to rise. "Help me up before you drown me," she pleaded, voice trembling. Debra's grunts and groans made Mike worry as he gently leaned her forward, trying to comfort her.

"Now, help me tuck that peashooter of yours nice and tight like I taught you," she said, her eyes dancing with mischief as she caught his bewildered gaze. "This ain't the mountain, and we certainly aren't them folks," Debra instructed with a confidence that steadied Mike. Nodding, he followed her commands, fully aware that this was Deb's family, Deb's Mountain, and Deb's war; above all, he was Deb's soldier.

In a playful gesture, Debra glanced up at Mike's baseball cap, encouraging him to relinquish it. A smirk crossed his face, and his brows furrowed as his eyes looked up at its curved brim. Mike flushed with nostalgia, reversed the cap before placing it on her head, ensuring it faced backward the way she always did to him during target practice at the rifle range. With a few tugs, Mike secured it snugly. Debra's lips curled as nostalgia demanded another smile. Their shared glance lingered, spoke of many treasured moments together, creating a connection that transcended words. Deep in thought, Mike felt a pang at the prospect of leaving his mother behind. Yet, in this fleeting moment, the reasons he had burst from Debra-Ann's arms to race for those train tickets at the bustling Mississippi station became as clear to him as the urge to leave her now. Mike had always been Debra's soldier, and he understood that even more now. Memories flooded back—countless afternoons, trips to the gun range where he learned to handle a firearm before learning his ABCs—bringing a deep sigh. He knew those lessons were meant to prepare him to survive on the street alone if necessary. The truth was that Mike would not lead, but he would not be alone in this fight. Debra looked down the mountain with fierce determination, deftly loading a round into the chamber and adjusting the dials on her sniper scope. She kept her gaze focused, refusing to look up at her eldest child, as she needed to clear her mind for the task ahead.

"I'm going to take these motherfuckers down, Sergeant York style," Debra ordered. "And Mike, do your thing."

Debra's breathing was shallow and labored when Mike gently touched her shoulder. He stood there, a heavy weight of longing pressing against his chest, staring at his mother's still form and wishing fervently for her to turn around. He craved the warmth of her eyes and the comfort of her voice, yearning to hear her speak even a single word. Yet, deep down, he understood that everything meaningful had already been expressed; still, he couldn't bear the thought of leaving her alone. It felt as if he had just discovered her at that moment. Debra's gaze, however, remained fixed and unwavering on the distant rifle scope, while Lancelot, their loyal dog, observed Mike's frantic departure with calm vigilance. There was no need for a command; Lancelot instinctively understood his role as protector and wouldn't abandon her; he was her ol' hound dog.

Mike's eyes snapped open, then swiftly shifted from the slow-spinning ceiling fan to every corner of the room, as if trying to catch a glimpse of some trickster lingering in the shadows from the night. The alarm clock rang a second or two before Mike hit the button, yet his chest continued to heave as if a lost race had just ended. The vivid nightmare left the scent of crisp autumn air lingering in his nostrils; his mind debated whether to believe it. Distressed Mike lay in a clammy bed, the sheets soaked in sweat. The intensity of it served as a haunting reminder of the early days following the Vietnam War, with feelings of loss and despair crashing over him like crashing waves on the shoreline. Though he could remember little, his dream, if that is what it was, left his sheets sweat-soaked. Inching his way to the edge of his bed, he sat. *The undertaking was much like* Vietnam, *him crawling through the dirt, foxhole to foxhole.* Mike's heart still raced as he stood Unsteady. The fog still clouded his mind as he stepped hesitantly into the dim hallway.

"Lancelot, Galahad, Percival," he called out, his voice cutting through the stillness, then paused, straining to hear the familiar pitter-patter of eager little paws.

Upon entering the bathroom, he pursed his lips and let out a piercing, high-pitched whistle—a sound perfected over many years—to call the Knights to him quickly. However, the three pups, his cherished brother, named after his sister's country hound, and the other two who shared in the legendary adventures—remained quiet, their absence felt especially deep, as these were the holiday gifts his sister had given him because he was off fighting the war, and they were nowhere to be heard. Mike, still lost in a fog of uncertainty, stared out the bathroom window that faced the backyard. This Christmas morning brought a light snowfall that covered three headstones he gazed upon a hundred yards away from the house, which caught his attention. '*The Knights.*' He rushed to the sink with urgency and doused his face with cold water to wash away the remnants of his troubling dreams. Mike stared confusedly at the seemingly doppelgänger in the mirror as if it were a first meeting. The grey streaks of hair in his beard marked the passage of time for both, a testament to the years that had passed, including the forgotten Knights. Pressing a wet hand against his chest, he sought to steady the frantic beating of his heart. As his chin fell to his chest, a fragment of the forgotten dream surfaced—a moment crafted by Gabriel that flickered like a faded film. *The devil ain't got time* stirred in his mind as he recalled the grinning faces of the preacher and his wife, their joyful expressions framed by the front seat of their weathered Buick.

Yet, amidst the nostalgia, an ache filled him, marked by the stark truth of his childhood; he had never met any black people who spoke of fairy tales—only those who shared the burdens of heartache that life had relentlessly thrust upon them. In this fleeting reverie, his head bowed as if under the weight of revelation. Glancing down, Mike noticed a glimmer of gold—an unexpected sparkle shining through the damp, matted print left by his hand on his T-shirt. Dangling from a delicate golden chain was a tiny cross, its size almost concealed by the expanse of his broad, chiseled chest. Mike's furrowed brows knitted together in surprise as he raised the cross into the light, studying it with disbelief and amazement.

Not seen for decades, the cross and its precious memories shrouded Mike in a profound sense of peace and comfort. Its amazement was like a rare flower blooming in the harshness of winter or the delicate grace of a butterfly gracing the window-sill when hope seemed lost—reminding him that love has its ways of sending messages, blessed by God. During that tender moment, Debra, overcoming her fears with faith, pressed the small cross into Mike's hand before he could object and then boarded a train to boot camp. He hasn't worn or seen the cross since, but now it feels like a meaningful connection to a woman's faith that has helped him overcome his fears since birth. Mike massaged the cross between his thumb and forefinger while sitting behind the wheel of his car. The moment spent traveling from the bathroom to his current seat was forgotten; his thoughts about the origin of the cross and how it came to be around his neck were swiftly replaced with his sister and a rush of emotions.

Scott's eyes lifted as he stood in the haze of the gray clouds while thunder shook the sky around them. He looked at Gabriel. Scott's breathing grew faster and shallower as the reverie in Gabriel's hand, which had suddenly stopped pulsing, affected him. Smiling, Gabriel moved closer to Scott as he raised the paused reverie before him; Scott's creased brows showed his discontent. "This bears no less significance than the rosebush or the butterfly," Gabriel calmly reassured him. Frustrated grunts escaped Scott as his biceps strained to hold the weight of the reverie being passed to him. Gabriel chuckled. Recognizing the seriousness of their situation, Gabriel continued. "Sometimes heroes must say goodbye to their heroes, even if it's just a dream so vivid it might feel real.

"Gabriel, what about the cross around Michael's neck? It was lost during that dreadful war. Unlike a flower's bloom or a misguided insect—which can be seen as natural anomalies—the cross had spiritual significance, he added. Scott stared intently at his superior. "Gabriel!" Scott exclaimed, tilting his chin defensively, eyes widening as he faced his superior. Gabriel observed Scott's hand lightly resting against his breastplate, a gesture suggesting both helplessness and determination. Scott's expression quickly shifted to suspicion. "Sir," Scott said softly, "you now present a 'cloud soft' miracle and a false vision to this offspring of the courageous soul. Scott added, 'He will continue to suffer deeply after his mother's passing." Gabriel let out a deep sigh, softly clasped his hands across his stomach, then gently patted Scott's hand while meeting his gaze and replied,

"You understand the language and metaphors of these times well, but there's still much you need to learn about the souls around you." What you see as a false vision is how this child has always viewed his mother—not as an action that will be taken, but as a possibility that could be taken. The courageous soul will defend her family to her very last breath, which is what is in his heart, Gabriel confirmed.

"And what exactly is there left to learn?" Gabriel's gaze drifted toward the heavens, a serene smile gracing his lips before he returned his attention to Scott, whose focus had shifted to the distant, looming clouds, heavy with portent.

"This offspring has the Word in his heart, so there is hope. It is what the courageous soul wanted to confirm. Also, the next encounter with the courageous soul will be her last in her earthly body," Gabriel established. Disbelief wavered Scott's head as his eyes fell to his feet. "If the actions were not blessed, there would have been nothing to witness and nothing for him to experience," Gabriel reassured the young angel, then confessed, "I patiently watched over the courageous soul, and then Michael as he struggled with fear, pain, and loss after the war." Sighing loudly, Gabriel's words enveloped Scott like a dense fog.

Scott responded, quoting Romans 1:9: KJV "For God is my witness, whom I serve with my spirit in the gospel of his Son, that without ceasing, I make mention of you always in my prayers."

Mike sat in his car with gifts stacked on the seat beside and behind him, singing along with Nat King Cole on the radio about chestnuts roasting. He gently rubbed the tiny gold cross between his thumb and forefinger, finding comfort in it, as he watched snowflakes dance and melt on his windshield. Although he remembered nothing of his morning, he always felt this type of joy during Christmas with his family, thanks to his sister, who had brought him happiness since birth. Approaching a stop sign, he slowed and nodded, offering a childlike smile to his elderly neighbors as they crossed in front of his car. That smile quickly vanished as sweat formed under his arms, and his grip on the steering wheel tightened, turning his knuckles white; he felt a deep, heartfelt longing to see Debra, almost as if his heart was calling out for her. Quick, jerky movements had Mike shifting up and down along the expressway before he ventured into the familiar shortcuts through the back alleys and streets of Philadelphia.

From the edge of the gray clouds above, Scott watched with focus as Mike sped through traffic, resembling a police car in pursuit. A smirk spread across Scott's face as he emerged from the thick mist and stepped into the settling fog surrounding his feet and Gabriel's.

"Is there anything that comes to mind?" Gabriel inquired, his voice calm and reflective. Scott's wings flared open like a nervous twitch, catching the delicate light before settling back against his back as he sighed.

"Who comforts us in all our tribulation, that we may be able to comfort them which are in any trouble, by the comfort wherewith we ourselves are comforted of God." 2 Corinthians 1:4, he recited softly, the words resonating in the tranquil air like a sacred melody. Gabriel's brows furrowed as he gazed intently at Scott.

"Interesting scripture you've chosen. Is there anything else that comes to mind about what you have witnessed?" Scott squeezed his eyes shut as if summoning hidden memories. "The cross—it was not a miracle," he said softly and uncertainly. Gabriel's brows knitted together, his eyes sparkling as he grinned.

"Yes, that gold cross... Although my young angel," his voice was steady as he took hold of Scott's shoulders. Gabriel added, "It was tucked away in the bottom of a box to be

223

discovered in the coming days." Scott's eyes opened, and he instantly glanced at his feet. His shoulders drooped forward as soon as Gabriel released them. "I see there is still doubt," Gabriel sighed.

"I do," Scott exclaimed in frustration, his voice hurried, like a confession being chased. "But does he wear the cross because of the courageous soul?" Scott's hand clenched into a fist, pressed against his chest, his eyes looking upward as he pulled back and then turned away from Gabriel. He walked back and forth along the cloud, passing Gabriel repeatedly. "What is happening to me? I have thoughts that captivate. The offspring's reverie brought me sadness. Am I not an angel? Have I turned into a human?" he said quietly.

Finally, Scott stopped pacing and faced Gabriel; his eyes widened as fear traced the outer limits of his face. "And you... You seem to be preparing to return to Earth," he gasped. Gabriel calmly pressed his palms together. Thunder echoed overhead. Gabriel shimmered with a brilliance as bright as the sun. When his palms separated, he presented Scott with the Word, glowing with divine purpose.

"Whether an angel or a human, the power of belief and the teachings of the scriptures will always light your path," Gabriel asserted. Scott's eyes drifted to Gabriel's exhale; he suspected a flicker of distress behind Gabriel's closed lids. "And no, Scott, it is not I that is returning to Earth... it is you," Gabriel admitted, offering a soft smile of comfort gracing his lips.

"Returning?" Scott's brow furrowed in confusion after a hard gulp. "I steer the cloud; souls board, souls disembark. I... I don't go down there." His voice trembled as he looked helplessly at Gabriel. Turning his back to Gabriel, he pointed over his shoulder. "And I have small wings," Scott admitted with a sigh, his wings drooping as Gabriel remained unconvinced. The cloud carrying Gabriel and Scott floated to a stop, hovering over the Hunter house, its color deepening to a dark, heather-gray, indicating the seriousness of what's to come. "If I need you, come at once," he urged, grasping the Word and nodding firmly before slowly vanishing as he was pulled to earth, the weight of destiny on his slender shoulders.

CHAPTER THIRTEEN
CHRISTMAS WITH AN ANGEL

OSCAR NOTICED THE sudden shadow covering the streets in every direction, a deep contrast to the white glistening ground. He squinted at the turbulent skies above. "We might have that white Christmas this year, just like the kids wished for," he grumbled, a hint of hope breaking through his gruff tone. Oscar's wife, Jackie, glared at the threatening clouds circling overhead.

"Mmm-hmm," Jackie agreed, letting out a heavy sigh that spoke volumes as they worked together, unloading their family and a mountain of colorful presents from the car trunk. Eager young feet raced up the front steps, and the childlike excitement filled the chilly air. They repeatedly pressed the doorbell, hoping to catch last-minute gift wrapping. Slippers skidding across the hardwood as they rushed to the front door, "It's like she's sandpapering the floors with every step." Oscar giggled, ears perked, eyes glinting with mischief.

"Pick up your feet, Mom!" he called out. His voice was cheerful as familiar footsteps approached. The door swung open with a creak, releasing the scent of Balsam fir mixed with hints of cinnamon and pine that brought smiles, but it quickly faded upon seeing that Grandma was not there.

"Merry Christmas...Auntie J.!" the children exclaim joyfully, rushing to her with a flurry of hugs, then pause for quick pecks of affection in return, her cheerful squeal echoing through the vestibule. After the lively exchange, Oscar and Jackie leaned in to share a hug and kiss with Sandy J., whose presence was a soothing balm. As he stood back to his full height, Oscar's gaze shifted over Sandy J.'s head toward the kitchen, curiosity mingling with concern.

"Where's my mom?" he asked, a cheerful smile masking his worry as he hung the coats of his children, as Jackie passed them. Sandy J. glanced toward the staircase, a hint of sadness shadowing her features.

"Deb's resting," she replied softly. Friends and family alike were momentarily stunned by her absence, as they didn't find the woman of the house who always greeted them with holiday cheer. Body tingled with anticipation as they caught the delicious aroma of their favorite Christmas dish wafting through the air. *Where's Mom,* everyone would ask, eyes darting in the direction of the kitchen, voices filled with curiosity. However, Mike needed more than whispered speculation – he yearned to see his sister. So, after a warm embrace and a kiss from Sandy J. at the front door, he bounded up the stairs. Sandy J. watched as Mike leaped up the stairs, skipping two and three steps at a time, his excitement unchecked. He didn't slow down until he stood just outside Debra's bedroom door.

In the same space, Scott appeared in Debra's bedroom, caught between a flash of light and its gentle glow. He froze in place, overwhelmed by doubt. The flash of light from beneath the door drew Mike's attention as he raised his hand to knock. Inside, Debra sat patiently beneath a reading light, her hand pressed firmly against the Bible resting on her lap, across from her bed. Scott and Debra exchanged a long, steady stare. Scott gave a hesitant nod to Debra's soft smile.

"Beautiful eyes; soft and … peaceful," she marveled. "Been around, gone through some things, you entertain me before?" Debra asked calmly, her voice stained with a hint of recognition. Scott stood silent, his eyes drifting to the Word, chapter, and verse as she struggled to her feet. Debra's knees nearly buckled under the strain as she inched toward her bed. Scott remained silent, watching her steps as she passed.

A shadow of sorrow crossed the angel's brow when the back of Debra's hand brushed against the soft feathers of his wings; it stirred his voice.

"It is time, my child… This world and its burdens have been lifted from your heart," the angel declared, his voice carrying the comfort of a mother's lullaby. Debra sighed as her steps hesitated, then continued until she came to rest on her bed. Closing her eyes, Debra mumbled a prayer of thanks as a wave of peace washed over her. Scott took her hand, sharing a smile that seemed to offer the comfort of forgetting the pain and suffering of this world. Debra's attention raced to the wall clock, and as the second hand ticked agonizingly slowly, it froze.

"You have visited my past… Witnessed the horrors I've hidden even from myself and the fleeting moments of happiness in my life," Debra murmured, vulnerability threading through her voice. Regret lined her features as she turned her gaze up to the angel. "I have tried to bury the heartbreak that comes with being born black in this world so my children can live without fear. I've marched to protest injustice, fought for the right to vote, for a woman to have choices, to be seen as a human being, to watch others come to this country and enjoy the rights I still yearn for." "I still wonder why so many strived to see me unhappy.

"Was it a wonderful life...?" Debra asked, her heart heavy.

Scott's eyes closed softly in contemplation before he opened them again, his voice imbued with comfort.

"The difference in the world you were born into was you, and the difference in the world you leave will be the family God has blessed through your union." "It is written, and it is time, my child," he repeated gently. Debra gazed at the angel's hand, which she continued to hold, warmth radiating through her. Her heart fluttered, and her brown eyes sparkled with newfound hope as she closed them momentarily. Debra held her breath and then slowly exhaled.

"Yes, it is," she said, before a knowing, almost sly smile spread across her face. Scott's eyes widened before he looked upward, filled with urgency. "Gabriel!" he called; his voice even fell silent to him.

Mike knocked harder, more desperate on the door this time, his chest pounding as his nerves turned his stomach. The rush up the stairs left little time for contemplation. Once he reached Debra's door, he knew he needed to calm down. Closing his eyes, Mike bowed his head, focused on deliberate breaths; he braced himself for pain and sorrow on the other side, but his hands trembled. Another flicker of light crept out from beneath the door, only more intense, igniting his anticipation, holding his sister, Mike's only thought. The door, warm to the touch, opens slowly, and Debra, giving off a cool warmth herself, stands in the archway. She clears her throat as if stalling, giving herself time to register the person in front of her. Her bright smile, awkward yet beaming at her brother, is full of energy, her heart fluttering with excitement. Her eyes sparkle like polished chestnut-brown gems, full of life. She pinches her brother in a tight embrace without hesitation, wrapping her arms around him so securely that Mike cannot move. The embrace causes Mike to question his strength. After a moment, Debra releases him as quickly as she had hugged him and hurries down the hallway. "Hey, sis," he replies, curiosity in his voice. Mike watches how his sister walks. It starts clumsily, like a baby's unsteady first steps, then becomes more confident, taking bold strides that fill the space with newfound confidence, and finally transforms into spirited young Debra, ready to chase after him for his mischievous deeds. This was more than Mike expected, but he happily welcomed her youthful energy as if time had given her a new lease on life.

The laughter in the dining room overflowed with holiday cheer, and the shared memories of Christmases long past filled the air, each voice weaving more embellished Christmas stories than the last. As friends and family with their dedicated jobs, they busily set the table. In the kitchen, the last of the splashes and dashes were added to complete the holiday feast. The conversation shifted to 'chitlins,' the once-a-year dish, as soon as the lid was lifted, then laughter and the story of Louie and Earl's first encounter with the dish quickly filled the dining room. As both Louie and Earl exited the kitchen, guilty of taste-testing their new favorite side dish, the room erupted with playful banter and jokes that danced like fireflies through the festive atmosphere. The air suddenly grew heavy with silence as frantic, thunderous footsteps raced up the basement stairs, evoking a drumroll that announced an unexpected climax. "I don't want to play with you blockheads anyway!" squeaked the meek voice of young Lyneé, her frustration cutting through the moment before the basement door slammed shut with a decisive bang, reverberating against the walls.

"Stop that noise before your grandma gets that pumpkin!" Eddie's commanding tone bellowed, effortlessly demanding attention and slicing through the festive chatter. The only granddaughter, little Lyneé, is six years old and the youngest grandchild; her curls bounce as she pouts, scrunching her face in annoyance.

"But, Dad... they won't let me play darts with them," she huffed, her voice thick with irritation. Instantly, the scraping of wood against the floor signaled someone lifting themselves from a chair, sending a jolt of anxiety through Lyneé. It quickened her heartbeat and made her eyes bug out like a startled deer as she tiptoed toward the living room doorway, her tiny figure silhouetted by the flickering lights of the Christmas tree. Only the dazzling lights of the Christmas tree and piles of opened — and unopened — gifts below captivated her. Each box was a promise of joy waiting to be opened, hers as well as her brother's. Lyneé smiled at the possibilities. Suddenly, her uncles' raucous laughter erupted, startling her and quickening her pulse.

Lyneé's breath became quick and shallow as she dashed

to the shelf where the prized gold medal belonged. Her body jerked with nervous energy, and she whimpered as her fingers struggled with the clasp. Frustration brought beads of sweat to her forehead, unlike the sweat pouring from her young uncle Kevin in the photo she glimpsed, a beaming boy whose grin captured the innocence and triumph of the day he won gold, sending a sharp pang of pride through her heart.

"You need help, child?" A soft and gentle voice found its way through the chaos building in Lyneé's mind from a shaded corner of the room. Lyneé spun around, unstable, her eyes brightening, still filled with terror at the familiar sight.

"Grandma!" she exclaimed, relief flooding her, though the looming threat of getting her pumpkin beat still hovered. "Oh no, I'm sorry," she stammered nervously, her hands raising, the gold medal hanging from her neck, her gaze locked on her grandmother, who was sitting uncomfortably in her favorite chair. Without hesitation, Lyneé sprinted over, her movements timidly clumsy, as she turned around, and lifted her hair off her shoulder and neck. Her words faltered before she managed to say, "Thank you, Grandma." Lyneé took a deep breath and exhaled slowly as the clasp finally released, the weight of the gold medal resting solidly in her hand. She hurried back to the shelf, carefully placed the medal in its rightful spot, then struck a triumphant pose—just like her Uncle Kevin on the Olympic podium, arms raised high, as if she could almost hear the crowd cheering for her. But at that moment, her exuberance froze in mid-air.

She was suddenly curious as she scrutinized the figure resembling her grandmother. With a grim line set across her mouth and her brow furrowed in confusion, Lyneé edged nearer, her heart thundering in her chest. "What are you, and where's my grandma?" she growled, the tremor in her voice betraying a mix of defiance and concern as she braced herself for the answer.

The Angel-Debra's eyes glazed over with an otherworldly softness, a gleaming innocence shimmering within. "I am an angel; my name is Scott. The courageous soul…your grandma is with me," he said gently.

"You're an angel? And your name is… *Scott?*" Lyneé questioned, skepticism lining her tone. The angel chuckled lightly, amusement dancing in his eyes. "Where is my grandmother?" she snapped, her determination unwavering.

"Your grandmother is laughing; she thinks you are adorable. It was her wish for me to wait here until you called for Christmas dinner; her request to witness this family celebration was granted," he explained. Lyneé's hands dropped defensively to her hips. "Tell me, child, why do you not have that natural fear of the unknown that children often do?" the angel asked, watching Lyneé as she stepped closer, curiosity sparking within her as she reached out to touch him.

"I have the Word in my heart and Jesus' name on my lips," Lyneé declared with the conviction of a child wise beyond her years as her hand rested softly on the angel's lap. She felt a quiver wordlessly rising within her; Lyneé wanted to fight, but instead, she felt surrounded by a sense of truth and love. Sighing heavily, she raised her chin, a gentle smile spreading across her face. "I believe you're an angel, which means my grandma and grandpa are together." A confident nod rocked her head back and forth; Lyneé continued, "If you were evil, my grandma would have burned you with the Word, because she don't play!"

"Yes, lean on the Word," the angel grinned warmly, his expression warm, his stare steady and unblinking. Oscar poked his head around the corner into the living room. His sigh extended the time it took him to absorb the cozy, festive Christmas scene. "Dinner!" He announced, fingers drumming against the doorframe multiple times as Uncle Mike slowly descended the creaky wooden stairs, his heavy footsteps pounding in the stillness.

"Dinner's ready, Unc!" Oscar called out impatiently, his voice bouncing off the walls, as Mike rushed up from behind to give him a bear hug and a kiss on the cheek.

"Man, you've been announcing dinner since you were a little butterball running around here in diapers," Mike chuckled. Oscar joined in the laughter as he cringed, a little boy giggling in his uncle's arms. As Mike started to walk, Oscar, still in a bear hug, into the dining room, Oscar replied,

"Well, now, Unc., you need to reach up to kiss me, shorty. You've been getting more neck than cheek for years, old man." The two of them, laughing joyfully, rolled down the hall. Lyneé looked up in wonder, smiling broadly, her bright eyes shining with excitement at her playful giant uncles. Angel-Debra, always perceptive, quickly examined Lyneé's face, noticing her happiness. Uncle Mike, walking by, pushed open the basement door, its hinges creaking in protest.

"Feet should be moving up these steps; time to eat!" he shouted urgently, annoyed and shaking his head.

"You read my mind, Uncle Mike," Oscar huffed. "They're lucky... Pop be throwing threats against the well-being of your body about now. We'd be farting around when dinners on the table." Kevin glanced at his watch just long enough for everyone to notice, a teasing grin spreading across his face as he looked at Oscar, then surveyed the room. Laughter breaks out, bouncing off the walls as everyone joined in, good-naturedly teasing Oscar's irritation. "Yup, that's Oscar," they said. "Every time someone's late to the table, he's like Pop when it comes to his food." Darryl's amusement boomed the loudest; *maybe it was that he remembered more about Pop, or perhaps he missed him the most.* Eddie, through tear-filled laughter, added,

"Ever since Oscar got that first Chiclet in his mouth!" The dining room erupted into even more chaotic laughter; a familial joy heightened by the holidays.

As the lively sounds surrounded her, Lyneé first focused intently on the familiarity of her Uncle Oscar's footsteps; *she had suffered the repercussions of him backtracking to retrieve stragglers during dinner time.* Yet, she intentionally waited until now to turn her attention back to Angel-Debra, who stood waiting to be summoned for dinner. Reaching for the angel's delicate hand, Lyneé felt a rush of determination. "You hear that? It's always been about that with her; I need my grandma, my uncles need their mother... let her be with us," Lyneé begged, gently tugging at Angel-Debra's hand, urging her to rise, *hoping her grandmother heard if nothing else.* Looking deeply into the mirrored image of her grandmother in the angel's face, she searched for her grandmother in those eyes, seeking any trace of the twinkle she had sought out in times of trouble, the protection only a grandparent could provide, even as she acknowledged the differences in Debra's appearance.

Lyneé's brothers Devon, Keith, and her cousins were a whirlwind of energy as they burst through the cellar door, racing down the hall. The framed photos adorning the walls danced precariously, caught in the chaos of their enthusiastic footsteps. Their sneakers squeaked in rhythmic madness, bouncing through the house like a lively game of basketball. Debra's brows creased together in irritated frustration as her eyes shot imaginary house slippers at her grandsons. "I have told you boys not to run through my house!" she roared, a firm reprimand that held an underlying harsh consequence. Instantly, the boys, stunned, walked stiffly, knees wobbly, transforming their roughhouse playing into an orderly parade into the dining room, each trying to appear more unruffled than the last.

Lyneé's mouth moved silently, her eyes remaining fixed. *The tone and attitude stunned her.* "It's you... Grandmom!" she cried, a fluttering sensation in her belly as she leaped onto the balls of her feet. Debra's eyes shimmered, absorbing every bit of joy from the moment as she looked down at her granddaughter.

"I heard you," Debra replied. Tears pried at the corners of her eyes. "You are something special, my little Lyneé."

"From the rooter to the tooter," Lyneé whispered with conviction. Her hand was halfway covering the hushed words from her lips as if pulled from a secret file. Debra chuckled, her laugh familiar, filling the hallway with a comforting introduction to her presence. She tenderly stroked Lyneé's shoulder,

"Sweetheart... now, you city folk, your parents' city folks... leave the country sayings to country folks... because you're not good at it. The silent stare was exchanged for a moment before an outburst of knowing giggles, the two always shared. Bending at the waist, Debra gathered her granddaughter, cradling her with the gentle care she has over her lifetime, only a loving grandmother could provide. Lyneé found her comfort on her grandmother's shoulder, that soft spot where she always rested her head, the place where she had always felt safe and protected, her tiny lips pressing a warm kiss as her arms wrapped loosely around Debra.

"I love you even more, baby," Debra replied, with tears welling in her eyes, as she gently rubbed Lyneé's back. Debra continued her careful steps toward the dining room as Oscar's voice broke through, filled with urgency and playfulness.

"Dinner's getting cold!" Lyneé turned her head, softly pressing her lips against her Grandmom's ear, her quietly lowered voice hushed but urgent.

"Grandma, wait!" Lyneé called out. Debra's steps slowed as curiosity gradually appeared on her face, her eyes searching Lyneé's, whose head tilted, though her eyes stayed fixed.

"Grandmom… you ain't been this strong in a long time," Lyneé breathed, a hint of spirited nostalgia teasing in her soft, swishing tone. Debra grinned as she welcomed her granddaughter's words.

With a slow, knowing nod, Debra's gaze paused at the entrance of the dining room as she lowered Lyneé. "How could I have forgotten? I'm not in here alone," she confessed, a subtle smile breaking through as they continued to join the family.

Lyneé sat alone at the children's table during dinner, her plate half-filled with a colorful assortment of untouched food—a sectioned arrangement that seemed to lose its appeal amid the lively voices around her. The noise of her brothers and cousins had only echoed through their small section of the dining room where they sat, as they wolfed down their meal, their laughter shining like a spotlight into the dark corners of the house before they dashed to the basement, their sanctuary of play, just as their fathers had before them. Lost in her world, Lyneé leaned her chin and cheek against her palm, her large, curious brown eyes wide with wonder as she absorbed and imagined the rich tapestry of family history being relived through the lively, joyful, and sorrowful conversations among the adults. Lyneé's heart clenched at her father's dejected tone when mentioning those who passed, still blended seamlessly with her uncles' joyful laughter and the gravelly tone of her great-uncle Mike. It created a comforting backdrop that made her feel a mix of happiness, sorrow, and a deep connection to those who came before her. She especially loved listening to stories about her grandpop, Kevin Sr., a man she had only heard snippets of, but whose spirit seemed alive in the memories that floated around the table. She also cherished tales of Dr. Walker, a family friend whose brutally truthful, yet tender demeanor, along with his radiant smile, lingered in the eyes of those around the table — a testament to a man who bore the pain of his final years with grace, ensuring that no one would worry about him.

The family's adventures spun and whirled like bright autumn leaves in Lyneé's imagination, a treasure trove of cherished memories she filed away for the next generation of family gatherings. The joyous reminiscences held dear by everyone around the table needed a larger audience. *Lyneé's heart cried out to be heard; only she knew tonight would be the last time they listened to the imaginatively recounted tales from her dear grandmother, the main storyteller.* The laughter faded, and the room settled into a warm hum, Debra's eyes fixed on her granddaughter as she quietly and unnoticed slipped her hand into Darryl's on her left and Vincent's on her right.

The two moved closer; their faces tense with focus, and their playful banter briefly quieted. "I know I've repeated this to you boys every day since before you were born, along with my daughters-in-law, and all my grandchildren, but it's just..." Debra paused, a soft sigh escaping her lips, her heart swelling with emotion. "Everyone, together now... God loves you..."

" ...and we do, too! Yay!" The chorus of voices rang out, fading like the last notes of a cherished lullaby. Debra's eyes twinkled as she looked at Lyneé.

The smile was familiar; the look was that of her grandmother. Lyneé assured herself, yet the moment seemed staged — just for her, somehow. I reminded my boys of God's blessings, Debra continued, because it's a wonderful gift, and a simple 'thank you' will be enough, it's good enough for the Lord, it should always be good enough for you. Lyneé stared, wanting more.

An endearing wink passed between mother and son. A playful wink passed between Debra and Eddie, and Lyneé couldn't help but giggle at the endearing sight of her father, humbled and more like her grandmother's little boy than her father at that moment. "It's important to remember, sweetheart, that you understand, God gave you to us, just as much as He gave us to you," Eddie said, his voice sincere and steady, prompting Lyneé to beam up at her daddy, a sense of needing to own this moment washing over her. Lyneé looked from one person to another, her face devoid of expression. *But how? She knitted her eyebrows together.* Then, in a burst of excitement, Darryl stood, still holding his mother's hand. *A wide smile gradually appeared, indicating that what came next would be lighthearted.* He looked at the faces of those gathered.

239

God blessed my Uncle Mike, my brothers, and me with two wonderful parents: Sandy J. for us and Auntie J. for you young folks, Dr. Walker—may his soul rest in peace—Louie, Earl, and all our friends, just as He gave our parents the Hunter boys here. Lord knows they got the short end of the stick… if this house could talk." His words triggered guilty laughter from Mike and the Hunter boys, louder than the cheers and applause that erupted, making Lyneé's brothers and cousins rush back from the basement, eager to see what was causing the ruckus. Chins tipping down and heavy sighing overcome the boys as they quickly return to their sanctuary of play in the basement.

A remote-controlled car rushing into the dining room disrupted the calm filling the space. Unable to sit still, many bounced in their seats as if it were real, zooming around the table with playful energy. Suddenly, Keith Lyneé's brother dashed in, the antenna on the remote in his hand bent, his confusion hidden behind a silly smile amid the excitement his chaos created. The remote-controlled car sped between legs and over shoes, its lights dimming, veered wildly, bouncing off walls and chairs, leaving plastic pieces in its wake before crashing into Aunt Alyssa's foot. A flicker of pain flashed behind her closed lids as the car made a loud thud that echoed through the room. As the laughter roared, Lyneé's attention returned to her grandmother; she, by chance, caught a glimmer of the angel's brilliance in her eyes. Lyneé's fork dropped from her hand. Its clatter raised eyebrows around the room, drawing curious glances toward Lyneé. She coughed, her distraction. The unwanted attention closed the walls around her, and her heart raced with a mix of nerves and anticipation. Lyneé cleared her throat and sipped on her juice as her eyes darted to each corner of the room, stopping on her mother as she rose. "I'm okay, Mom. The greens are a little spicy," she managed with an awkward smile, prompting raised eyebrows around the table and a lopsided grin that fought against the bubbling, unconvinced laughter from Auntie J.

"What?" Auntie J. asked curiously, sampling the greens on her plate. After a moment, she cleared her throat. "Well…" Only her raised eyebrows in protest remained. The laughter erupted like popcorn in a hot pan.

Suddenly feeling overwhelmed, Lyneé jumped to her feet. "Prayer and a Wish," she declared boldly. Grand Michael, her affectionate name for her Great Uncle Mike, playfully steadied himself by grabbing Kevin's arm.

"Oh!" Eddie howled, his cackling laughter ringing the loudest through the air. Kevin, noticing chicken grease staining on Eddie's forearm, glanced at him, then glared at Uncle Mike, who was enthusiastically clapping; he also had grease staining in the same place as Eddie's.

"The floor, baby girl, is yours. You called it," Grand Michael supported, his head nodding, reassuring and inviting. Everyone joined hands and closed their eyes as Lyneé cleared her throat again, and heads bowed. A hush settled over the room as Lyneé gathered her thoughts. She remained silent, searching her heart, and then, with forceful authority, she began.

"Father God," she roared, *"I pray you never forsake this growing family. Help us find peace when overcome with pain."* Lyneé's eyes opened as her voice briefly cracked with emotion, scanning the still-bowed heads in front of her. Tears streamed down her cheeks, which she quickly wiped away, determina-

tion fueling her resolve as she continued. *And God, I pray you keep us in love and prayerful in gatherings forever. Amen.* When eyes reopened, hands erupted into applause, filling the room with a warm sense of community.

"How old are you, taking us to church up in here?" Sandy J. joked, teasing, lightening the mood after Lyneé's heartfelt prayer. Misty-eyed, Alyssa stepped forward, wrapping her arms around Lyneé in a comforting hug as she rested her cheek on the top of her head.

"What's your wish?" Alyssa inquired softly. Through squinting eyes, feigning them closed, she watched her grandmother, before scanning the room. A gentle nudge from Alyssa urged her to share her wish. *If only.* Lyneé nodded slowly as her head rose; she beamed; her eyes charming theirs.

"I want to see my dad and uncles dance with Grandma like they used to when they were young, just like me." Auntie J. stood up, bustling about as she cleared the table.

"That's a good one, sweetie," she replied, her smile warm. "I can't remember the last time I've seen these boys dance without cleaning the floor with their clothes ... what do they call that mess, Break dancing?" Lyneé's mother joined in to help, and Auntie J. continued, her voice laced with nostalgia. "Remember that joke you told Deb?" Debra grinned at Sandy J, her face lighting up with the memory. "Remember? We peeked through the spindles on the stairs and watched these boys flailing around on the living room floor... Ah, what did you say? All they need is a little floor wax." Lyneé's brows furrowed, and her eyes widened with anticipation as laughter erupted again, this time from everyone except her grandmother, who seemed to be slipping away.

"Let's go," her heart raced, "Dance; it's my wish," Lyneé insisted, her tone earnest and her desire hugging each syllable. Everyone froze, staring at Lyneé unblinking. Eddie looked at his wife's face with a gentle and curious expression.

"Hmm... she's tired. My baby don't act out?" he speculated, chuckling softly. Uncle Mike pushed away from the table, ready for whatever came next.

"Let's go, family; you know the rules," he demanded with a playful authority. Vincent stood just inside the kitchen, with pie in hand, shaking his head as he passed by his uncle,

"Uncle Mike's a pushover. When did this happen?" he teased. Darryl chuckled; his eyes grew wide as they surveyed the room, a smirk danced on his lips, as Uncle Mike whisked by, grabbed hold of Lyneé's hand, and headed into the living room. Eddie drummed his fingers on the table, as chuckles escaped him like a fast-pouring drink. His eyes lifted to the ceiling while tapping his chin. "Let's see, six years ago, the day after Thanksgiving, around noon," he replied. His wife chimed in,

"Yup! Lyneé was born at eleven fifty-nine, I was there," she chuckled.

Uncle Michael released Lyneé's hand as they crossed the threshold into the living room, pausing to take in the vintage record player, its wood gleaming under the soft glow of the lamps. Hundreds of albums neatly lined up beneath, as if it were his first time seeing them, each offering a glimpse into a different time, struggle, and love. With a smile of satisfaction much like his brother-in-law's lighting up his features, Mike began sifting through the records, eager to capture that special memory for his sister. Meanwhile, Lyneé hurried to her grandmother's favorite chair, knowing she would join her. Its worn upholstery was familiar and comforting to both of them, as she watched the scene unfold with great anticipation and interest. Michael recalled how he and Lyneé's grandfather began building his album collection when he was about her age, the same year they moved into this beloved home. The air thickened with warmth and familiarity, wrapping around them both like her grandmother's comforting hugs as he shared his stories. The determination in Lyneé's nerves quickened her heart as she felt a surge of anticipation bubble up inside her; her feet began to tap against the polished wood floor like the steady beat of a percussionist's drum roll. She looked around the empty living room, and it made her little body tense all over. Grand Michael's face suddenly lit up, and he turned to Lyneé, exclaiming, "I found it, baby girl!" Grand Michael stared at Lyneé and asked, "Where is everyone?" he probed. Lyneé sighed. *Time was slipping away.* She struggled to keep her lips sealed, and it became unbearable. Lyneé raised her eyebrows, staring back at her uncle, knowing silence was the wiser choice. As Grand Michael turned towards the dining room, her jaw fell slack, like a fish caught on a hook. Frustration creased his forehead as he snapped, "Hey, get a move on!"

"Coming!" responded echoes from down the hall, their voices harmonizing as they marched in single file; the trickle of family members and friends seemed endless. Lyneé's head bobbed and weaved through the crowd, searching for her grandmother; her heart ached with hope that there would be no sign of an angelic glow within her grandmother when she laid eyes on her. "Those knuckleheads in the basement, they have ten seconds, I better hear footsteps coming up!" Grand

Michael exclaimed, his eyes brightening as he eagerly looked at Lyneé.

Everyone filtered into the living room in a single file; her grandmother, Angel-Debra, remained missing. It sharpened Mike's gaze, and his displeasure was clear as he barked, "Where is that sister of mine?" As the final waves of family and friends filtered into the living room, Lyneé's mother gave her a side-eye as she came over and sat beside her, "I'm here if you start falling asleep, Miss. Cranky," she said. Lyneé's attention was on her grandmother as she entered the room, holding Kevin's hand, and she noticed the angel's glow was now intensifying around her. Kevin's nostrils flared as he took in the rich, fragrant scent of the Christmas tree.

"This tree...," he breathed out, feeling a sense of weightlessness fill his heart. "Mom, that first Christmas here, for me... it was like God decided to answer every prayer I had made in years past all at once... he gave me love, family, and a minibike." As a tear rolled down his cheek, he kissed her gently on the forehead. Just then, the boys, led by Keith—Lyneé's big brother and the oldest of them, bounded up the stairs from the basement, exuding the aura of restless energy. They let out an exaggerated sigh as they lifted their chins and cast weary eyes upon her before rolling them with practiced indifference as they strode past. Lyneé bit her nails, attempting to see around her brothers and cousins. "Sit... down!" she demanded, the urgency of her voice breaking through the commotion, startling her mother.

"Grand Michael, dance with Grandmom first," Lyneé insisted. Her mother quickly nudged her to calm, as her pleading eyes immediately tamed his furrowed brows.

"Lyneé," her mother scolded, "Uncle Mike comes for that pumpkin, you are on your own."

"Please, Grand Michael," Lyneé hurriedly persisted, as sad images of her heartbroken family filled her head, while Keith, exhausted, sagged into his chair, folding his arms in response to his little sister's continued dramatics.

"This girl, it's always something with her," he mumbled with annoyance. The other boys flowed onto the couch and plopped down like minions, yawning loudly before closing their eyes, *a clear message that they were already tuned out of the joyful chaos around them.*

"There are enough beds upstairs if you boys want to act out," Oscar roared.

Mike delicately placed the needle on the vinyl, holding his breath as he slowly turned around. The anticipation built as the needle created a soft rustling sound. A wide, contented smile blossomed on his face as Sam Cooke's velvety voice floated through the air with the sultry refrain of "Darling... You Send Me." Amid this musical reverie, a vision caught his eye—his sister Debra, standing gracefully by the twinkling Christmas tree, its lights casting a warm glow around her. He reached out his hand, and Debra returned his gaze with a hesitant smile before moving toward him like a beam of light. "Every time Kevin played this song," Mike said, grinning into her eyes, "I knew he was in the doghouse." Debra's laughter rang out like a giggling schoolgirl as her hands relaxed with a sense of ease and affection.

"Oh yeah!" she exclaimed; her eyes sparkling. "That man always knew just what to say—a lesson you Hunter boys picked up from him very well," Debra teased, emphasizing her point. Mike chuckled, shaking his head.

"Well, sis, I had a front-row seat watching Kevin tame the queen of the jungle with his words." Debra hugged him tightly, and the music's rhythm swayed them side to side like leaves in the breeze. Rolling her eyes, she playfully patted his back,

"You were such a mischievous little boy sometimes," Debra replied, amusement dancing in her eyes. "Kevin and his father tamed the jungle boy you were becoming, too,". Mike let out a hearty laugh. "I didn't realize how these two black men could show so much love for each other and still be the baddest men on the planet. Freedom. And they passed it down to you, and you to them. How else could you 007 around the world and hold your nephews when they're scared? Mike smiled, "Smooth ol' Pop Hunter didn't like it when I called him 'grandpop,' chased me around the room every time," Mike reminisced. Debra rested her head on her brother's shoulder.

"He absolutely loved hearing you call him grandpop; that was just his way of getting you to say it a lot." They both chuckled.

Lyneé marveled at the sight. Sagging against her mother, the tension in her shoulders dissolved, and a sense of satisfaction settled on her face as her mother adjusted to support the extra weight resting against her. Darryl rushed to the stack of albums, grunting softly as he rifled through them, reading the back covers before returning them to the pile. "I only remember us being shipped next door to Sandy J.'s house soon after this song was played," Vincent sighed, nostalgia pulling at the corners of his smile. His wife kissed his pouting lips, linking her fingers through his before tugging him toward the dance floor. Darryl examined the next album cover in his hand, a grin spreading across his face. He placed his palm on his heart, memories of happy days drifting through his mind as the song played in the background for all of them. He bobbed his head. "This is it!" excitement bubbling as he hovered near the record player. Darryl tapped his foot, anticipating the finale lyrics of Uncle Mike's selections to finish and the needle slowly rising.

Darryl carefully and quickly set the needle on his chosen record. The sound of the needle on vinyl sped up his tapping foot as he waited for the music to start. He smiled broadly, turning to the crowd and then to his mother, eager to see their reactions. An "Oh yeah" from every corner of the room, mouths fall open, and eyes go wide. Debra's hand flies to her mouth as she beams back at him, her eyes glistening with the memories the song stirred within her. "Come on, Momma! Let's show 'em how it's done!" Darryl challenged, looking around the room, his smile infectious as he beckoned everyone toward the dance floor. Heavy sighs and tender stomach rubs filled every corner, but slowly, family members and friends made their way to the center of the living room. Enticed by her husband's come-hither gaze, Lyneé's mother shifted her daughter's arms away from her, "One second, sweetheart," she said as she strode over to her husband. Debra smiled; the gentle way her head came to rest on her son's chest was a fond memory of her marriage.

Lyneé glanced over at her brothers' and cousins' expressions as they immersed themselves in the sight of their grandmother's joy, like never before, with heart-tugging tears streaming down her smiling cheeks. Concerned, Lyneé's mother hurried to her, leaning down to her level, "What's wrong, baby?" she asked softly. Lyneé's gaze lifted to meet her mother's furrowed brow.

Her mother glanced at her daughter's drooping eyelids and offered a warm, reassuring smile. Lyneé let out a deep sigh.

"Mom… How can I be happy …and sad?" Lyneé asked. Her mother hurried to sit beside her. Lyneé rushed to wrap her arms around her, anchoring her with love as her father, the preceding Hunter, chose a song and took his mother's hand as the song neared its end. Lyneé's hug tightened just as forcefully as her eyes were closed shut. After the last song and last dance ended, there was a stillness—no shuffling of feet from her brother and cousins for their favorite seat, no rush to the kitchen for more pie from her uncles. *Did the angel take everyone to Heaven?* A thought crept into Lyneé's mind—she leaned over and gently patted her daughter's arm, grounding her in that bittersweet moment.

"Baby, mommy's right here, but I need you to open those beautiful hazel eyes of yours," she whispered, as her heartbeat raced at a dizzying pace. Lyneé shook her head defiantly, "No, momma, if I open my eyes, everyone will be gone," she insisted. Lyneé's grandmother called to her; it touched her ears like a gentle breeze, enticing a fragile flower to blossom. "My dear butterfly," she said, her tone soft, comforting. Unsure, Lyneé's eyes opened slowly, her right eye, then her left. "See, everyone is here, little butterfly." She rushed toward her grandmother, stopping just inches away, her small frame radiating energy. She arched her back slightly, tilting her head back to gaze up at who she believed was her grandmother with fierce determination.

"Are you still here, grandmom?" Lyneé whispered between the two of them.

A big grin stretched across her face as she looked down

and said, "For the moment, my love." Lyneé rushed her grandmother, "I want everyone to call me by my first name, grandmom," she mentioned for her ears only. She grasped her grandmother, wrapping her arms around her waist and pressing her cheek against her stomach. "Grandmom, I love my name almost as much as I love you, I do," she said, her chin trembling, her voice filled with sincerity and affection. *They both knew this was goodbye.* Her grandmother gently lifted her into a warm hug.

"I love you more than words can say, Miss Debra-Lyneé Hunter," her voice beginning to fracture. Ears strained around the room to catch the voices beyond the soft music, as eyes widened with amazement at the feat of strength, their movements a graceful pirouette of a ballerina, each rotation sparking cheers and laughter. Debra-Lyneé's brother, Keith, grabbed his cousin's arm to steady himself. Mike's mouth opened in astonishment, his eyes nearly popping out of his head as he watched his sister cradle Debra-Lyneé just as she once held him as a baby.

Still, he lingered by the record player, waiting for a nod from his sister to spin the vinyl of her favorite Stevie Wonder song. When the music began to play, Debra-Lyneé gazed into her grandmother's eyes, soaking in the warmth and love that covered the entire Hunter family and friends. She watched as the last flickers of her grandmother's essence in the angel's eyes dimmed, feeling the bittersweet rush of emotion as her grandmother smiled at Michael. "I dedicate this song to all of you because you're special," she said as the music continued. Now… there will be extraordinary moments when you smile, and it's because you just heard me whisper, I love you," she continued as Stevie Wonder reassured, 'I'll be loving you always,' her gaze sweeping over the room as she caught everyone's eye. "I'm going to rest, but you all keep dancing and enjoy yourselves." As Debra-Lyneé was gently lowered back to the floor, she scanned the room once more, where laughter and joy erupted like fireworks against the night sky, and the radiant light of love emanated from the angel. However, Debra-Lyneé was the only one to witness it and instantly closed her eyes. She weaved through the crowd, almost invisible, her heart thrumming as she slipped away toward the stairs, peering through the delicate spindles. From her vantage point, Debra-Lyneé watched as Scott, the angel, still embracing the image of her grandmother, flickered in and out of her view. Scott hugged Sandy J. with the familiarity of Debra; he affectionately called her by her middle name for the first time. "Mary, don't you weep, the family you have is the one you prayed for, my child," Scott said softly. He gently kissed her cheek. As Sandy J. looked up at the photos on the mantel, Scott moved gracefully around the room, his ethereal presence drawing her gaze, then back to the mantel, which was decorated with cherished family photos of her with her family spanning the decades, memories etched in time. He touched everyone's heads or shoulders, a tender gesture that drew a furrow between Debra-Lyneé's brows, yet no one seemed to find it strange. The silence was filled only by a grandmother's serene smile; although a mirage, it was an endearing farewell before she bid them goodnight. Debra-Lyneé's eyes flitted around the room, landing on everyone Scott had touched. Her hand instinctively covered her mouth in awe. "Comfort," she whispered, a prayer for solace. Scott's gaze caught hers from across the room, and she instinctively sank into the shadow's embrace as he approached Alyssa. The angel's touch lingered on Alyssa's shoulder and then gently on her abdomen. *Blessings.* Scott turned and ventured toward the stairs, drawing nearer to Debra-Lyneé. Her heartbeat quickened, each thud reverberating in her chest as she instinctively stepped back and upward a few paces.

Debra-Lyneé stood firm, crossing her arms defiantly and locking eyes with him. "I want my grandma; I need her," her expressive almond-brown eyes said, filled with fierce longing and certainty. As Scott reached to touch Debra-Lyneé's head, she tightly shut her eyes, her shoulders lifting instinctively as if bracing for something unknown. "Do you understand where this comes from?" he asked softly. Debra-Lyneé kept her eyes shut, struggling with her feelings. "Yes... No... Thank you," she said, her voice trembling as Scott's hand hovered above her, in a moment that felt both timeless and tumultuous.

CHAPTER FOURTEEN
CROWNED ON CHRISTMAS

BLINKING AWAY THE lingering haze from her eyes, a profound sense of loss and loneliness began to grip Debra-Lyneé's thoughts. Despite her yearning to hold onto every fleeting moment, she braced for her uncertain fate. As her breath slowed and her shoulders relaxed, she wrapped her fingers around the cool, polished wood of the banister. Blinking the haze from her eyes and moving with deliberate slowness, Debra-Lyneé looked down at her shoes as she placed both feet on each step as if each served as a reminder of her heart's weight. Her gaze was drawn toward the living room, where everyone stared sightlessly, and a heavy silence hung in the air. The soulful tug at the heart of "As" by Stevie Wonder held the room's attention, its tear-jerking lyrics weaving through the air like a spell that halted her movement. Having heard the song countless times—an enduring family favorite—it resonated more profoundly with her at this moment, each line striking a familiar chord deep within. As Debra-Lyneé made her way back down the stairs, her fingers brushed against the festive decorations she had helped put up just days earlier, which adorned the banister; their glittering colors were muted in the somber atmosphere.

"Christmas…" she murmured to herself, the word lingering on her lips. Upon reaching the bottom step, her fingers lightly skimmed a delicate bell tied with a bright red ribbon, its soft jingling sound a calming surge of holiday cheer. Suddenly, a burst of light flickered three steps from the top, snapping her attention upward. With his otherworldly presence, Scott turned to look at her, the melody pausing in his mind. A surge of heartache welled up inside of Debra-Lyneé as Scott continued his ascent without faltering. Her shoulder drooped, and she mumbled, "Nice wings." Scott paused for a moment, then turned to look at his wings and Debra-Lyneé. A broad smile spread across his face, showing his excitement and warmth.

"…Bigger," Scott confessed. And, if you should ever entertain this humble angel…I am Scott," he added warmly." Debra-Lyneé nodded slowly, her lips pulling down at the corners as a knowing expression crossed her face, and she shuffled into the living room. The soft sound of bells ringing gently as they settled echoed around her while she stood before her two brothers. Her eyes pleaded for some space. She was nestled between them, leaning her head on Keith's shoulder and resting her hand on Devon's lap. Eddie asked, "Were you playing with that hall light?" breaking the silence. Without hesitation, he added, "Didn't I tell you, kids, not to play with that hall light?" once more disturbing the quiet.

"Yes, Daddy," she softly responded, her voice quiet, tears

welling up, and avoiding eye contact. Kevin, to lighten the mood, played some old-school tunes, leading to hoots, hollers, and head bobbing. 70s funk music with thumping bass from the speakers, with its infectious energy, a Christmas party in full swing. Debra-Lyneé edged toward the archway, her heart lifting at the sight of Uncle Vincent strutting down the make-shift Soul Train dance line, with Uncle Oscar closely trailing behind, executing an enthusiastic *if not entirely coordinated* version of the robot. Earl encouraged his brother with animated gestures, and the infectious laughter from every corner of the room swelled around her like a soothing warm bath. '*This was exactly what Grandmom had hoped for.*' Gleefully raising her hands at her brother's encouraging call, she stepped through the doorway, ready to join the festivities. But in a blink, the room began to spin, and the kaleidoscope of joyful faces blurred in a rush as everyone seemed to drift past her like the steam gushing from the underbelly of an old locomotive train. Debra-Lyneé staggered back, her hand flying instinctively to cover her open mouth, disbelief washing over her as the laughter faded and the room cleared out. It was only then, as she watched each of her family members stampede up the stairs, that the Knight, resting by her grandmother's bedroom door soon after Scott's arrival, heard howls piercing her ears. The loud thud of the Hunter boys collapsing onto their mother's bed and dropping to their knees on the floor around them sent shockwaves through the house, making Debra-Lyneé look up at the ceiling in alarm. Yet, still, she remained frozen in her spot. Suddenly, the festive music came to an abrupt halt, replaced by the dreadful, heart-wrenching wails of grief from the upstairs hall. The noise amplified in her mind, then abruptly silenced as if someone flicked a light switch.

A shiver zipped up Debra-Lyneé's spine. The chill of despair was wrapping around her like a cloak. Breaking the uneasy silence, a record began to spin on the turntable, filling the empty air with soothing organ music reminiscent of a church service on a sorrowful Sunday. Then Curtis Mayfield's soulful voice whispered tenderly, "So in Love." Debra-Lyneé gazed at the Christmas tree, transfixed, as though Curtis himself were standing before her, trying to explain something her grandmother wanted her to understand. Debra-Lyneé's eyes drifted up to the wedding picture of her grandparents, a symbol of unity that hung above the others of her family who had wed. She smiled. "Oh, Grandmom," she teared up.

Debra-Lyneé slowly and steadily made her way up the stairs, her pace measured, her heart heavy with the knowledge of this sad outcome all day, as she reached the top. Her eyes widened as she turned the corner into a hallway filled with giants. The collage of family and friends gathered together seemed more meaningful than what was dancing in the living room just moments before. The walls now seemed to groan under the collective weight of sorrow, supporting hunched backs and shaky legs as hidden faces turned toward one another, draping themselves in arms that barely contained the heart-wrenching sobs that saturated the air. Debra-Lyneé frantically gazed down the hallway, arms folded across her body, her heart racing with each step as she inched forward through a sea of people. A steady stream of mourners closed in on her space, their hands pawed at her head and shoulders, each one desperate to offer solace. "Mom," Debra-Lyneé, tears shimmering in her eyes, her voice trembling as she searched for the shiny crushed velvet of her mother's dress amidst the moving tapestry of Christmas's colorful clothing. As the anguished moans of "Grandmom" from her brothers and cousins echoed, tears started to flow steadily from her eyes. Just then, her mother exited the bedroom of her grandmother, desperately searching for her baby girl, her face streaked and smeared from wiping away endless tears. As she walked down the hall through the crowd, their eyes locked in a shared understanding of grief. With an urgency born of heartbreak, Debra-Lyneé rushed into her mother's embrace, her arms lax at her sides as she pressed her tear-streaked face against her mother's soft fabric, weeping openly. "I'm still a crybaby, Mom... I thought I was a big girl, but I'm not," her muffled confession escaped her lips while her mother's gentle hand continued to soothe her back, each stroke a reminder of comfort amidst the chaos.

The Knights zigzagged through the crowd of sorrowful mourners, aggressively brushing against legs as they moved with purpose. The frantic, soft chatter—a mix of whispered prayers and quiet, traumatized conversation—went silent. The heads that had bowed in prayer suddenly raised and shifted, popping up like daffodils in springtime as the Knights emerged into view. Debra-Lyneé's mother noticed the awkward, jerky movements of the crowd as they parted, creating a visible path for the Knights—led by Galahad, with Lancelot and Percival flanking him. The Knights stood in formation tall and proud, much like their three disciplined Marine canine fathers before them. Her mother stared at the Knights, unblinking. "D-Debra-Lyneé," she nervously whispered. Debra-Lyneé's eyes lifted to her mother's cautious tone before a nod directed her attention. Debra-Lyneé's shoulders slowly rose to meet her ears as she timidly turned to face what shocked her mother and everyone else. Each Knight, one by one, knelt gracefully at her feet and remained. Confusion furrowed Debra-Lyneé's brows as she looked back at her mother. Her eyes begged the question. Her mother beamed, "Some things are just blessed to be," she said, the overhead light illuminating her tear-streaked face. Her mother sniffed as she dabbed tears from the corner of her eyes. "Well... your grandmother has spoken, sweetheart; you're their queen," she said, her voice filled with tenderness.

Debra-Lyneé's brows knitted together, "Their Queen?" she timidly replied. Her mother softly nodded as warm memories brought a smile.

"The day you were born, your grandmother held you, and the first words out of her mouth were This is my little princess, so yes, you're their Queen, she confirmed. The truth sinking in, tears squeezed from her smile and rolled down her cheeks as she turned to face the whimpering knights. Debra-Lyneé kneeled to greet them and extended her small hand to pat their heads gently.

"I miss her too," she said, as she hugged each of them close, their shared love and loss binding them together. With each comforting embrace, the Knights' bond sealed, she held them close, forming a tender, heartwarming cocoon of love amid the pain.

CHAPTER FIFTEEN
SALUTE

THE NEWSCASTER ON every channel issued urgent warnings about the plunging temperatures and the impending blanket of snow that threatened to cover the town throughout the morning. Yet, the biting cold and the promise of stormy weather did little to dampen the community's spirits. People united in respect of a dedicated colleague and cherished friend, all with a firm resolve to pay tribute to a woman whose life had inspired and touched many endearingly. Inside the grand church, the diverse crowd—a sea of faces from all walks of life—included doctors, lawyers, millionaires, the homeless, judges, and the convicted filling the aisles. Their hearts filled with fond memories were heartwarming, contrasting with the frigid air outside that slowed most of the city to a standstill. It was truly a testament to Debra Hunter's profound impact on this little part of the world she decided to call home; those who gravitated towards her quietly reflected on shared memories and heartfelt connections. As the somber procession of power blue hats, coats, scarves, and other items that represented her favorite color emerged through the church doors, many reflected on their lives without her presence, and a heavy calmness settled over the scene. The line continued from the church doors, down the weathered pebble stone steps, where heads rested gently on shoulders, a weary sign of their shared sorrow for families and friends. Seeing Debra's family, heartbroken but able to walk tall with heads high as they moved through the line, the burden of individual grief felt lighter as they found comfort in each other's presence. Each heavy-hearted breath was a visible puff in the cold air as they watched their beloved Debra Hunter begin her final journey. Tears slid down Mike's cheeks, and waves of sorrow rippled through the tightly knit crowd as he kissed his sister farewell and closed the casket. He was joined by the Hunter boys, Louie and Earl, who served as pallbearers, walking in step while reverently carrying Debra Hunter in her powder-blue casket down the church aisle. Carefully ascending the polished marble stairs toward the waiting, glossy gray hearse, its surface like a teardrop under the overcast sky. The constant ache in his chest grew heavier, adding to the gloom as they approached. Mike sighed, searching his heart; he found a place for the unforeseen memory that would stay with him for the rest of his days. It began and ended with that last kiss he gave his sister; his lips touched her cold cheek, yet it still warmed his heart. He didn't need to voice his love for her - she lived it... Yet he did. Whispering in her ear as he always had, "I love you," he professed for the last time. Only this time, he whispered what they both secretly hoped would have been the way they lived their lives together, "Mother."

Behind the hearse sat a luxurious black limousine. The chauffeur—a stocky, short, light-skinned black man—stood sentinel by the vehicle, immovable against the frigid winds that cut through the gathering. His tailored black suit, pressed with a sharp crease, fit his frame perfectly, highlighted by black leather gloves and a snug black fedora hat atop his head. Weariness weighed heavily in his eyes, even though he was still young, exhausted from hours of witnessing raw, unfiltered sorrow surrounding him and the horrors of his military service. As he exchanged brief eye contact with the mourners—offering a slow, comforting nod—the breadth of their grief solidified in that fleeting moment. To Sandy J. and the Hunter men, he tipped his hat before opening the door of the limousine, and heat rushed to greet them to a warm, inviting sanctuary. There was one more passenger he needed to greet before he could retreat to the warmth of the limousine's front seat; his focus shifted to a tall, stocky man, who stood as a statue, cloaked in darkness with sunglasses masking his eyes and a powder blue handkerchief that stood out against his black peacoat, fixated on the hearse as its driver gently closed the door. A deep, heavy sigh escaped Mike, bleeding through the silence like the exhalation of a stallion coming to rest after a hard ride in the frigid air.

The chauffeur observed Mike as he assisted two former nursing school classmates of his sister into their cars, feeling a prick of alarm as Mike removed his sunglasses to kiss each of them tenderly on the cheek.

It wasn't... It couldn't be that brother; the chauffeur mused internally that dude had to be as old as my pops. Mike's gaze fell to his midsection as he meticulously buttoned his suit jacket and peacoat, but the weight of his sorrow kept his gaze fixated on the ground beneath his feet. As he approached the limousine, he finally lifted his head, causing the chauffeur to blink hastily, trying to clear his vision. This man was incredibly built, yet wore the same burdened expression in his eyes, heavy with memories and unspoken grief. Although the chauffeur didn't know his name, he recognized him as the man who had wept for his beloved dogs, and his heart raced within his chest as he held the door of the limousine open. He was acutely aware that neither man was in the military anymore, yet a profound respect compelled him to salute, his right hand rising crisply and promptly in recognition. "As American as apple pie, sir," the chauffeur said, striving to stand tall, embodying the discipline ingrained in him from boot camp.

Mike paused at the entrance of the limousine, his eyes momentarily lifted to the overcast sky as though searching for solace in the clouds before they fell to the chauffeur's spit-shined military boots, gleaming like polished onyx beneath the razor-sharp crease of his dress pants. "Dubai," Mike replied, his voice a soft murmur that contrasted with the lively chatter in the distance.

The chauffeur's breath caught in his throat as he looked at Mike; he was again the terrified teenage soldier he was when they first encountered each other. He held his salute, and Mike lifted his eyebrows slightly as he nodded in acknowledgment.

A wave of pain moved in sync with the memory, sweeping over Mike and recalling echoes of past conflicts. His head bowed to his chest as he gently tapped the roof of the limousine in thought—a gesture of gratitude and familiarity. Turning to the chauffeur, he saw the same inner struggle; he studied the man's face for a moment before returning the salute—a silent exchange of understanding and respect. "Thank you for your service, Marine," Mike said. His mind was soon overwhelmed with thoughts of Dr. Walker, just before he knelt to step into the warm interior of the limousine, leaving the cold and sorrow behind, if only for a moment.

Mike glanced at his nephews, their wide eyes brimming with concern as he sank into the plush leather seat of the limousine. Beside him, Sandy J. radiated a quiet support. In that poignant instant, he longed to dissolve into the warmth of his aunt's embrace. Still, he fought against the urge for the sake of the innocent, searching gazes of the boys he had helped raise to manhood, not for the distinguished fathers and important men who watched their uncle closely with the eyes of lost children. Mike's heart pounded loudly in his chest. He let out a trembling breath, as if standing in the cold, fingers fumbling to unbutton his peacoat and suit jacket, each movement slow yet heavy with grief. Sandy J. instinctively raised her hand, her palm gliding softly across his back, as he leaned forward until it settled over the unrelenting thrum of his heart. His nephew's eyes shimmered with unshed tears as they looked at their uncle's face, desperately hoping to catch a glimpse of the brave facade he had put on after their father's passing. Yet their solemn expressions shifted as they noticed a delicate gold cross, jeweled with stories, cascading down from his tie—a stark contrast to his slumped shoulders, evidence of the cumulative toll of heartbreak as he began to yield to the weight of losing his sister. Unaware of their stares, Mike's attention was drawn to a neatly folded powder-blue blanket, its fabric a relic of tender memories on the seat across from him, and it quickly caught everyone's eye. Each of the Hunter boys shook their heads in a muted chorus of 'no,' responding to an unspoken question before they all turned to Sandy J, who also shrugged, pretending not to notice the blanket's presence. Mike's jaw appeared to unhinge itself as his breath quickened, becoming uneven and shallow. Hand trembling, he reached for the blanket, struggling to lift it as if it had weight, raising it to eye level. Mike carefully examined every thread of the blanket with great attention to detail, his eyes moving from left to right as if translating some ancient scroll. Nah... this can't be... This is the cover Deb brought me from Mississippi. Sandy J.'s eyes shimmered with tears. She set her hand on Mike's back again, this time firmly, her warm touch acting as an anchor amid the chaos in his heart. Leaning in closer, she whispered,

"That amazing woman was always a force, a true force. She told me she would plan her funeral down to the last detail, didn't want her boy to have to face something so painful. She never spoke of your father's funeral, but I think that played a big part in it. Still, she was so young, I didn't think she would follow through with it." A bittersweet smile touched her lips as she continued, "Funny thing, Deb confided this to me unexpectedly, while we sipped coffee in her kitchen, the air thick with the aroma of brewing beans and sweet memories. We listened to music crackling—I think it was a song playing through that old puke-green radio under the window. Kevin Sr.'s mother gave it to them as a wedding gift, which struck a nerve..."

"What did we call her again...? Sandy J. asked.

"The dragon," Darryl murmured from his seat, gazing out

the window with his powder blue handkerchief in hand—used to absorb tears—pressed to his chin, muffling his voice.

"Right, right, that woman was a piece of work," Sandy J. chuckled softly. "It was your first day of high school, and we watched you spend ten minutes fixing your afro in the mirror, then head out the door." Mike lowered the faded, powder-blue blanket and made eye contact with five pairs of thoughtful eyes, each reflecting a spectrum of emotions. "All of you Hunter boys are going to be okay. It's God's plan; it was your parents' plan, the Hunter family was put here to change the world," Sandy J. added as she turned to embrace her nephews, her admiration and determination clear. Everyone was gazing at Mike with hearts laid bare. Darryl leaned closer, placing a steadying hand on his uncle's knee,

"You have never let us down, Uncle Mike, you are not alone. Kevin instinctively offered his hand upon Darryl's shoulder, followed by Oscar's gentle touch on Kevin and then Vincent's hand finding Oscar's shoulder, with Eddie last, resting his hand atop Vincent's in a protective stack of support.

"We got you, Uncle Mike," Darryl said, his voice a soothing anchor in the turbulent sea of grief. The Hunter boys sat draped in heavy silence, the only sounds filtering through the tinted glass being the distant hum of the city bustling outside. Mike sat absorbed in the melancholy of the moment; his head turned toward the window. The powder-blue blanket nestled securely across his lap. The dark-tinted partition separating the chauffeur from the somber interior of the limousine squeaked as it descended slowly, letting in the overwhelming scent of burning rubber that abruptly pierced their moment of quiet reflection. The slow, steady flow of the funeral procession was

265

upended by the sound of the flat tires wobbling violently, forcing everyone to adjust in their seats.

"Sir, the hearse popped two," the chauffeur said as he slowed to a stop behind Alyssa, who was driving the '69, with Debra-Lyneé nestled in the passenger seat, sat up as tall as she could. A deep sigh escaped Mike's lips, heavy with anticipation.

"Sergeant," Mike said calmly, his gaze fixed on the blanket draped across his lap, which wafted with memories he wished to revisit—if only for a moment. The Sergeant squinted at the world outside while searching for street signs. A moment of stillness passed before his eyes rose to the rearview mirror, and his voice boomed with clarity.

"Sir! Three klicks out, sir!" Mike's hand gently caressed Sandy J.'s. He lifted his head to look at his nephews, who met his gaze with wide eyes filled with curiosity and unease. A smile broke through Mike's solemn demeanor, much like their mother would when she wanted their hearts to take over their rationalizing.

"I've cried on that lady's shoulders more times than I care to admit, and that's after my time in Vietnam," Mike confessed, leaning forward in the luxurious confines of the limousine. The squeak of leather on leather filled the silent void as Mike wiggled his fingers in each of his gloves before exiting the limousine and stepping into the gusting winds.

The air was frigid and biting, an unforgiving chill sweeping through the streets on this first Sunday of the new year. As Mike buttoned his tailored suit jacket and peacoat against the cold, he took a moment to absorb the scene around him. The strong gusts whipped around him, causing the rustling signs above storefronts to creak and sway uncertainly while empty cans and newspapers danced along the sidewalks like lost souls. Women bundled against the wind clutched their hats and shopping bags tightly, their dresses fluttering in the chill; they fought, digging in their heels against the hard gusting airstream. He double-tapped the passenger side window for the chauffeur's attention. The tinted window's slow descent dramatically exposed the seriousness of Mike's expression that the chauffeur had long committed to memory. "Point, Sergeant," Mike instructed, his tone resolute. The chauffeur's nod was gentle as his gaze shifted from the passenger-side window to the front windshield, following Mike, and observing his steps as his nephews exited the limo in close formation, their pace matched their uncle's determination. The chauffeur's eyebrows raised,

"Still leading soldiers," he murmured, smiling, his words barely escaping his lips. Sandy J., the only passenger still seated in the limousine, heard the chauffeur through the partition and let out a soft chuckle,

"Son," she replied, "Michael's mother always told me he was raised not just as a lion that other lions would fear, but from activation to annihilation; a lion that would lead other lions bravely through their most faith-challenging battles... and by the grace of God, you can witness this moment." Eddie struggled to keep his facial expressionless. Oscar's eyes quickly shifted toward Vincent ahead of him. " 'Take point' means go to the front of the line, right?" he whispered. He matched every step his uncle took.

"Yeah, something like that," Vincent said with a grimace, stepping a little behind him. He turned away from the gusty wind, which billowed like sheets in the air, as it pushed up the lapel of their peacoats toward his brother. An unspoken tension hung in the air—did anyone truly grasp what was about to unfold? The Hunter brothers exchanged amused glances, their chuckles cutting through the somber atmosphere with an understood purpose. The chauffeur shifted into reverse, then swiftly drove the limousine around Alyssa and positioned himself in front of the hearse, as onlookers marveled at the limousine's smooth maneuvering. Across from Alyssa, Debra-Lyneé sat quietly, clad in a little black dress and black stockings, with a delicate powder blue ribbon accentuating her afro-puff ponytails. She sighed deeply; her tear-clouded eyes gazed out the window, desperately wanting to join her grandmother for as long as she could on her last great getaways. Blinking furiously to clear the blurred shapes of towering giants outside, she wiped her damp cheeks with her sleeve, her gaze shifting to Grand Michael, her father, and her uncles, along with Louie and Earl, who walked toward her, their silhouettes becoming more distinct in the side mirror. Grand Michael caught her eye and flashed a reassuring smile, his wink stirring a whirlwind of emotions within her—her stomach twisting and her hands trembling uncontrollably. Summoning courage, Debra-Lyneé slowly turned and tentatively touched Auntie Alyssa's hand, her tear-filled eyes pleading for understanding before she uttered a word.

"Sweetheart," Alyssa nervously giggled, as the Knights rose and sat up straight in the backseat, their presence a silent show of loyalty.

"Auntie Alyssa," her eyes pleaded, then squeezed shut, "he needs me," Debra-Lyneé insisted, anguish seeping into her voice.

"Your daddy... he'll be alright," Alyssa brows raised as she reassured.

"No, no, no," Debra-Lyneé responded desperately. The bat of her lashes rushed tears streaming down her cheeks as she continued. "It's my Grand Michael, I can't explain how I know, but... I saw a little boy looking back at me when he passed. Auntie ... he's scared. He needs me out there with him," she pleaded, her voice quivering with desperation. *The soft whimpering of the knights in the back drew Alyssa's attention away momentarily. "Your parents would kill me for letting you walk out in the middle of the street by yourself,"* Alyssa snapped, her tone more authoritative than she intended. Debra-Lyneé's brows furrowed as she turned to gaze out the front windshield, her hand instinctively moving toward the car door's latch.

"You could tell them I just got out," she replied cleverly, a hint of mischief dancing in her eyes.

"Girl, don't you play with me!" Alyssa grunted low in her throat, exasperation and affection swirling within her. She sighed deeply, realizing that if she closed her eyes tightly enough, the woman—who had swiftly found her way into her heart—would take form. The lady she adored and referred to as mom was in the car with them now, a gentle reminder of family ties. Alyssa's gaze drifted back to the front windshield, her heart sinking as she noticed her husband Kevin's worried expression, mirroring Debra-Lyneé's sense of foreboding, which grew stronger. Meeting her worried eyes in the rearview mirror, she let out another sigh, feeling like a parent caught between her faith and her fears.

"Go ahead, sweetheart," Alyssa relented, the weight of her words lingering as Debra-Lyneé eagerly unbuckled her seatbelt and swung the heavy door of the '69 open, letting in the bitter bite of winter wind. She hesitated before stepping out, turning to her aunt with a bright smile that briefly lifted the heavy atmosphere.

Alyssa's brows creased, her eyes studied Debra-Lyneé's hand, which subtly slid across to the driver's side and gently placed it on her barely visible baby bump. Alyssa's mouth fell open gradually; only her mother, Mrs. Hunter, and Sandy J. knew.

The anxious lines on Alyssa's forehead asked many questions while her sealed tight lips resisted.

"I'm glad to have a girl cousin, finally," Debra-Lyneé said, her eyes dancing with delight. She giggled, her gaze locked onto her aunt's, bridging a connection that transcended their shared worries.

"Uhh... say what?" Alyssa asked, pretending to be surprised. Debra-Lyneé's grin grew wider as she got out of the car, tilting her head and shaking in disbelief. "Snitchin' brush up against a few feathers, angel tell all your business, child." A broad smile stretched across Alyssa's face as she pushed the passenger seat forward.

"Knights, protect," she commanded, her voice firm. The knights sprang into action, rushing from the back seat, out the door, and standing in a stair-step formation at attention, waiting for Debra-Lyneé to move.

Mike carefully opened the hearse's back door, the cold metallic creak punctuating the thick air. The driver, visibly trembling from the sound, met Mike's gaze with a blank look in his rearview mirror, creating a fleeting connection that showed his startled surprise. As Mike stared down at the sky-blue casket, a violent surge of sadness washed over him. *Alone, he let out a heavy sigh that revealed the difficult times ahead for him, which his sister knew would come. The vibrant color of the casket almost seemed soothing, as if his sister was telling everyone she was comfortable in this space, amidst the somber occasion, highlighting both the beauty and fragility of her life and life itself.*

"God blessed us with you, Mrs. Debra Hunter," Mike began, his voice trembling and cracking as tears streamed down his cheeks like cold raindrops on a winter's day. "Of course, you would find a way to give me a hug from Heaven." He chuckled as he slid his hands over the casket's polished surface; the smoothness of it cooled against his fingertips. "My brother-in-law always looked to the Heavens when you did things like this. Where is he placing his gaze now, I wonder?" Mike grinned. Treasured memories swirled in his mind, each cherished Aretha Franklin song Debra adored, played like a nostalgic melody in his head. Mike nodded as he received the gift, a fleeting smile broke through his sadness as 'You're All I Need to Get By' danced into his thoughts. First, the whole family stopped their weekend chores to rush into the room for a sing-along. The metaphorical needle of a record player dropped gracefully onto the familiar chorus, as if the universe had paused. *"At the same time, you danced alone, thinking about your husband, honoring the love and laughter you shared."*

Behind Mike, his nephews, along with Louie and Earl, hesitated to speak as they waited, enduring the now occasional blistering gusts of wind. Carefully, Mike's gloved hands gradually rolled the casket out of the hearse, the fabric of Mike's peacoat brushing against the sides as he slid the casket from handle to handle. "You were an answer to prayers, a guiding light to the lost, and a divine gift to all," he continued, his voice cracking under the weight of the truth in his words as each black-gloved hand grasped a handle. Mike glanced behind him at the gathering crowd, then to his sweet little niece and the knights as they walked up, their presence creating a sense of unity amid the heartache. Debra-Lyneé pointed with purpose behind her father, her voice resolute.

"Galahad, Percival, six!" she commanded. Eddie's brow furrowed momentarily in confusion before comprehension softened his features. Uncle Mike smiled gently in response, feeling the comforting presence of Debra-Lyneé and Lancelot standing beside their Grand Michael, a steadfast anchor in this turbulent sea of emotion.

"You impacted so many greatly," Mike continued, his heart swelling with gratitude as he glanced at the casket again. "It would be our honor if you rest on our shoulders and allow us to carry you, as you have cuddled all of us." "Lift on Hunter. One. Two. Three, Hunter," Uncle Mike huffed, and with a gentle, steady movement, they raised the casket onto their shoulders.

Their labored breaths produced condensation, like fog escaping from the underbelly of a locomotive when it comes to rest, merging with the thunderous roar of the pallbearers' voices — a powerful affirmation of the fierce determination this black woman chose to face every facet of her life. As they fought against the gusting wind, each step became a small battle; the pallbearers were resolute, while inspired mourners parked their cars and joined the procession on foot behind them. Debra-Lyneé's attention darted to scraps of newspaper underfoot, catching in the corner of her eye. She halted abruptly, squinting to scan the growing crowd of onlookers lining the sidewalk, her gaze darting upwards in search of the angel Scott. Frustration tightened in her chest as she scanned the clusters of unfamiliar faces and pavement for any sign of him before exhaustion crept in, forcing her to sigh, realizing it was merely the wind brushing against her. The pallbearers marched solemnly toward the cemetery, their feet tapping the ground like a steady drumbeat, their arms swinging in unison with the flare of Debra Hunter, each carrying memories of the woman resting on their shoulders. The honor of it comforted them on their tireless journey. The once powerful winds had subsided, leaving behind a hushed stillness and pockets of leaves scattered like a paisley carpet of memories laid near the cemetery's open gates. "Break," Mike said as they stopped just outside the cemetery entrance, the weight of the moment settling in quickly.

Mourners and the curious walked past, nodding slowly with raised eyebrows, then continued on their way to the gravesite, stepping over the fragile flowers left by grieving visitors in their path.

"Why did we stop, Grand Michael?" Debra-Lyneé inquired, her eyes wide with concern as she gazed into his eyes.

"Let your uncle gather his thoughts, baby," Eddie murmured as he touched his daughter's shoulder with his free hand. He understood it was the collective's need for space and a moment of reflection; goodbye was real all of a sudden; the raw emotion created an unspoken bond.

Debra-Lyneé followed suit, kneeling peacefully and gently caressing the knights, offering them comfort. As her eyes gazed into the distance at her family standing on the hill at the gravesite where her grandmother would be buried—and where her grandfather is buried—she remembered a visit to this somber cemetery with her grandmother. The memory unfolded in Debra-Lyneé's mind like a captivating movie, capturing every sight, sound, and emotion. The family celebrating Uncle Vincent's new dental practice was a big deal, as it brought jobs and free dental care to the community. The news turned grandma's expression wistful as she became lost in her memories, wishing her husband were there to share the moment with her. Then, a smile spread across her face, unmistakable in its warmth. Grand Michael, having seen this smile before any of them were born, assured everyone that his sister loved deeply and still profoundly missed her beloved husband.

Grandma casually walked over to the bowl where everyone placed their car keys upon entering the house. The keys rattled like coins sliding around in a tin can as she fished for and retrieved hers; she quietly slipped out the front door without a word, but no one dared question her departure. She was the head, Hunter. "Only, I was always with my grandma, a faithful companion akin to Robin at Batman's. My brothers and cousins teased, calling me a bit of a stalker when it came to her, a bond that had taken root since before I could remember."

As she gazed across from the driver's seat of her car to voice a protest, I quickly slipped into the car before she could refuse. She gave me the piercing looks that made my dad and uncles shake in their boots to this day. Only, I met her gaze unflinchingly, flashing a confident smile that painted my face, reflecting her spirit. Despite her potential to scold, there were no visible signs of anger; her heart softened under the weight of our shared resemblance. Grand Michael explained it well: when confronted with someone who mirrored them, it was hard for anyone to refuse a request. As I looked up for what would ultimately be our last adventure together, I noticed a distant look in Grandma's eyes. The radio played 'The First Time Ever I Saw Your Face,' a song by Roberta Flack that deeply resonated with my grandmom since my grandfather passed away. After giving a slow nod accompanied by a crooked smile, she began to hum along with the familiar tune as her mind drifted to distant memories before we arrived at the first traffic light.

Grandma's frown reflected nostalgia and sadness as she smiled and said, "Those were the days." I could see that her eyes were gradually dimming, and her voice echoed the same emotion she felt the first time she realized my grandpop was gone and would never come back.

"I've seen this look," Debra-Lyneé frowned, contemplating my Grandpop, their love oozing as she recounted their bond, often saying, "Child, if he told me the sky was purple, I'd believe him." She was straddling the line between the past and the present, closer to him now than to the world where she stood. Grandma often told me that their love blossomed at first sight, but neither of them confessed it until they were about to get married. There were times when her flood of stories left me stifling yawns, battling sleep as my mind filed her tales away under "blah, blah, blah." Then there are moments when Grandma's eyes sparkle with excitement, like this one—her last of many—when her eyes light up with youthful enthusiasm, eagerly gesturing toward an abandoned building that stands as a relic of lost dreams, still her eyes danced, with the wonder of a child staring at the lions, bears, and tigers at the zoo.

"Ooh! Look Lyneé, your grandfather and I danced until

sunrise in there," she began, her eyes sparkling with untold stories that lay in wait. *If I were older, her eyes twinkled at me.* A girly giggle escaped as her hand rushed to her mouth, accompanied by a subtle raise of her brows and a gentle press of her lips to hold back the things that made her blush. She carefully surprised me, sifted through her memories, and searched for the perfect story to share. I glanced toward the building—a towering structure marred by fire and with boarded windows, it was imposing, with two stories of dilapidated decay standing out like a rotten tooth in an almost empty mouth. When I turned back to my grandmother, she was already lost in her memories, her eyes glimmering with the vibrant neon lights of a long-gone past as she imagined stepping through its doors again. The honking of car horns brought her back into the present, and she glanced at me and then into the rearview mirror, an expression of quiet loneliness flickering across her face before she offered me a warm smile.

Out here, at the cemetery? I mused after Grandma navigated two left turns and a right turn down the road. "What happened to the ice cream parlor?" I inquired, curiosity bubbling as we stepped out of the car to traverse the gravel path leading into the cemetery.

"Hush your mouth, child, you gonna wake the dead," Grandmom teased, grasping my hand as she smiled. Just then, Percival snapped Debra-Lyneé's reverie with a gentle lick to her face, bringing warmth back into the moment.

Mourners gathered solemnly around the gravesite, their breath caught in awe as the casket rested on the strong shoulders of Grand Michael and the other pallbearers, who had given the signal, and the march continued. Debra-Lyneé watched as they followed the long, winding path he had chosen, which was used by cars—but she felt an instinctive pull to stray from it. The Knights surrounded her in a protective cluster, and together, they took a shortcut across the frozen grounds. As she made her way up the hillside, the names of the dead etched on headstones filled her darting glances. She couldn't help but wonder if their lives had seen even a glimmer of daylight. Standing beside her mother and brothers, Debra-Lyneé's thoughts lingered on the names carved into the stone as the mourners' attention drifted from her grandmother's covered headstone to the black rope toward the open grave beside her grandfather's. She gazed down the hillside at the casket, which appeared to float weightlessly above those who bore its weight. The heaviness of the moment pressed down on her, and she felt the soft, plush grass beneath her feet, reminiscent of a comforting pillow, contrasting sharply with the dead, brown turf that was now crushed beneath her feet. Permitting himself by the occasion to share his true feelings, Devon noticed how his little sister shifted her weight nervously. "Are you okay? Do you have to go to the bathroom?" he whispered, bending down, his face leveled with hers, their cold cheeks touching. A subtle pressure on her shoulder drew her attention to Keith, who met her gaze with concern. Despite the tremor of uncertainty in her cheeks, she offered him a fainthearted smile. Keith's brows knitted together as he peered over the rims of his glasses, smiling down at his sister's sad eyes,

"Hmm, Grandma's thoughtful look, like when she's thinking about Grandpop," he remarked, his voice laced with warmth and a touch of concern. Devon touched her other shoulder, nodding in shared purpose. Slowly, a gentle, warm smile crept across her face as she felt comforted by their presence. The Knights moved in measured tactical circles, their eyes probed the surroundings every few seconds before fixing on Grand Michael, eager to serve and protect. Debra-Lyneé knelt, embracing the knights with warmth, just as she clutched her teddy bear when stormy nights rattled her nerves. A thought whispered only to the Universe:

Could it be something more than just a passing daydream or fleeting thought that has happened to me?

She tightened her grip on the Knights, her gaze fixed on her grandfather's headstone, the world around her blurring into a swirl of emotions. Blades of grass and dandelions swayed gracefully in the summer breezes of yesterday while Grandmom's chin tilted toward the sun, basking in its golden rays as they approached Grandpop's grave. It was just as it had been when she took the trip with her grandmother; now, she and the Knights were there as observers of everything. For Debra-Lyneé, it was like *Elmo Through the Looking Glass*. The simplest moments for Debra-Lyneé and her grandmother became special. Debra-Lyneé sensed that the angel was near; she needed to return to the present. Her heart pounded as the Knights whimpered, sensing her concern, lost in reflection, with the bond of love woven intricately between the past and the present.

Her mother gently rested her hand on the crown of Debra-Lyneé's head as if offering a silent blessing. Bewilderment clouded Debra-Lyneé's eyes, and her breath came in heavy, trembling gasps beside her mother; the knights around them seemed to share in this anxiety, heaving forcefully against the tension in the air. The casket slowly and deliberately descended as a dark, coarse rope pulled tight against the black cloth covering her grandmother's headstone. The mourners' attention, initially focused on the formality of the covered headstone—knowing Debra Hunter's family legacy and the indelible mark she left on everyone she touched—now shifted their gaze to the slow drag of the ominous black rope tied to the descending casket, their collective anticipation rising like a swell before a storm, filled with great promise and expectation for what was about to be revealed. Once again, Debra-Lyneé searched the crowd for the angel Scott as the knights gracefully escorted her through the sea of faces to where her Grand Michael stood. Standing beside him, her eyes drifted, scanning the crowd for family and friends among the many strangers who marched solemnly alongside them. As the knights moved to stand by the descending casket, Debra-Lyneé gripped Mike's finger; suddenly, it grew tighter, becoming a lifeline in the whirlpool of emotions. She felt his startled gaze drop toward her, and he smiled down at her with a warmth that contrasted with the chilly heaviness of the moment. But still, Debra-Lyneé stood frozen, her attention ensnared by the angel's captivating presence. The twinkle in Scott's eyes, shimmering with a mystical resonance, caused him to stumble back when his gaze fell on Debra-Lyneé and Mike's joined hands. His brow furrowed in confusion as he followed her gaze, struggling to reconcile and grapple with the logic of what he was witnessing: not only the spark of life twinkling in the man's eyes, but also a vibrant green patch of healthy summer lawn beneath his feet. Mike snatched off his sunglasses, but he still couldn't reconcile the stark contrast against the desolate, dead grass surrounding them. "Did I see a tear roll down his chin and bring that grass back to life?" He knelt, first looking for others' reactions before whispering with a mixture of excited wonder and disbelief. A slow, triumphant nod of satisfaction escaped Debra-Lyneé's lips as she raised their joined hands in front of him, and a smile blossomed on her face, brightening the somber atmosphere around them.

"He was Angel-Debra, now he's just Scott. He's an angel." *No one could see what they saw or hear their conversation, but she still whispered into Mike's waiting ear, her gaze fixed on the angel in earthly form.* Mike stared from his bent-over position, his mouth hanging open.

"Say what?" Mike exclaimed. His voice was tinged with astonishment as the crowd around them turned to search for the source of the unexpected voice. But Debra-Lyneé felt no doubt; it was Scott, as sure as the heartbeat in her chest. Their gaze seemed to stretch into eternity, forging a connection that transcended the moment until it sparked a breathtaking vision in Scott's mind—a little girl's delicate hand entwined with his. Mike watched as Scott smiled down at her, the girl's dark brown eyes reflecting an innocence that tugged at his heartstrings, reminiscent of familiar faces from the past that had faded from the memories of every angel. A memory fragment was woven for this occasion: a country girl dressed in overalls... her bare feet dusted with earth. Gently, she pressed Scott's hand against her cheek in a tender exchange, and in that fleeting moment, Scott wept, tears mingling with the promise of renewal and hope.

CHAPTER SIXTEEN
SAY GOODBYE

DEBRA-LYNEÉ STOOD WITH her heart pounding, watching as Scott's eyes shimmered with unshed tears, reflecting the profound grief surrounding them. She felt a current of energy coursing through her veins, her body instinctively rocking back and forth on her heels as if bracing for the moment's weight. Her gaze flickered to the neatly covered headstone as the breeze teased an early reveal, the slow, steady tug of the thick rope connecting the cover to the grave, and the polished casket of her beloved grandmother being gently lowered into the earth as the rope was pulled. She recalled her grandmother's wise words: *Leaps of faith are not truly leaps if you don't leap and don't have faith.* With that mantra parading around in her mind, Debra-Lyneé focused on Scott, feeling her vision blur with emotion. She reached out, grasping Mike's hand between her own, holding it tightly as if their bond could defy the sorrow surrounding them. "Close your eyes, Grand Michael, you're coming with me," Debra-Lyneé assured as her eyes blurred.

Scott's body quaked; his legs became unsteady beneath him as he swayed between memories and loss. He wiped at warm tears drizzling down his cheek, each droplet a testament to the depth of his love as he watched the casket being lowered. Memories of the courageous soul rushed Scott; crawling, first steps, the joyous laughter at play, her unforgettable toothless smile. He clutched at the tightening in his chest like a pain he could harness, desperate to contain the anguish bubbling just below the surface. The silent cries escaping his lips morphed into the heart-wrenching whines and whimpers of the Knights, their loyal bodies curled at the edge of the grave, sharing in the somber ritual. Choking back the regurgitated sorrow that had long been sown, its fruit deeply rooted in the blood-soaked soil of Mississippi. Scott's gaze bolted to the sky, pleading and desperately searching for Gabriel's presence. Slowly, his breathing eased, a gentle calm beginning to surround him as his eyes met Debra-Lyneé's, then blurred, intertwining in that moment and forming a delicate bond of grief and shared hope.

"Get! Get!" A burly voice commanded his mule as a towering brute of a man stepped forcefully behind the plow, carving through the earth with rhythmic grunts that pushed man and beast forward, stirring up dirt and rocks under the sweltering Mississippi sun. The heat was oppressive; a heavy blanket of air made it shimmer in every direction. Hand blistered from decades of hard labor, the broad-shouldered old man raised his arm, flicked his wrist, and cracked his whip to urge his mule onward. Scott stood nearby without a shadow; he winced as he raised his blistered hands that mirrored the old man before his gaze. Brows knitted together; he slowly acknowledged a shared pain as he reflected the old man's frail gestures. The wavering air surrounding them heated until it was hard to breathe; the old man and Scott sagged under the relentless sun. The mule, tethered to the plow, trudged forward as if frightened by phantom lashes; echoes of its laborious strides rumbled through the countryside. Scott's and the old man's weary bodies were dragged as one across the field, leaving behind a haunting trail of dust that swirled and settled like whispered secrets in the late afternoon air. From her grandfather's creaking rocking chair on the shaded porch, young Debra-Ann rose, her bare feet whispering against the cool wooden boards.

Making her way down the stairs, shading her eyes with her hands, Debra-Ann still squinted, scanned the twenty acres behind the cloud of dust that billowed like a ghostly apparition, searching for her grandfather or that stubborn old mule. Shielding her eyes from the glaring sun, she strained to discern the approaching silhouette. The mule zigzagged full steam across the field, her heart swelling with a mix of concern and amusement. Debra-Ann laughed as she made out the mule's image, "That ole mule's gonna get sold, he keeps running off." Lancelot, their spirited hound dog, heard stress in the mule's whine and rushed to Debra-Ann's side. His barks rumbling through the still air calmed and directed the mule toward the barn. Soul-bound to the old man, Scott was towed behind the mule as it dragged the plow and its master until they reached the closed barn doors.

Debra-Lyneé and Mike, wide-eyed and paralyzed by shock, stood rooted to the spot as Scott's heart beat faintly, like the old man's, looming over his near-lifeless body. A wave of nausea churned in Scott's stomach, and his foggy mind began to clear about who he was and why he was here. His trembling hands betrayed his panic as he struggled to catch his breath, the air thick with an overwhelming sense of dread weighing heavily on him. Debra-Ann repeatedly screamed for Grand Michael as the dust settled and his body came into focus, slowly revealing the somber scene. Lancelot, the loyal hound dog, emitted worried barks, his ears perked as he sensed the moment's gravity, while Debra-Ann desperately rushed to her grandfather's side. Scott's eyes widened; his heart was heavy with the weight of existential questions that clawed at his mind. "That's Grandmom and my great-grandfather," Debra-Lyneé whispered to Mike, her voice trembling with grief.

Tears traced lines down the old man's weathered face, carving paths through the dust that had camouflaged his entire body, pooling on his earlobes before falling to the ground. His gentle, sorrowful gaze to the sky stalls over Debra-Ann's shoulder, as if searching for answers beyond. The old man's eyes locked with Scott's; a silent question hung between them—a desperate plea for life itself. "I beg you, please let me see my little girl happy," he beseeched, his voice a ghost of its former strength, contemplating the embrace of Heaven. The old man's weary eyes fell on his granddaughter, and he smiled as they grew paler. Debra-Ann collapsed to her knees and draped herself across her grandfather's lifeless body. Lancelot's mournful howl pierced the air, and it rushed Debra-Ann's mother from the house. Her elbow locked instinctively as she leaned over the porch handrail, a picture of misery, her lips pressed tightly together, frustration etched on her features as she stared at the worn soles of her father-in-law's boots, then cast her gaze down the stretch of unplowed land that seemed to stretch endlessly before her. With a heavy sigh,

"Damn!" Helen exclaimed before stepping back, the door slamming behind her in her wake, the sound booming loudly in the quiet. Lancelot's growl rumbled in his throat, displaying his canine teeth in a fierce snarl. He jittered with tension as he climbed the porch stairs and lunged at the door, his instincts compelling him to protect his family even as Helen struggled to keep the heavy wood door closed against the tumult of emotions swirling around them.

When Scott jolts back to the present, bringing Debra-Lyneé and Mike with him, he is met by a swirling carousel of grief-stricken faces parading before him. Debra-Lyneé and her uncles' eyes cleared as they stood in the same place, resolute, with a resounding "Amen" rising around them. The two wasted no time looking for Scott among the gathered. They watched as mourners, comforted by Debra Hunter's final display, filed away from the gravesite, their cheeky smiles squeezing tears from the corners of their eyes as they passed. Instantly curious, Debra-Lyneé, Mike, and Scott's eyes darted away from mourners blocking their view of the headstone. Their gaze fixed on the inscription, "Thank You," etched boldly into the stone. Confused, Scott's expression morphs as he glances from one person to another, a profound stillness washing over him, halting his human heart and angelic essence. In an instant, the moment's weight overwhelms him, causing his face to sink into the shelter of his palms, with the unanswered question searing in his mind: "Was this a wonderful life, or merely relief from pain?" he wondered. His entire being, human and angel, paused. Scott's face remained in his hands, tears flowing through his fingers and nourishing the dull, dead brown grass that was now a vibrant green beneath. Mike focused on the angel and gently lifted Debra-Lyneé, whose eyes glistened after reading the inscription on the headstone. As Scott looked toward the sky, tears continued to streak down his cheeks, a testament to the unyielding sorrow pulling at the human soul still within.

Debra-Lyneé, weakened by the step back in time, furrowed her brows when she caught sight of Scott, a flicker of hope and sadness dancing in his eyes. "He's ... still family, right?" she whispered, her voice soft and shaky as she wrapped her arms around Mike's sturdy shoulder, resting her head warmly against him. "Grandmom never spoke of seeing her grandfather die."

Mike sighed, questioning his memories, then patted her back and replied with a solemn, "Yeah," before falling silent, studying Scott, whose brows were knotted together, weighed down by grief and uncertainty. Debra-Lyneé sighed as their concern for Scott grew deeper. Mike nodded in acknowledgment as a familiar voice, sweet yet distant, cut through the crowd's murmur — only they could hear it, calling out to Scott.

"I'm happy, grandfather," the voice whispered. Scott leaned in the direction he believed the voice was coming from, eager to hear it again. Desperately, he searched the crowd for Debra-Lyneé, Mike, or any of his family, longing for comfort or to be with family while still human. His eyes widened, and he fought for breath, pushed along by the crowd like a pinball bouncing off bumpers. Debra-Lyneé saw Scott, her eyes brightening as they made contact. Their gazes connected with deep emotion. Mike smiled at Scott.

"Yes, he's family... That's my great-grandfather," he said, beaming with admiration and a sense of belonging. Debra-Lyneé's brows furrowed briefly, an honest mistake she brushed off, before she radiated joy, her smile brightening the heavy atmosphere.

"Thank you, Father," Scott cried out, his voice quaking with emotion as he acknowledged the answered prayer his earthly being received. This fervent praise emanated not from his lips but from the very core of the majestic angel he had become. Scott struggled, his steps pausing, and he gently closed his eyes, surrounded by an angelic glow that enveloped him like a soft shawl. Both Debra- Lyneé and Mike's hands flew to their open mouth in awe. The Knights rushed to their side, fully aware of the spirit's presence, their gazes fixed on the angel as he began to ascend toward the heavens, liberating himself entirely from his earthly form. Mike's memory of the angel started to blur and fade slowly.

"I'm not going to remember any of this, am I?" Mike smiled. Debra-Lyneé, the courageous soul anointed, remained silent, keeping an eye on Scott as he soared through the sapphire-blue sky until he vanished from sight. She slid her hand into her uncle's huge paw, knowing that even the question would be forgotten. *Debra-Lyneé, a tapestry of smiles, looked up into the eyes of her hero, knowing everything was now completely forgotten.*

"It will always be in your heart, Grand Michael," she whispered. His brows furrowed, and he tilted his head to the side.

"Huh? What was that?" he nonchalantly replied. Then, as his brows remained knitted together, he pointed to their family down the hill by the cars, waiting for them. "When did that happen?" he chuckled. Debra-Lyneé's brows lifted as she stared unblinkingly.

"Am I too old for piggyback rides?" she quickly asked, shooting her eyes up to her uncle. Mike grinned. "As long as I can give them, you can get them," he said, stooping down. Mike pranced down the grassy hill like a proud black stallion. Debra-Lyneé's cheek pressed against her uncle's ear as she bounced, giggling in his comfort. Her dad and uncles at the bottom of the hill smiled up at them, reminiscing about their youth, and yelled, "We got next!"

High above the clouds, the once-bustling city of Philadelphia faded away, replaced by an expansive sea of white. Scott inhaled deeply, nostrils flaring as he caught a faint scent of baby powder. It wasn't a brief, passing whiff through soft clouds, but rather sharing the same space as his great-great-granddaughter, holding onto the memory of the next courageous soul in his family for as long as it lasts. He reminisced about her smile and her scent, then both vanished in an instant. A feeling of loneliness shriveled Scott's wings and slowed his journey. Like a kite stilled in the wind's grasp, he momentarily felt the pangs of loneliness, until they vanished as swiftly as they had come, making room for an overwhelming sense of agape — *love without measure,* which returned in a flood. His form, now defined by rippling muscles and magnificent wings, flapped once and was launched to heights he'd never been. Scott had transformed into a new angel, embodying the divine essence from head to toe.

ALPHA – OMEGA

Archangel Gabriel casually lifted his gaze to the vast heavenly skies, where the sound of mighty wings beating against the winds resounded like music all around him. His sharp eyes scanned the horizon searching for a familiar figure gliding toward him—only there was Scott anew. A warm grin from Gabriel greeted Scott as he welcomed the angelic warrior returning to Heaven, changed and with newfound confidence. *Scott's eyebrows knit together before his feet touched the cloud beneath him. He studied the brave one standing before him. A space Scott knew he was supposed to fill with words was left empty; instead, he inhaled a familiar* scent that transcended the bounds of earthly existence. *His curious eyes met Gabriel's, whose gaze never left Scott. Only now, they were fixed on the Herculean wings Scott had received, admiration shining in his eyes.*

"The courageous soul's prayer has been answered," Scott questioned, *his tone tinged with curiosity in his youthful voice. Gabriel first nods to the expansion of his wings, then smiles at the youthful tone in the young angel's voice.*

"In part," *Gabriel replies, as his eyes meet Scott's. Their gaze at each other would have lasted an eternity if not interrupted by a soft giggle from the little girl in a powder blue dress, suddenly appearing before them.*

"I don't understand," Scott admitted, studying Gabriel's angelic expression. *Scott's head turned forward as if pulled by an invisible thread, joining Gabriel's, and his eyes slowly traced the breathtaking sight of Heaven's Gate rising majestically before him.* "Although many people she met on her life's journey are waiting to welcome the courageous soul, her prayer was also to thank God, so we wait," *Gabriel whispered, his voice carrying deep wisdom.*

The soft howl of a hound caught the little girl's attention, and their eyes met; an instant connection blossomed, though familiarity danced just out of reach.

She reached for the pinky of Scott's left hand, and as her tiny fingers made contact, a sensation of warmth surged through him, causing his wings to unfurl into two glorious plumes behind them before settling into their natural grace. Turning toward Gabriel, Scott faced the grandeur of Heaven's Gate, a majestic sight that took his breath away. The approach of panting canines interrupted the serenity, drawing the courageous one's eye as Lancelot, the country hound, galloped over with the three *Knights who emerged from the gentle mist. Though her touch was tender, like someone greeting a friendly animal, their tails wagged wildly as they welcomed the little girl, showing they carried warm memories, as if they had just played together yesterday. After the dogs' excitement calmed, they arranged themselves neatly, two by two, like rooks on a chessboard, standing watch beside Gabriel and Scott.*

Was It a Wonderful Life?

AUTHOR BIO

DAVID HUNTER ELLIS was born and raised in Philadelphia, PA. He found his way back to his love of writing after a wrongful termination of his job resulted in the writing of his first novel, 'Trial By Fired, You Bear Witness.' Soon after, he stepped through the doors of Wilmington University, where he studied Digital Film Directing. Eager to learn all facets of his newfound storytelling medium, he took on many roles on film crews throughout the years. Finally, in 2013, David formed Hunter/Ellis Productions, LLC, ready to take the lead.

When not thinking creatively about novels and movies, David, the admitted sports fanatic, gets his fill of boxing, baseball, football, and basketball by watching his hometown teams, the Philadelphia Phillies, Eagles, and 76ers.